Splintered Emerald

JANE BLYTHE

Acknowledgments

I'd like to thank everyone who played a part in bringing this story to life. Particularly my mom who is always there to share her thoughts and opinions with me. My wonderful cover designer Amy who did an amazing job with this stunning cover. My fabulous editor Lisa for all the hard work she puts into polishing my work. My awesome team, Sophie, Robyn, and Clayr, without your help I'd never be able to run my street team. And my fantastic street team members who help share my books with every share, comment, and like!

And of course a big thank you to all of you, my readers! Without you I wouldn't be living my dreams of sharing the stories in my head with the world!

CHAPTER One

July 28th
3:30 A.M.

She could barely breathe she was sobbing so hard.

Emerald Hatcher stared at her sisters for as long as she could, but as the five of them were dragged out of the back of the van they had been transported in, they were split up. Her seventeen-year-old sisters Ruby and Amethyst were taken off to one side of the huge building, while she, her sixteen-year-old sister Sapphire, and eighteen-year-old sister Diamond were taken to the other.

As they entered the front door and were dragged up a flight of stairs, she was split up from her remaining sisters as Diamond was taken off down a corridor, Sapphire was taken down another, and the man whose hands were holding her so tightly it felt like he was turning her biceps to mush, dragged her down a third.

"Ooh, she's a pretty one," a man loitering in the hallway drawled as they stopped outside a door. "How old?"

"Fifteen," her escort replied. "She's not to be touched though, she needs to be processed."

"Any specific buyer in mind?"

"Not yet. She'll be kept in here for a couple of days and then depending on what we're going to be doing with her, she'll either be sent to training or sent off with her new owner."

It was odd to be talked about as though she were less than human.

No, not odd, more like horrific.

Because she knew that to these men, she *was* less than human.

To these men, the only value she had was to bring them in a truck-load of cash. Her parents had just sold her and her sisters for nearly a quarter of a million dollars, if these men had paid that for them then she could only imagine the amount of money they would receive when they sold them on.

Sold.

To think of that word in relation to her and her sisters, to people, was ... was ... well she couldn't even think of an appropriate word.

She was a human being. She had feelings, she had likes and dislikes, she was terrible in math but great at history and creative writing, she had been doing gymnastics since she was two-years-old, she often got in trouble for daydreaming at school, and while she didn't really fit into any of the social groups at her school, she was liked by almost everyone. She had a life, she had hopes and dreams for her future, she wanted to move out to the country when she got married, live on a farm surrounded by animals and nature, and she wanted to work with injured animals to help rehabilitate them.

Nowhere in her plans for her future had there been anything about being sold to human traffickers.

These men didn't care about what she liked and didn't like, they didn't care about her hopes for her life, they didn't care if they hurt her, they didn't care about anything but getting their money.

Fresh tears began to flow down her cheeks, they blurred her vision but not enough that she couldn't see the mountain of a man standing before her. He was bald, had tattoos all over his arms, and enough muscles to make him look like a rock. She wondered whether he took steroids. A boy from her class—a boy she'd had a crush on—had taken them, and while they had helped him develop enough muscles to make him the toughest guy in their class, he had started having mood swings and became aggressive. Aggressive enough that he had tried to attack her and two of her friends when they'd turned down his advances. Unfortunately, the boy had ended up committing suicide. He was the first person she had ever known who had died, and it had shaken her up for months afterward.

Did this man take steroids?

Was he going to make advances on her?

Her escort had told him that she wasn't to be touched, but she wasn't convinced that this man would listen.

He looked like bad news.

He looked scary.

Actually, he looked downright terrifying.

"She sure does cry a lot," the man-mountain noted.

"That's not an invitation," her escort reminded him.

Was crying a turn on to the man-mountain? That seemed weird to her, but she didn't know a lot about men, she wasn't very experienced, she'd only had her first kiss last Christmas. She'd been fourteen then, she was kind of a late bloomer when it came to developing an interest in the opposite sex, but she had a boyfriend now, and he certainly didn't think that tears were a turn on.

But who knew what kind of things these depraved men were in to.

Emerald made a gallant attempt to get her weeping under control, but it didn't do any good. She didn't think she could stop crying right now if her very life depended on it.

"Come on, kid." Her escort tugged on her arm as he unlocked the door and led her into a bedroom. The room was simple and yet nicely furnished, but her eyes bypassed the huge bed, and the dresser, and the armchair by the window, and zeroed straight in on a metal ring embedded in the wall.

She knew what it was for.

Just as she expected, the man walked her over to it, then unsnapped the chain that was attached to the metal collar that had been put around her neck, and attached a longer one, snapping the other end onto the ring.

She was trapped.

Emerald knew it was silly to feel trapped just because she was chained up, when she was in a house, surrounded by armed men, no doubt the bedroom door would be locked, but this made her feel claustrophobic. And it made her feel like an animal. People chained up their dogs, they didn't chain up teenage girls.

And yet here she was.

"Bathroom is in there," the man told her, pointing to a door on the adjacent wall. "The chain will let you move about anywhere in here, but it doesn't reach outside the door."

Having given her the rundown, he left her alone.

Alone.

She hated being alone, as the baby of the family she had been coddled by her older sisters, and as such, she hadn't outgrown some of her childish fears. The dark and being alone were two of them. She and Sapphire shared a bedroom—well, they had—and it was only just over a year ago, when she started high school that she had finally given up using a nightlight. Still, knowing her sister was asleep in the bed across from hers had always been a comfort, it had been nice knowing that if she got scared or had a nightmare, that someone else was there.

But now she was really alone.

There were no sisters to count on.

There was no one.

Just her.

Or not ...

The door to her room swung open, and the man-mountain stood there, leering at her. She shuddered and shrunk backward into the wall, letting it support her as her legs began to shake.

She wished she could shake so hard that she would shatter herself into a million pieces. Anything was better than being here and enduring what was coming next.

"You got gorgeous eyes," the man said, taking a step toward her.

Emerald knew she had pretty eyes, she had been told it a million times before. They were a bright green, emerald green, and she had always thought that it was cool that they matched her name, but not today. Today she wished her eyes were a plain, simple brown, nothing that would further attract any of these horrible men.

"A gorgeous figure too," he added, giving her a once over, his gaze lingering on her breasts. She might be fifteen, but just as she had been a late bloomer developing an interest in boys, she had been a late bloomer in developing her womanly attributes as well. She had been as flat-chested as a child up until a few months ago, and even now, she knew she wasn't anything special. She doubted that he cared much about her body, she was just an easy target.

"Y-you, you're not, h-he said, the man, he said you're n-not allowed to t-touch me," she stammered, trying to disappear into the wall as he approached her.

The man winked at her. "But I'm not going to touch you, *you're* going to touch *me*. No rules about that."

He stood before her, towering above her, and she knew she didn't stand a chance. She could weep, she could beg, she could lash out in anger, but nothing she did was going to stop it from happening. She was at his mercy, and she was as helpless as a mouse being played with by a cat.

The man unzipped his pants, then put his hands on her shoulders and shoved her down onto her knees.

Emerald sobbed.

He touched his fingers to her wet cheeks then put his finger in his mouth. "I love the taste of tears," he told her. Then he freed himself from his boxers, curled a hand around the back of her neck and shoved her head forward.

Emerald felt like the world had fallen away from underneath her.

She was falling ...

Falling ...

Falling ...

Only there would never be a landing.

She would just keep spinning through an empty world filled with nothing but pain, humiliation, and fear forever.

CHAPTER *Two*

August 4th
12:21 P.M.

"It's your lucky day, kid."

Emerald lifted her head off the pillow as the door to her room swung open, and the man-mountain that she had come to know much better than she wanted to over the last few days stood there.

She didn't know what he meant by it being her lucky day, but she was sure she didn't want to find out.

Her experience with this man had taught her that in this new life, she had to accept whether she wanted to or not, that the worst was to be expected at all times. And not just the worst, but worse than the worst. She had been shattered into a million pieces day after day, so many times that she wasn't sure there was any possibility that she could put herself back together again, even if by some miracle she was rescued from this hellhole.

Every day things seemed to get worse.

Most of the time, she was left alone in this room, she had free use of the bathroom, she could take a shower or a bath, and she had even been given clean clothes to wear. Meals were brought to her three times a day, the food was plain but good, and although she had resolved to not eat or drink and just let herself starve away or die from dehydration, it was a whole lot harder to do that than she'd thought. She hadn't even lasted more than a day before her stomach was growling at her so badly she couldn't help but eat a little. She'd lasted less than that before caving and drinking some of the water that was always left for her.

But every now and then, she heard the sound that chilled her to the core.

The sound of a key sliding into the lock.

It always signaled the same thing.

That this man was coming.

He had done things to her, made her do things to him that she hadn't even known existed. You would have thought with four older sisters that she would be a little wiser to the ways of the world, but she wasn't, and this wasn't the way she should be enlightened about them.

One thing she had learned during her short stay here was that when this man entered the room, she was to stand and be waiting for him to do to her whatever he pleased. Although she didn't like making herself so available for him to use as his own personal toy, it was definitely easier this way. It saved a lot of pain to just go along with it, although she knew that he'd been told he wasn't to hurt her, he was obviously well-practiced in hurting someone without leaving a mark.

"You're going to do great, kid," he told her as she stood waiting to see what fresh hell he had planned for her today.

Since she knew better than to ask what he was talking about and what she was going to do great with, Emerald just kept her mouth shut and waited.

She hated waiting.

It seemed to have become the center of her life.

She waited for meals to be brought to her, she waited for this man to come in and do something to her, she waited to find out what was going to happen to her next, who was going to buy her, where she was going to be taken, what was going to happen to her there, and when she would die.

Her life expectancy had just dropped dramatically.

Now she no longer expected to live well into her seventies or eighties, now she doubted she would make it to her twenties.

The man—whose name she didn't think she would ever know and who to her would always be just the man-mountain—walked over to her then pulled out a key and unsnapped the lock fixing the chain to the ring in the wall. Then he unlocked the chain from the metal collar and put on a smaller one, holding on to the end of it as he led her from the room.

As much as she hated being walked around like this, as though she were a dog, she knew it wouldn't do any good to complain about it. She now lived in a world without rules, without laws, without rights, she was nothing here, and she had no say in how she was treated.

They walked through the house, past door after door, and she wondered how many were occupied with kids like her. How many young women were being kept prisoner here? Were her sisters still here or had they already been sent off to their new owners?

Try as she might she couldn't get used to that word.

Owner.

People didn't have owners, dogs and cats did, but people were supposed to be their own person, free to make their own decisions and choices.

Not here though.

She was going to have to keep reminding herself of that.

The man stopped her outside a door, unlocked it, and then led her down a set of stairs into the basement. While her room upstairs had been nice, this place was dark and dirty, and smelled bad. There was a row of rickety-looking beds lined up against one wall, she could see a toilet down one end of the large room, and a showerhead on the wall beside it.

Down the other end of the room were several weird looking pieces of furniture. She might not know what they were, but she could guess. There was a table that held a variety of what looked like whips and paddles, and she stiffened.

What was this room?

"I'll miss you, kid," the man-mountain told her, then crushed his mouth against hers, shoving his tongue between her teeth. She just stood there and took it, let her mind go blank, wander away into a different place. Maybe if she did that long enough her mind would just stay there and never come back.

Or maybe it wouldn't.

"She's all yours," the man called out before heading back off up the stairs.

Another man stepped out of the shadows. This man was different, he *felt* different. He was smaller than the one who had just left her here, but he was still much bigger than she was, she wouldn't have stood a chance at fighting him off even if she intended to try.

And she wouldn't try.

She was too scared.

One wrong move and these men would crush her.

"I hear you're already starting to learn what's expected of you here," the new man said, his voice was cold, dark, evil. "That's good because we only have one month to get you trained ready to be sent off to your new master. A few basic rules you need to know; never speak unless given permission, never make eye contact unless asked to, your role from here on out is to let your master use you for whatever he wishes. You are to do whatever is asked of you immediately, without resistance of any sort. What you want is not only unimportant it is irrelevant. No one cares. You are replaceable, you are nothing."

Emerald just stood there staring at him.

It wasn't like he had told her anything she didn't already know, but hearing him say it so bluntly took that last little piece of hope that was still living inside her and extinguished it.

She was nothing.

Who she was before was irrelevant.

Who she might have become was irrelevant.

She was here now, this was her life, and in this life, she was nothing.

"Strip," the man ordered. "We don't have a lot of time to get you trained so we must start immediately."

Strip?

Take her clothes off in front of him?

Not just in front of him, as her eyes roamed the room, she saw that there were at least four other men in here, and maybe a dozen girls.

She couldn't stand naked in front of all these strangers.

Emerald gasped as the man was suddenly standing only an inch away from her. His hand curled around her long chocolate brown locks and yanked her head back hard. "You were given an order, and you did not fulfill it. There are no second chances here, I gave you the rules, you chose not to follow them, so you will be punished."

Punished?

She shuddered as she wondered what it would be.

Grabbing hold of her around the middle, he pulled her up against his side, his arm snaking around her back so she was bent over with her back facing the same way as his front. He took hold of the hem of the simple white cotton dress she had been given to wear the first day she had been brought here, and shoved it up so it was bunched around her waist.

Her underwear had been taken, and she hadn't been given a new pair so her backside was now bared for all to see.

His hand rained down against it in a bevy of slaps that left her bottom stinging with a tingling sensation.

"Next time I won't use my hand," he warned as he released her. "Now strip."

What choice did she have?

In this new world into which she had been abruptly thrust, there was only one option.

Obey.

With tears streaming down her cheeks, and hands that shook so badly it hurt, Emerald removed her clothes and let them fall to the ground at her feet.

Obedience.

If she didn't want to die, then she had to learn how to hand control of herself over to another human being.

CHAPTER
Three

September 4th
4:42 P.M.

Emerald sat with her back ramrod straight, and her hands folded together and sitting on her lap. She held herself tightly, like a coiled spring, ready to bounce into action at a split-second's notice.

No hesitations.

That was something she had learned the hard way over the last month.

Hesitations led to punishments, it was so much easier to just go with the flow, block out what was happening around her, let her mind go blank, and pretend that she was anywhere but here.

She liked to pretend that she was out in a field, on the back of a gorgeous white horse, riding through the grass. The sun was shining, the sky was a bright endless blue, birds were chirping, there were flowers everywhere, and her hair was fluttering in the breeze. She could ride a horse, she'd been taking lessons since she was four, she'd competed and won a lot of first-place trophies, and even if she didn't end up with her farm full of animals she had always planned on at least owning her own horse.

But like all her other dreams, it would never come true.

Some days she wondered why she was going to such great lengths to remain alive if this was all she had to live for. Why not just let these men get angry enough with her that they killed her because she was more hassle than she was worth? That way, at least her suffering would be over. It would certainly be easier, and it certainly seemed like the better option, and yet ...

She couldn't.

Maybe it was because she was afraid.

Afraid of being dead and afraid of the pain that would precede her death. She knew that after spending fifty thousand dollars to buy her, they weren't just going to let her die a peaceful and quick death, if they killed her, it would be something horrific and painful.

So she was stuck.

She didn't want to be alive and yet she was too afraid to die.

The limousine she was sitting in the back of pulled to a stop, and she began to tremble. She tried to control it, she didn't want to get into trouble, but she couldn't help it, she was terrified. This was it, she was about to come face to face with her fate and find out what her future was going to look like.

Bleak.

Her future was bleak, but how bleak?

Would her new owner be nice? Well, as nice as someone who bought another human being to use for their own pleasure could be.

"Remember what you've been taught," one of the trainers who was sitting beside her in the back of the limo told her. "This man has paid a lot of money for you, and I expect you not to disappoint. We have a seventy-two-hour return policy if he's dissatisfied with you, and I can promise you this, if I have to come back here and pick you up, you will not like the punishment waiting for you when we get back to the mansion," he warned.

The threat was enough to have her straightening her spine even more and making another attempt at stilling the tremors rocking through her body.

It wasn't that she got some sick sort of pleasure from pleasing these vile men, it was merely about self-preservation. She was doing what she had to do to survive.

The limo door was opened, and the man climbed out, Emerald slid along the seat and followed him. The day was gray and dreary, and besides leaving the house earlier, it was the first time she had been outside since the day her parents sold her.

As she was prodded in the direction of the house, Emerald surveyed her surroundings. The building in front of her was a large old farmhouse, it was painted a bright white, and there were rocking chairs on the front porch, giving the place a relaxing look. There were open fields around them, she could see horses and cows, and goats, and there was a red barn off to one side and behind the house.

A farm.

It looked like she was getting her farm after all.

Only she had never imagined getting it like this.

At the front door, the man escorting her rang the bell, then turned to her, giving her a once over, before reaching out to move her ponytail so it was in front of her shoulder instead of behind it. "Feet together, arms by your sides," he reminded her. "You've been taught how to stand, don't think you can relax your standards just because someone chose to buy you. Make sure you listen to your new master's instructions, some things he likes might be different than what you've been taught, but it's your job to do things the way he wants you to. Remember you're his now, your sole purpose in life is to cater to his every whim," he gave her last minute instructions as they waited for the door to open.

When it did open, there was a man standing there, dressed in a pair of smart black pants and a white shirt. He had a head of gray hair, and small beady brown eyes hidden behind thick-rimmed glasses. Emerald let out an internal sigh of relief, this man didn't look so bad, maybe things wouldn't be quite so awful as she had been expecting.

"Good afternoon, sir," the man at the door greeted them. "Mr. Curtwood has been delayed, but he gave me instructions on getting our new guest settled. He also said that the money had been transferred."

"We received it before we left the property as per policy," her escort said. "Please ask Mr. Curtwood to contact us when he gets the chance just to confirm that everything is as he hoped. Remember, he only has seventy-two-hours to express any displeasure."

"Mr. Curtwood is aware of the rules, I'll have him call you this evening. He might want to spend a little time with his new pet before he makes the call," the man in the doorway said, throwing her a quick glance.

"That's fine. Tell him I hope he enjoys his new purchase." With that, the man nudged her forward where her arm was grasped by the man in the doorway, and her escort turned and departed.

As the limousine drove off, Emerald felt a pang of loneliness. It wasn't that she wanted to go back to that hellhole, it was just that that was the last place she had seen her sisters, and at least, as awful as it was, she knew what to expect there, but here there were so many unknowns.

"Come along," the man said, pulling her into the house and closing the door behind her. "Your master should be home shortly, I'll show you where you'll be spending most of your time. Mr. Curtwood works a great deal, and he doesn't want to be bothered with you every day."

All of this sounded better than she could ever have hoped for.

The man who had bought her worked a lot and wasn't even interested in seeing her every day, maybe she could spend most of her time on her own. It would be lonely, and she had no doubt that when the man did want to spend time with her it wouldn't be pleasant, but it was better than things could have turned out.

Instead of leading her upstairs like she had been expecting, or through to a bedroom down here on the first floor, she was led all the way through the house and out the back door. They crossed to the side of the yard where there was a fenced-off area that appeared to be filled with several large dogs.

Was this where he intended her to stay?

"Mr. Curtwood doesn't like to share his home with strangers. The fence is electrified," the man told her as he unlocked the gate. "The dogs are friendly, there's a doghouse for shelter, meals will be brought to you twice a day when the dogs are fed."

With a slight nudge, she entered the yard, the gate was closed and locked behind her, and the man was gone.

She was alone with dogs.

There were six of them, and they came rushing over, darting about her, smelling her with their cold, wet noses, and licking her as their welcome.

This wasn't what she had been expecting. If she'd had to make a guess, she thought she would have been locked up in a room much like the one she had been in those first few days at the mansion. While this had probably been intended to be something that would make her feel humiliated, being treated like the dogs, it was actually a blessing in disguise. She loved animals, she was comfortable with animals, and she would gladly be part of this pack if it kept her out of the house and away from her owner.

Emerald patted the dogs' heads, and walked around her new home, avoiding the bouncing creatures as they followed her. He'd said the fence was electrified, but she would check out every inch of this place looking for weaknesses. Who knows, maybe she'd get lucky and find a way to escape.

The sun was just starting to set when she saw a man approaching.

Her owner.

He was coming for her.

It was time to find out just how bad things were going to get.

CHAPTER

Four

Two and a half years later

February 1st
7:32 A.M.

It was cold out.

There was snow on the ground, and he never bothered to give her anything warm to wear in the winter months.

In his mind, there was no need to. She was just a disposable toy that you threw away when you were bored with it because you knew you could always get a new one. A bright, shiny new toy that you could break.

Despite the snowy weather, Emerald wasn't all that cold, curled up in the large doghouse with her furry companions snuggled around her, they were protected from the conditions, and their combined body heat made the six-foot by six-foot wooden shack reasonably cozy.

She loved these dogs.

Loved them just as much as she had ever loved any human being.

They were her life.

Over these last two and a half years, they had been the one good thing in her life. They played with her every day, they slept beside her at night, they let her wrap her arms around their necks and bury her face in their furry coats and weep until she felt empty inside. They never complained about anything, they never got angry with her, they never hurt her or said mean things to her. They loved her, they wagged their tails whenever she came near them, they showered her with wet kisses, and they were always there for her.

Always.

Whenever she was brought back out here, they always came running straight over, hovering close by as though they understood that she had just endured something horrific and she needed them.

And she really did need them.

Without them, she wasn't sure she could have made it this long.

But Emerald feared that she wouldn't last much longer.

Richard Curtwood was starting to lose interest in her. He no longer came for her every day, now it could be three or four days, maybe even a week in between his visits. While she wasn't upset about that, she suspected that the reason was he was bored with her.

She was sure she knew why. It was because he didn't find her attractive, she lived out here with the dogs, she was never given a bath or a shower, she was fed a couple of times a day, but the food was hardly what one would call nutritious, and she had lost weight, she was so thin now that her ribs were visible, and when she lay down on the hard wooden floor of the doghouse at night she hurt because she was too bony. Her hair hadn't been brushed since she arrived here and was such a knotty mess that there was no hope for it, it would have to be cut off and grow back again.

She was a mess.

No longer desirable.

While she hated to admit it, knowing that Richard no longer thought she was attractive, hurt.

It was messed up, it was sick, it was twisted, it was wrong, and yet it was what it was.

Richard was her owner, he did horrible, despicable things to her, things that killed a little piece of her every time he did them, but he was the only other human being she saw besides the man who she had met that first day who brought her her meals. Richard never said anything nice to her, he never treated her nicely, he simply came for her, took her inside and up to his bedroom, did what he wanted with her, then threw her back in here, and yet ...

She wasn't really sure.

Her feelings for him were complicated, she hated him, she was terrified of him, she was repulsed by him, and yet at the same time, it had been drilled into her that her job was to please him and that he wasn't pleased with her made her feel like a failure.

What good was she when she couldn't even make her owner happy even though she let him do anything he wanted to her body, even though it messed with her mind?

Emerald knew the answer to that.

She was no good.

She was useless.

She was nothing.

The first light of a new day began to shine outside the doghouse, and she decided she couldn't be bothered getting up to wait for her meal. She didn't feel like eating, she hadn't had an appetite for a while now, and she suspected it was because she was waiting on tenterhooks to find out what was coming next.

Change was in the air.

She could feel it.

She didn't know how long she had, but she was sure that she would be dead before her eighteenth birthday.

It was only ten days away.

Ten days.

She should be planning a big party like other girls her age, she should be getting excited about graduating high school and starting college in the fall. She should be doing a lot of things, but instead, she was living in a cage with dogs.

What about her sisters?

What had become of them?

If they were still alive, Diamond would be turning twenty-one in a couple of days, Ruby and Amethyst would be twenty in the middle of the month, and Sapphire would be nineteen at the end of February. Some days it was hard to believe that it had been two and a half years since she had last seen them. Were they dead already? If they weren't, they were no doubt suffering at the hands of their masters.

Emerald pushed those thoughts away. She didn't like to think about her sisters, it was too depressing. It hurt too much. She loved them, and she hated knowing that they were either dead or stuck in a version of the same hell she was trapped in.

Part of her prayed for death, a quick and painless one, but part of her wanted to survive. She had come this far, and she wanted to see how much longer she could last because the longer she lasted, the more chance that one day she would be rescued.

In reality, she knew it would never happen.

She had long ago given up hope, and yet at the same time, she *did* still have a tiny glimmer of hope left. She knew it wasn't possible for both to be true and yet it was.

"Come," a voice commanded, and Emerald rocketed up. The dogs bounded up alongside her, thinking it was time for their feed, but she was filled with a sense of foreboding.

Careful not to linger too long, Emerald crawled out the door, then stood up straight, her head dipped forward, eyes fixed firmly on the man's shoes. She didn't speak, she simply waited for her next instruction.

"I have orders to bring you into the house, clean you up." Richard's butler or assistant or whoever the man was, spoke in that cold, detached voice he always used. He may never have laid a hand on her, and yet he was complicit in everything Richard had done to her because he hadn't done anything to stop it.

Although she wondered why she was to be taken inside and washed, she kept her mouth shut as she followed him out of the cage and toward the house. Was he going to clean her before he killed her to eliminate any forensic evidence that might have been on her body so that when they dumped her corpse, the police wouldn't link it to Richard and this farm?

She couldn't think of any other reason for her to be bathed. She had never been before, and she didn't think that Richard would simply decide to start now.

A blast of warm air hit her as she entered the house, and instead of making her feel warmer, it made her start to shiver, as though her body remembered that it was cold outside. She was led upstairs and into a bathroom where a bath had already been filled.

"You have fifteen minutes," the butler told her. "There's shampoo, conditioner, body wash, soap, combs, and scrub brushes. You're to clean yourself and tend to your hair, then put on the clothes that have been left for you. I'll be waiting outside the door."

With that, he exited the room, closed the door, and she heard a key slide into a lock and click.

Emerald was surprised he'd left her alone, she was half expecting him to have washed her himself, but apparently, those weren't his orders. The bath looked like heaven, she could see the steam rising off it, and it would be amazing to scrub every nook and cranny of her body, and under her nails, to wash her hair and try to detangle it, and shave her legs and armpits. She'd be clean, and after two and a half years of being filthy, that was a dream come true.

But why?

Why was she getting a bath?

Why today?

What was so special about today that she was allowed to come inside and take a bath?

Emerald couldn't come up with a single reason why, but one.

Today was the day she had simultaneously been dreading and longing for ever since the night she was sold. Today was the day that Richard was going to kill her.

As she stripped out of her filthy sweats and folded them neatly, setting them on the chair beside the clean clothes, and stepped into the steamy hot water, she decided she better make the most of this, one last moment of normalcy before her life came to a premature end.

~

9:53 A.M.

. . .

Once again she was sitting in the back of a limousine.

And once again she was on her way to meet a horrible fate.

Only this time, the fate was death.

Emerald was sure that she was being taken somewhere, probably some remote spot in the middle of the woods or something, where she was to be killed, her body buried in a shallow grave that no one would ever find.

Her sisters would never know what had happened to her just like she would never know what had happened to them.

Now that she knew her ordeal was drawing to a close, a sense of peace was settling over her. It was nice to know that there would be no more pain, no more suffering, just death, and then everlasting rest. She wasn't afraid, what was there to be scared about? The fear of death was that you had to give up your life, that you left family and friends, pets and jobs and hobbies, it was leaving behind the life you loved that made you terrified of death's clutches. But her life was a nightmare, she didn't want it, which made death something to be craved, something to be welcomed.

The only thing Emerald wished was that she could know what had happened to her sisters. Would she be meeting them when she walked through the door of death into the afterlife? Or would she be there waiting for them when they came to join her? If she could just know their fate, then she could walk out of this world without a care.

But there was no way to know.

Maybe they had been rescued, maybe they had escaped, she hoped that if they had, they were moving on with their lives, finding happiness and joy, and forgetting all about her.

If they survived, then she didn't want them wasting that second chance at life by worrying about her. She was already a lost cause, she would soon be dead, and if her sisters were alive and free then she wanted them to focus on themselves and not on her.

The limousine pulled to a stop, but she couldn't see through the blacked-out windows where it was that they had stopped. She didn't really care, what did it matter where they took her to kill her?

It was just the butler in the limo with her and the driver. Richard hadn't even bothered to come and see her one last time. She was upset about that, it was no use denying it, it bothered her that she had failed at her only purpose in life. And it bothered her that it bothered her.

If someone had asked her three years ago whether anyone could twist her own mind and turn it against her, she would have given an emphatic no. She was a free spirit, she knew who she was, she knew what she liked, she knew what she wanted in life. She was the kind of girl who stood up for anyone being bullied, who looked for the good in everyone even if it was hard to find, who wanted to take all the hate and negativity in the world and turn it into a place that was full of love and peace and joy.

Now she was ...

Nothing.

That was the only word that seemed to fit.

She had certainly heard it hundreds of times these last couple of years. From the men who had trained her, drilling into her each day that she was worthless, that she was nothing, from Richard who screamed it at her in frustration each time she failed to meet his expectations.

After being told it so many times, she believed it.

Emerald one hundred percent believed that she was nothing.

The limo door was opened, and she waited while the man got out before sliding out behind him, she was the obedient little lamb right up to the very end. As she blinked in the bright light, she was surprised to find that they weren't out in the middle of the woods somewhere, instead, they were standing in front of a mansion.

She had always believed that mansions were gorgeous places, filled with wealthy people who lived their lives happy and carefree because they didn't have to worry about money.

But that view had changed.

Now she thought mansions were horrible dark places, filled with wealthy people who used their money to fulfill their own sick desires and cared little for their fellow man.

Emerald wondered what they were doing here. This wasn't the kind of place she had expected to be brought to for them to kill her. Maybe a hitman lived here. How much did someone pay to take a person's life? Was it enough to be able to afford a huge house like this?

"Come along," the man snapped irritably like he had more pressing things to attend to today.

She trailed along behind him as he walked toward the house, up onto the porch, and across to the front door. The door was oak, and it had a knocker in the shape of a skull. If that wasn't a foreshadowing of what was to come then she didn't know what was.

The door was opened promptly by a woman in a maid's outfit, and without uttering a word, she ushered them inside. The foyer was grand, there were paintings on the walls, and two suites of armor stood on either side of the impressive staircase. The maid led them across the foyer and into one of the rooms leading off it. This room was just as grand, the walls were papered in dark greens and maroons. There were a number of portraits hanging along the walls, some looked to be hundreds of years old while the newest one, a picture of a young blonde man with a square jaw, looked recent.

Since she knew better than to sit without permission, she remained standing while the man who'd brought her here took a seat on a large leather sofa. Although she wasn't scared of being dead, Emerald couldn't deny that she was still scared of dying. If this was the house of the hitman who was going to take her life, then surely since he had no personal stake in her, he would kill her quickly. It was only when you hated someone or were otherwise passionately involved with them that you wanted them to suffer. Right?

"Good morning," a rich, deep voice spoke, and although she knew better than to look at anyone without being given permission, Emerald's head snapped in the direction of the voice. A young blonde man with a square jaw, who looked to be in his mid to late twenties, walked into the room. She'd seen him before, he was the man in the last portrait hanging on the wall, this was his house no doubt.

Was he the hitman?

He was wearing a crisp white shirt and a pair of black pants that looked like they were half of a suit. He was certainly overdressed for killing someone. Didn't you get messy when you took a life? Wouldn't he wear something simple like old jeans, or sweatpants or something?

"Good morning, Mr. Landry," Richard's butler said, standing to greet the man. "I take it she meets your approval?"

They both looked at her, and she quickly dropped her gaze to the floor. Why did it matter whether she met this man's approval? She was here to be killed. Wasn't she?

"She's a stunner," Mr. Landry agreed, walking over to stand before her. Emerald fixed her gaze on his shiny black shoes so she didn't look up at him. His voice was so smooth, so rich that it drew her in.

She didn't agree with him. She was hardly a stunner with her bony limbs, and the plain green dress she had been given to wear. And she didn't know why it mattered, but the longer she was here the less she believed that she'd been brought here to be murdered. So why was she here?

"The finances have all been taken care of, so if you don't have any issues then she's all yours."

All his?

So she wasn't here to be killed, she'd been resold.

She no longer belonged to Richard Curtwood, now she belonged to Mr. Landry.

Was that a good thing or a bad thing?

He couldn't be worse than Richard. Could he?

"Thank you," Mr. Landry addressed Richard's butler. "Cynthia will see you out."

Alone with Mr. Landry, he reached out and touched the back of his knuckles to her cheeks. Before she could help it, her eyes darted up to look at him, then quickly skittered away when she saw he was looking right at her.

She would be punished for that.

Her new owner wouldn't be any better than her old one had been, she was sure of it.

"Come this way," Mr. Landry said, taking her hand and leading her through the house.

No punishment?

That should make her feel good, but it didn't, she was too nervous, too unsettled to feel anything but anxious. She didn't know the rules here, she didn't know what to expect, and that was terrifying.

After walking up two flights of stairs and down several corridors, they stopped outside a door. "This is your room," Mr. Landry told her.

Well, at least she had a room in the house, that was an improvement on her last place.

Mr. Landry opened the door, and her eyes grew round when they walked inside. The room was large, there was a bed, and some pieces of furniture she recognized from her training, but that wasn't what had captured her attention. In the middle of the room was a golden cage with a large gold pillow inside.

That was where he was going to put her, she didn't need to be told that to know it was true.

"You'll change out of the dress, leave it for Cynthia who will wash it, and you can put on this," he said, holding out a skimpy piece of black leather lingerie that was less about covering her up than it was about highlighting her small breasts and giving Mr. Landry easy access to the part of her that was supposed to be private.

She shivered as she took the lingerie and began to change into it, no longer embarrassed about being naked in front of a stranger.

What was the point of being embarrassed?

Her body wasn't hers anymore, it was just a vessel for wicked men like the one standing before her, watching her like a hawk to use for their own pleasure.

Her pleasure didn't matter because she didn't matter.

She was nothing.

But who was Mr. Landry, and what was he going to do to her?

CHAPTER *Five*

Eleven Years Later

November 25th
10:13 A.M.

"Why is it so cold?" Detective Sapphire Hatcher-Barlow asked no one in particular as she tugged her coat tighter around her and shoved her hands deep into her pockets.

"Because it's late November," her partner replied.

She rolled her eyes at him. "I know that."

"You asked." Elijah Newton grinned at her.

She rolled her eyes again. As much as she liked her partner—who also happened to be her brother-in-law—and enjoyed working with him, it didn't mean that he didn't get on her nerves sometimes. He knew just how to annoy her, and he sometimes took great pleasure in getting her all riled up.

In a good way.

Sapphire trusted him with her life, and more than that, she would trust him with her son and husband's lives, and that was saying something. Although she had been concerned when Elijah started dating her oldest sister, Diamond, that things would become awkward between them, they hadn't. They made sure that when they were at work they were partners, and when they saw each other for family functions they were family.

"Do we know anything about the body?" she asked as she sidestepped a giant muddy puddle. It was nearly December, and although they hadn't had any snow yet, they'd been having a lot of rain, a lot of rain made for a lot of puddles, and she was not in the mood to get these new boots ruined. Although she wasn't much of a clotheshorse, she did love boots, and these had been a gift from Gideon on her thirtieth birthday last February.

"Just what the 911 caller said. They were out walking their dog when they stumbled upon the naked and badly beaten body of a woman," Elijah replied.

"Why do people always have to leave bodies way out here in the woods?" Then before her partner could offer an answer to what was clearly a rhetorical question, she added, "I know, it's so that no one sees them dump the body."

"Yet this guy didn't bother to bury the body," Elijah said thoughtfully.

"He wanted it to be found," she said, her own face going thoughtful as she considered this. "So he didn't want anyone to see him dump the body, but he did want it discovered. And fairly promptly, this is just at the edge of the woods, only fifty yards or so from the tree line, and it's a popular spot for dog walkers, and joggers, he knew that it wouldn't take someone long to find it."

"The question is, *why* did he want the body discovered."

She nodded her agreement. The majority of their job was working out why people did the things they did. Forensics was always helpful, and witnesses could lead them in the right direction, but in the end, it was usually finding out why someone might commit a crime that led them to the who. "Who was the 911 caller?" she asked.

"Older couple in their early seventies, they're waiting on the scene for us to speak with them."

"Good," she said as they approached the scene that had already been marked off with bright yellow crime scene tape that seemed incongruous with the dreary gray day. "As soon as we take a look at the body we'll speak with them, I doubt that they saw anything, but you never know."

The medical examiner wasn't here yet, and the crime scene unit hadn't arrived either, so they couldn't touch the body, but at least they could get a look at it, see anything obvious that might help them start piecing a story together.

As she stopped beside the body, the first thing she noticed was that the face had been beaten so badly that it was unrecognizable, they wouldn't be identifying this woman by her face. The second thing she noticed was that the woman's hands were missing, they wouldn't be identifying her through fingerprints either. The third thing she noticed was the red mark around the woman's neck, it looked like strangulation was the most likely cause of death.

"We assumed he left the body out in the open and close to where people walk and jog because he wanted her found, so why go to such lengths to make sure we can't identify her? He didn't need to beat her face like that, looks like he strangled her, he did it, and cut off her hands, to try to make it harder for us to identify her. It's almost like two different people, someone killed her and tried to hide who she was, the other dumped the body and wanted her found. Do you think we could be looking for two killers?" Sapphire asked.

"That's a definite possibility," Elijah agreed.

"What's that?" she asked, leaning over the body and pointing at a pink mark on the woman's stomach.

"Looks like a scar from surgery, appendix maybe," her partner replied.

That's what she'd thought.

Taking a step back, she took in more general things about the woman. Her skin was a pale, pasty white like she didn't spend much time outdoors, her hair was long and a pretty chocolaty brown, and she looked approximately five foot three.

Something felt wrong here.

If there was one thing she had learned in her years as a cop it was to always trust her instincts, and right now, her gut was telling her to look closer at the woman.

Moving around so she was near the woman's feet, she crouched down so she could see better.

"Are you looking for something?" Elijah asked.

She was, but she ignored him, she had an unsettling feeling brewing in her stomach, and she had to find out if she was right or just imagining things.

As she leaned in she saw what she'd been looking for.

A small star-shaped scar on the sole of the woman's right foot.

Panicked now, her heart hammered in her chest, and she was no longer cold, now she felt like someone had stuck her in a pot of boiling water.

"Sapphire? What's going on?"

This time she didn't ignore her partner on purpose, she was just focused on one thing and one thing only. Getting confirmation that this was who she thought it was.

Straightening, she moved back up near the woman's head and saw something gold catching the light.

A necklace.

Without even thinking, she reached down and undid the clasp.

"Sapphire, you shouldn't be touching that until crime scene, and the medical examiner take photos," Elijah said, but his voice suddenly sounded very far away.

Hanging from the simple gold chain were five gold charms.

A sun.

A music note.

A paint palette.

A book.

And a horse.

The world rocked beneath her feet.

The necklace with the charms dropped from her hand, landing with a small clink at her feet.

She probably would have joined it on the ground if Elijah hadn't appeared behind her, wrapping an arm around her waist and pulling her up against his chest so she remained on her feet.

Only now her feet were tingling.

The tingling went all the way from her toes to the top of her head.

"I think I'm going to pass out," she murmured.

And then she did.

When she slowly came to, she was being cradled in Elijah's arms as he walked somewhere with her.

Back to the car it turned out because someone opened a car door, and then he was laying her down on the backseat.

"Just stay put, we'll call an ambulance," he told her when he saw she was awake.

She didn't need an ambulance.

What she needed was what she had just seen to have been nothing more than a horrible nightmare.

"Are you okay?" Elijah asked as he squatted beside the open door. "Are you sick? Pregnant?"

When she'd been pregnant with Leo, who was two years old now, she'd suffered with some pretty bad morning sickness, but that wasn't what this was about.

"The body," she said, her voice strained and shaky. "I know who it is."

"Who?" he asked, his brow crinkled in a combination of confusion and concern.

"Emerald," she whispered as tears blurred her vision. After all these years of hoping that her little sister would return to them it was finally over. Emerald was dead. She was never coming back.

"Emerald?" Elijah echoed. Since he was her partner and married to one of her sisters, he knew about their past. How their parents had sold all five of them to human traffickers, and how only four of them had ever returned. "Are you sure?"

"Emerald had her appendix out when she was thirteen, it was right before Halloween, and she was upset that she wouldn't get to go trick-or-treating because she was meant to be going with a group of friends including a boy she liked. When she was nine, the two of us were playing down by the creek one summer, and while we were playing hide and seek she stepped on a rusty piece of metal, it cut her foot open and left a star-shaped scar. That body has both of those scars, and the woman was wearing Emerald's necklace. The necklace that she was wearing the night that we were sold. It's Emerald, that woman in the woods is my sister."

~

11:58 A.M.

"Dada Dada Dada."

Amethyst Hatcher bounced her one-year-old daughter on her knee. "Lucy, you've been saying Dada for over a month now, when are you going to start saying Mama?" she asked.

Her daughter was such a daddy's girl, much to her husband Zeb's delight, he spoiled her rotten, and she was already wondering how they were going to make it through Lucy's teenage years when she already had her dad wrapped around her little finger. Zeb had lost his parents and little sister in a house fire when he was eight, and when they found out that they were having a girl, there was only one name they could have chosen. Lucy had been named after the aunt who had never made it to her third birthday, and she knew it meant a lot to Zeb to be able to honor his sister in this way, it was like a part of Lucy would live on in their daughter.

The toddler cocked her head and looked at her with inquisitive golden brown eyes, the same color as her beloved Daddy's. "Dada," she said firmly.

She rolled her eyes at her little girl then laughed, she knew that Lucy loved her to pieces and she wasn't jealous of her husband's relationship with their baby girl, she knew that there was enough love to go around in their little family.

Her phone buzzed, and she picked it up, assuming it was a text from Zeb, he usually texted her a dozen times on the days she was off. Her husband was a cop, and she was a firefighter, they both worked crazy schedules, and when she had returned to work a few months ago they'd hired a nanny. Actually she, Diamond, Ruby, and Sapphire had all hired the same nanny to care for their kids because they wanted the cousins to grow up to be close. The nanny cared for Diamond's sons four-year-old

Archie and two-year-old Oscar, Ruby's two-year-old daughter Chloe, and Sapphire's two-year-old son Leo, five days a week, but Amethyst looked after Lucy herself on the days she wasn't on shift.

When she picked up her phone, she saw that the text wasn't from her husband, instead, it was from Sapphire. It was a short message, saying only that she was on her way over and that she'd also texted their other sisters to meet them here.

Bad news.

Amethyst knew immediately that the only reason her sister would gather them all together in the middle of the day was because she had bad news to break.

And there was only one kind of news she imagined her cop sister had to break.

If Sapphire had texted the others first, then they would no doubt be here soon. Standing up, she settled Lucy on her hip and carried her over to the playpen, popping the active little girl inside to play with her toys, then she began to tidy up the family room. Not because she was worried about the mess—it wasn't particularly messy, especially considering they had a toddler—but because she suddenly felt the need to be doing something.

Once the room was straightened up, Amethyst went to work making lunch. Lucy would be eating soon, so she may as well make something for herself and her sisters as well, although she wondered if any of them would have an appetite once they heard whatever it was Sapphire had to tell them.

A couple of minutes later her doorbell rang.

"Dada?" Lucy called out hopefully.

"I don't think so, munchkin," she told her daughter as she went to answer the door. Although this was the house she had shared with her sisters before they all got married and the others moved out to live with their spouses, they all insisted on ringing the doorbell instead of just walking in, even though she had told them on several occasions that it was fine for them to use their keys.

"Hey," she said when she opened the door and found both Diamond and Ruby standing on the doorstep.

"Hey," Ruby returned.

"Tillie asked if you wanted her to come and pick up Lucy," Diamond said as both her sisters stepped inside and she closed the door behind them.

"Just how bad is this news of Sapphire's?" she asked.

"Sapphire didn't say it was bad news," Ruby reminded her.

"She didn't say it was good news either," she muttered. "Are you expecting it to be good news?"

"No," Ruby admitted. "I'm expecting it to be ..." she trailed off, but there wasn't a need for her to finish the sentence, they were all thinking the same thing.

"Maybe I'll keep Lucy here," she said. "In case I need baby cuddles after we hear what Sapphire has to tell us."

"Dada?" Lucy asked again when they all entered the family room.

"No, baby, Dada is at work." Amethyst picked up her little girl. "Give Mama some kisses." Obediently, her daughter smooshed baby kisses all over her face. "You want to give me a Mama?"

The little girl just stared back at her, with her honey-colored eyes, and her dark brown hair that curled all over her little head, she was the spitting image of her daddy, right down to the half-smile she was so fond of giving.

"She still won't say, Mama?" Diamond asked.

"No, the stubborn little thing won't budge." As though offering an apology of sorts, Lucy wrapped her chubby little baby arms around her neck and slapped another kiss on her cheek.

"I was lucky, Chloe said Mama before she said Dada," Ruby said.

"Both Elijah and I missed out on being Oscar's first word, his was cookie," Diamond said with a roll of her green eyes.

Amethyst laughed despite the tension in the room. "I remember that. Kids, hey, they drive you crazy, but you love them anyway."

"Judah and I have been talking about adding another one to our family," Ruby announced. "Chloe is two now, and we only want to have two so we'd like them to be fairly close in age."

"I think one is all I can handle," Amethyst said. As much as she adored her daughter and wouldn't trade her for anything in the world, she wasn't sure she could go through pregnancy, labor, and a newborn again. She was happy with her family just the way it was. If Zeb had his heart set on more kids, she'd consider it and come to a compromise, but she thought he was pretty happy with the way things were too. They had a little princess on their hands, and she wasn't sure she could risk getting another little diva.

"With Brooke, we already have three, and I think that's enough for us," Diamond said. Brooke was Diamond and Elijah's sixteen-year-old foster daughter, she'd been with them for two years now and was just as much a part of the family as Archie and Oscar.

"I asked Sapphire the other day and ..." Ruby trailed off as the doorbell rang again.

It was time.

No more idle chitchat, trying to distract themselves from the black cloud that hovered above them.

"I'll get it," Diamond said, disappearing down the hall.

Amethyst set Lucy back in the playpen and tried to prepare herself, but of course there was no way to really do that.

How did you prepare to hear the words you had been dreading for almost half your life?

"Are you okay?" she asked as Sapphire and Elijah entered the room with Diamond. Her little sister's face was paper pale, and even from across the room, Amethyst could see that she was shaking. "Did something happen at work? Is that why you wanted to see us?" She scanned her sister from head to toe, searching for an injury that might be the cause of the sick look on Sapphire's face.

"No, I'm fine," Sapphire assured her. But when Diamond slipped an arm around Sapphire's waist, she could see that her sister leaned into her as Diamond led her across the room and over to the couch.

"She fainted at a crime scene this morning," Elijah told them.

Sapphire glared at her partner. "You didn't need to tell them that."

"I'm also going to tell Gideon if you don't," Elijah warned.

Sapphire aimed for another glare, failed, and just looked miserable. "Gideon, Zeb, and Judah are also on their way here."

Amethyst didn't want to wait for the others to arrive, she needed to know now. "It's what we're all thinking, isn't it?"

Sapphire looked at all of them and then gave a single nod of her head.

It was like the bottom dropped out of their world. That hope they had all been clinging to was gone.

It was over.

Emerald was no longer missing, she was dead.

"You found her body?" Diamond asked, slipping an arm around her husband's waist and resting her head on his shoulder.

"Out in the woods," Sapphire replied. "She was badly beaten, her face unrecognizable, but she had a scar on her stomach, right where Emerald did from when she had her appendix out, and a scar on her foot like the one Emerald got that summer out by the creek. And she was wearing this." Sapphire held up what looked like a gold necklace in a plastic evidence bag.

She knew the necklace.

It had been Emerald's gift on her fifteenth birthday, she, Diamond, Ruby, and Sapphire had saved for months to buy it for her, choosing each charm carefully to represent something that Emerald loved.

If the body was found wearing the necklace then there was no doubt about it.

It was Emerald.

Her baby sister, the youngest Hatcher sister, was dead.

"I'm sorry," Sapphire said, dropping her head into her hands. She said it like she believed that Emerald's death was her fault, and knowing what her sister was like, Amethyst wouldn't be surprised if she did blame herself. "I'll find who killed her, I promise you I will."

"Shh," Ruby said, dropping down onto the couch beside Sapphire and wrapping her arms around her. She and Diamond joined them, and the four of them held onto each other. Without Emerald, it was like a piece of them had been missing, but part of her had always believed that one day she would come back to them.

Now that would never happen.

The front door opened and then closed, and footsteps sounded through the house, a moment later Zeb, Judah, and Gideon appeared.

"I'm so sorry," Zeb said, coming to her and pulling her into his arms, crushing her against his chest. She hung onto him, needing something solid in her world right now.

Diamond went into her husband's arms, Ruby into Judah's, and Gideon sat on the couch, drawing Sapphire onto his lap.

Her family had grown over the last few years. First Sapphire had fallen in love with and married Gideon, then Ruby had married Judah, Diamond had fallen in love with Elijah, and he had brought Archie with him into their lives, then Brooke had joined their family, followed by Leo, then she'd fallen for Zeb, Ruby had given birth to Chloe, then Diamond and Elijah had adopted Oscar, and she'd had Lucy. So many new members of their family, and each one had brought with them a bundle of love, and through it all, she had believed that one day Emerald would be back, she'd fall in love too, and there would be more little babies joining their ever-growing family.

But Emerald was dead.

She was never going to return, and that meant that the Hatcher family would forever have a hole in it. A hole that could never be filled no matter how many people joined their family.

Burying her face against her husband's strong chest, Amethyst let her tears fall.

～

3:04 P.M.

"You should have stayed home."

Sapphire glanced over at her partner. "I'm fine, I just have a headache."

"No wonder you have a headache after you got such a shock this morning."

It had been a shock.

Every time she went to a crime scene where a body had been found, she wondered if it would be her sister's, but maybe she had never really been prepared for it to happen.

Because today *had* been a shock.

A horrible shock.

One that she still hadn't recovered from and doubted she ever would.

She didn't think that any amount of time would wash away the memory of seeing her sister's naked, beaten body lying out in the elements. Sapphire couldn't help but shudder as the image of Emerald in the woods flashed through her mind.

"You really should have stayed at home, like your sisters wanted you to, like your husband begged you to," he added.

"I can't stay home," she objected, the very idea was unacceptable. Gideon hadn't wanted her to come back here today, he'd wanted to take her home, ask the nanny to drop off Leo, and for the three of them to spend some time together. She got that he wanted to help her deal with the news that Emerald was gone, and she appreciated that he loved and cared about her, but right now there was nowhere else she could be. "Someone killed Emmy, she's my sister, I can't just sit on the sidelines and let someone else work this case."

"There's something we have to talk about," Elijah said, pulling his chair over so he was sitting beside her.

Something in his expression told her she probably wasn't going to like what he was about to say. "Out with it."

"We need to talk about the body—"

"*Emerald's* body," she corrected. That body in the woods wasn't just some stranger, it was the sister who had been a part of her life since before she was a year old. When they were kids, despite the fact that all five of them were close in age, it had always been Diamond, Amethyst, and Ruby, and her and Emerald. They were the two youngest, they had shared a room, and they had been friends, not just sisters. That her sister was dead still hadn't sunk in, this wasn't the type of closure she had wanted. She'd wanted Emerald back, not dead.

"Well," Elijah said slowly.

"Well, what?" she asked, narrowing her eyes at him. There was clearly something he wanted to tell her so why was he hesitant to just say it?

"I was thinking, the scars on the body, the ones that you said were scars that Emerald had, they seemed a little ... fresh."

"What are you saying?"

"I'm not sure that the body we found today is your sister's," he finally just blurted out.

Her eyes grew round as saucers. "You think that it wasn't Emerald we found in the woods this morning? But the scars, okay you think they look fresh, but that's just your opinion. And she was wearing Emerald's necklace. What are the chances that a woman around the same age as my sister would have the same scars and an identical necklace? Of course it was Emerald." It wasn't that she *wanted* her sister to be dead, it was just that she truly didn't see another option.

"I asked the medical examiner to run the DNA of the woman in the woods and compare it with your DNA. Sapphire," he said gently, taking her hands, "it wasn't a match. That woman is not your sister."

Her mouth hung open, unable to process what her partner had just told her.

How was that possible?

How could the woman have Emerald's necklace if she wasn't Emerald?

"I don't believe it," she said, snatching her hands out of his grip. "There must have been a mistake with the test. Maybe the sample from the woman got mixed up, contaminated somehow, that's why it didn't match mine."

"Or, it didn't match because that isn't Emerald," Elijah said firmly. He was obviously sticking with his theory.

"They should run the test again," Sapphire said. She still didn't believe this. It was too crazy.

"Okay," he nodded. "I'll ask them to run the test again. But I don't think we're going to get a different result."

"You really believe that it wasn't Emerald?" It was clear her partner was convinced, but there were too many questions that the possibility that the body was someone else's raised for her to be on board with this theory.

"I do."

"Then how do you explain the scars? The necklace? If it wasn't my sister then why did she have the same scars and the same necklace?"

"Because someone wanted us to believe that it was Emerald Hatcher," he said simply.

Sapphire gasped. "You think someone deliberately gave that woman scars, and gave her Emerald's necklace so we would believe that it was Emerald?"

"Could be why her face was so badly beaten and her hands were cut off. You would have known right away if it was your sister or not if you could see her, but take that away, and the scars and the necklace is enough to convince you that it was."

"But that would mean that someone had been planning this for a long time, you said what tipped you off was that the scars looked too fresh, but they *are* scars. They're not open wounds, they've healed and scarred over, which would mean they're at least a year or more old."

This was preposterous.

Crazy.

Insane.

Completely ridiculous.

It made so sense whatsoever.

"And why?" she demanded, still perplexed. "Why would anyone do this?" She had been feeling sick to her stomach ever since she'd realized the body was her sister's—although now the first inklings of doubt were creeping in—but now she felt like she might actually throw up. If someone wanted her and her sisters to believe that Emerald was dead that couldn't be good.

"You okay?" Elijah asked, placing a steadying hand on her shoulder.

"No," she said, shaking her head wildly. "I don't know what this means. Those were Emerald's scars, and that was Emerald's necklace, and if what you told me is true and DNA says that it's not Emerald, then someone sure went to a lot of trouble to make us believe that the body was hers. Why would they do that? They had to know we could still use DNA to verify her identity."

"Maybe they thought that they'd given us enough to believe that it was her and we wouldn't see a need to do a DNA test."

"We thought that the body was left in a fairly high traffic area because they *wanted* her found, which means that they *wanted* us to believe that Emerald was dead. I can't figure out if that's a bad thing or a good thing for my sister." The only good part of Elijah's scenario was that Emerald might still be alive. But in what shape? And did this new development mean that Emerald was in danger?

"Emerald was just a human trafficking victim, nothing important ..." Elijah trailed off as he realized what he'd just said. His eyes filled with regret. "I'm sorry, Sapphire. I didn't mean it the way it sounded."

"It's okay." She waved off his apology. "I know what you meant, and you're right. We were all human trafficking victims, easily replaceable, nothing that anyone should go to so much trouble over. And yet, someone did go to an awful lot of effort to make sure that the cops believed Emerald was dead. We have to figure out why."

"We will," Elijah assured her.

She knew that they would because she wouldn't rest until they had all the answers they needed.

Sapphire was so tired of people messing with her family. They had been through more than anyone should have to and yet it seemed like it never ended. Now she had to sit her sisters back down and explain to them that the body in the woods wasn't Emerald's, it was just a woman who someone wanted them to believe was Emerald. They'd have questions, and she would have to admit that right now, she didn't have the answers, but she would promise them that she'd get them.

Once she found who had killed that poor woman, no doubt after abducting her and keeping her prisoner long enough for the wounds they had inflicted to heal enough to make scars, she would make them pay. And maybe, just maybe, when she found them she would also find her sister.

Are you still alive, Emmy?

"Number one thing we need to do is identify that woman," she said, standing up and ignoring the nausea that lingered in her stomach. "Once we find out who she is we might find who killed her, and then we'll find the person who wanted us to believe that my sister was dead."

~

10:47 P.M.

. . .

It was a cold night.

Cold but beautiful.

The sky was clear, moonlight streamed down on the woods behind the house making the leaves practically glow in the dark. Out here in the countryside, with no lights but the one shining from the bedroom behind her, you could see all the stars in the sky, thousands of them, millions, and they were all twinkling so brightly.

She loved to stand out here on the balcony and enjoy the peace and quiet, the trees and the birds, the sunshine or the moonlight, but as beautiful as it was it always brought back memories.

Memories that stirred the ache in her heart.

Emerald Hatcher sighed and slumped down to rest against the pillar she was standing by. She should be happy, she *was* happy, she loved her life, after a long, hard battle and against all the odds she had managed to find her own version of happiness, and yet ...

There was always that little voice at the back of her mind telling her that there was something missing.

She had everything that she needed, she lived in a gorgeous mansion, anything she wanted—clothes, jewelry, shoes, bags—all she had to do was ask, and it was hers. She finally had her horses, and she spent time every day riding them, she also had dogs, a couple of cats, some cows, even a few goats. She had everything that her heart desired. Everything except the part of herself that had been lost along the way.

"It's icy cold out here, and you're dressed only in a nightgown," a voice rumbled behind her, and a warm shawl was draped over her shoulders. Large, strong hands began to vigorously rub her arms, and Emerald leaned back against the sturdy chest that had held her while she sobbed or woke screaming from a nightmare more times than she could count.

"You know I like to stand out here in the evenings," she said. It had taken a long time for her to gather enough courage to speak without express permission after her ordeal had finally ended.

"Winter is coming, make sure you put something warmer on tomorrow night, I don't want you freezing to death on me." Noah put his hands on her shoulders and turned her around so she was facing him. "I'd miss my favorite girl if she wasn't around."

"I'm your only girl," she said with a giggle. Noah had been so patient with her as she struggled to regain some semblance of the girl she had been before.

Before and after.

That was how Emerald thought of her life. There was the before she had been sold, back when she was a free-spirited teenage girl, and there was the after when Noah had helped her rebuild her life. He had been there with her every step of the way. He'd helped her learn to make eye contact again, to feel confident enough to speak up without fear of being punished for it. She had learned to make decisions for herself again, which after years of someone else telling her what she could do and when she could do it, had been harder than it sounded.

But Noah hadn't wavered in his support.

Not even once.

"Yes you are," Noah agreed, stroking his fingertips across her cheeks, then touching a kiss to her forehead. "Come inside now, its time you were in bed."

She allowed Noah to take her hand and lead her back into their bedroom, closing the double doors that opened onto the balcony behind them. She may not belong to anyone anymore, but she couldn't deny that Noah had a kind of controlling personality. He never made her do anything that she didn't want to, he just liked to look after her, and although she thought maybe it meant she wasn't as strong as she should be, his authoritarian attitude made her feel safe. There had been parts of her that had been lost that she could never get back and one of those was the ability to ground herself. Emerald often felt like she was floating about like a balloon in the sky, disconnected from the real world, and Noah gave her that grounding that she so desperately needed.

She loved him.

Completely and whole-heartedly.

She couldn't imagine her life without him.

Noah was wealthy, and they lived on his family's estate, just the two of them and a couple of staff that looked after the house and the grounds. She didn't need to work, which was a blessing because she wasn't sure that she could face a world full of people anymore. She hadn't been off this estate in over a decade, and Noah never forced her to, he took her for picnics on the grounds, in the woods or by the lake, he bought her beautiful jewelry and dresses even though they never went anywhere special. Sometimes they would get dressed up and eat in the large formal dining room, then dance for hours in the ballroom.

She knew how lucky she was that she hadn't been killed by one of her owners, and she treasured every second of the life she had because she knew that in a moment it could be gone.

"Come here." Noah paused beside the bed, curled an arm around her waist and drew her close, kissing her with the sweet passion of a couple who had been together for many years.

Sometimes it was hard to believe that this was her life. Emerald felt like a princess. A princess trapped in a castle, but an imprisonment of her own making. There was no longer someone keeping her captive, Noah was happy for her to come and go as she pleased, but she was afraid of the world. She was afraid of everything. This was the only place where she felt safe. This was her home, and Noah was her world, and in her own way she really was happy.

"What's wrong?" Noah asked, sensing her discontentment.

"Nothing," she said quickly, her gaze skittering away from his.

"There'll be none of that," he said firmly, grasping her chin and tilting her head back, waiting until she acquiesced and looked him in the eye. "What is wrong?"

His tone said there would be no wriggling out of answering his questions, so she might as well just get it over with. "I just feel ..." she struggled to name the right emotion. "I don't know," she said with a helpless shrug that said she wasn't trying to be difficult, she just couldn't put a name on it. "I just have this unsettled feeling. I'm sorry, I can't be more specific."

"Are you apologizing to me?" Noah demanded. "Because we've talked about that. Unless you have done something rude or nasty to me there is no need to apologize. Have you done anything rude?"

"No," Emerald whispered.

"Anything nasty?"

"No."

"So there's no need for you to say sorry. It's okay if you're struggling to decipher your feelings. Emotions can be confusing sometimes, especially for a woman who has been through what you have. Would you rather just lie down and go to sleep?"

When she and Noah had first become a couple it had taken him months—more like years—to break her belief that it was her job to give him what he wanted without any consideration of what she wanted. Even now, so many years later, she couldn't help the nervous butterflies in her stomach as she said, "I'd rather just go straight to sleep tonight." Emerald bit her tongue, so *if that's okay with you* didn't slip out.

"Then that's what we'll do." Noah touched a kiss to the tip of her nose, then reached around her to pull back the covers, tucking her in once she lay down. Then he stripped off his sweatpants, threw them on the armchair in the corner of the room, and slid under the blankets beside her. Noah was always hot, and she was used to seeing him in just his boxers, yet sometimes she was in awe of his body, he was so muscled, so strong, so chiseled, he could crush her if he wanted to, but he didn't.

Because he loved her.

She was safe here with him, Emerald knew he would kill anyone who tried to hurt her.

Stretching out beside her, Noah wrapped his arm around her and pulled her closer. She rested her cheek on his smooth chest, her head rose and fell with each breath he took, and she snuggled closer. Here in Noah's arms was her favorite place to be. Her fear of leaving this house meant that she had never gone back home to her sisters, but it didn't mean that she hadn't asked Noah to find out about them. She knew that they were all safe, alive, happy, they'd moved on with their lives, married and had children of their own now.

Her choice to stay here was the right one.

She was sure of it.

They'd moved on, and she had moved on.

There was no going back.

A decade passing by had cemented that.

CHAPTER
Six

November 26th
9:46 A.M.

"Did you sleep at all last night?"

Sapphire bit back another yawn, probably her hundredth for the morning, and said, "I slept."

"More than an hour?" Elijah asked.

"Probably not," she admitted. Gideon had pressured her into going to bed around eleven, but after tossing and turning for an hour, she'd snuck out of bed and downstairs to her study, where she had worked, completely losing track of time, until Gideon had found her in there at five. She was used to running on little sleep, before she had met and married Gideon she'd been a workaholic, okay so maybe she still was, but now that she had something else in her life besides her job, she tried to control her impulses. Gideon and Leo were the most important things in the world to her, and she didn't ever want her son to grow up and resent her for not being there for him.

It wasn't the lack of sleep that had her yawning all morning, it was the block of tension that was clamped to her stomach.

She hadn't been able to take a full breath since she saw the body that so closely resembled her sister, and her stomach had spun in a constant revolution of circles, nearly driving her insane. Sapphire hated living in this constant state of anxiety. She knew she needed to do something, but she didn't know what. She wanted to know who had faked Emerald's death and why, but she couldn't just snap her fingers and make it happen, and that made her feel like a failure.

"Don't let this case consume you," Elijah warned. "Try not to get too emotionally invested."

"How exactly do you propose I do that? Okay that body wasn't my sister, but someone wanted us to believe that it was which means they know about Emerald. That was her necklace, so at some point the killer was in contact with my sister." Although she had been skeptical at first, the second DNA test had confirmed what the first one said. The body in the woods was not her biological relative. It wasn't Emerald, but it was someone, and that woman deserved justice. She would work this case as hard as she could—as she did every case she was given—for the deceased woman and her family, and for Emerald and her own family because the two were interwoven together.

"Which means she's probably still alive," Elijah said. "If she was already dead then why would someone try to make another person look like her? They wouldn't. If she was dead then it would have been her body in the woods. Someone wants us to think she's dead so you stop looking for her."

"You think the killer knows that I still look into Emerald's case?" she asked as she parked the car. There hadn't been a day that had gone by since she joined the police force that she hadn't done something to look into her sister's case. She was a cop, she couldn't just sit back and let someone else do it. And who would do it anyway? Emerald had been gone for fourteen years, she'd be twenty-nine now, and although what Elijah had said made sense and Emerald really probably was still alive, she still belonged to some disgusting monster.

"I think so, and I think that they don't like it. They're trying to get you to back off, so you better give the impression that you've backed off."

"And walk away from this case?" she asked, aghast. There was nothing that would make her stop looking for her sister's captor.

"No, we work this case, but you need to stop specifically looking into what happened to Emerald. If you don't, you're putting your life in danger," he added when he saw he hadn't convinced her.

Sapphire opened her mouth to protest, tell her partner that she didn't care if her life was in danger because as long as she was someone's prisoner, Emerald's life was in danger, but he cut her off with a hard stare.

"You have a husband and a son now. A little boy who needs you, don't do anything to make him grow up without his mother. Be careful, play things smart and safe. I do not want to have to sit your husband down, or sit my wife down, and tell them that you got yourself killed."

Well, she couldn't argue with any of that.

She would never do anything to unnecessarily put herself in danger because she knew how much her death would hurt Gideon and Leo. "I'll be careful," she agreed.

"Good." Elijah nodded, obviously satisfied that she wouldn't do anything reckless. And she really wouldn't. She would work this case as safely as it was humanly possible to work it.

"I feel like this is probably going to be a waste of time," she said as they both got out of the car and walked toward a small but adorable cottage. Since she had fainted at the scene yesterday when she'd thought the body was Emerald's, they hadn't gotten a chance to interview the couple who found the body. That was what they were here to do this morning.

"You never know," Elijah said, and rapped on the door.

It was opened nearly immediately as though the occupants had been waiting for them. "Detectives?" Hugo Pickle asked.

"Yes, I'm Detective Hatcher-Barlow, and this is Detective Newton, we're here to talk to you about yesterday," she said.

"We've been expecting you," the man said grimly. "Come in."

They stepped inside, into a large room, there was a small kitchen in one corner, and a dining table in front of the window to the left of the front door. The other side of the room was the living area, a fire crackled in the fireplace, and Geraldine Pickle sat knitting in a rocking chair. The scene was very warm, cozy, and domestic, and Sapphire hated that this nice couple had been thrown into something so dark.

"What are you knitting, Mrs. Pickle?" she asked as she followed Mr. Pickle over to the sofa.

"A dinosaur," the woman replied. "For my little grandson, he loves dinos. Do you have little ones?"

"We both do," she said, indicating herself and her partner. "We both have two-year-old sons, and my partner also has a four-year-old son. All three of the boys love dinosaurs. Your grandson is lucky to have a grandma like you who can make him such special things." For obvious reasons her parents were not involved in her son's life, they were serving out their life sentences in federal prison, but Gideon's parents were fantastic grandparents and showered Leo with love and gifts when they came to visit.

"Nothing more precious in life than a grandbaby." The woman smiled. "All the love and cuddles of a little one and none of the responsibility of raising them."

"Sounds nice," she agreed. Cuddles and love were definitely the upside of parenting. Tantrums and teaching them patience, resilience, self-control, right from wrong, and all the other things she wanted her son to be were definitely the hard parts.

"We know that you spoke with officers at the scene yesterday morning," Elijah began, gently guiding their attention back to the reason for their presence here. "But we were hoping that after the shock had worn off a little, you might have remembered something."

Mr. Pickle shook his head. "We didn't see anything," he told them. "There were no cars in the parking lot when we parked our car, and we didn't see anyone else out walking. Our dog, he doesn't really like strangers or other dogs, so we always take him early before the other walkers are out."

"But there is something," Mrs. Pickle added, and she could feel her partner perk up beside her as she too straightened in her chair to hear what the woman had to tell them. "I didn't think of it yesterday, I guess what we saw ... I've seen dead bodies before, I was there when both my parents took their final breaths, but that was different, they were old, sick, in a hospital. That poor girl was ... what they had done to her ..."

"I'm sorry you had to see that, Mrs. Pickle." Sapphire reached out and took the woman's hands, which had fallen still in her lap. She had seen a lot of dead bodies in her years as a homicide detective, a lot of them in much worse condition than yesterday's, and every single one of them affected her.

The woman smiled, nodded her thanks, then steeled herself. "The last couple of weeks there was this car that was parked in the parking lot every single morning. At first we thought it might be someone who was homeless, living in their car, but there was never anyone in it, and we didn't see bags of clothes, or blankets, or anything else."

A car hanging around the dump site was definitely something they would look into. Especially since they believed that someone wanted them to find the body because they wanted them to believe Emerald was dead, it made sense that they had staked out the area to ensure it had enough foot traffic.

"Did you get a license plate?" she asked, hardly daring to believe that they might have an actual avenue to pursue this early in the investigation.

"We did," Mrs. Pickle replied proudly. "My husband said I shouldn't worry about it, that it was none of our business, but I got a bad feeling from the car, so I wrote it down." She nodded to her husband who picked up a sheet of paper and handed it over. "There it is. I hope it helps you find whoever killed that poor woman."

Sapphire did too.

The only way to find her sister was to find out who this woman was and who had killed her.

Anxious to get moving now, run the license plate, check out who the car was registered to, Sapphire stood. "Thank you so much for your time, and for this," she said, holding up the piece of paper.

"You're welcome, dear. Before you go." Mrs. Pickle stood, setting her knitting in her rocking chair, and disappeared into another room. She returned a moment later with three knitted dinosaurs. "For your little ones."

"I thought you made them for your grandson," Sapphire said.

"I can make more. I want your boys to have these."

"They're going to love them," she said, touched by the gift.

Family meant a lot to her, she knew what it was like to lose them all, to be completely on your own in the world. And when one by one she had gotten her sisters back they had been her whole world for a long time. Now she had her own little family, and she would do anything for them. But as much as she loved Gideon and Leo, and Diamond, Ruby, and Amethyst and their families, as long as Emerald was still out there somewhere a part of her family was missing.

She'd be careful, but Sapphire was more determined than ever to find out what had happened to her sister.

～

11:22 A.M.

"Hey, girl, you want a carrot?" Emerald asked her horse, Storm. The gorgeous gray mare whinnied and nuzzled at her shoulder, making her smile. There was nothing like spending the day with her horse to lift her spirits.

When Noah had first started working with her, it had been the horses that had finally cracked the wall she had been hiding behind.

Back then, she had been too terrified to believe that Noah wasn't going to hurt her. That he wasn't just trying to trick her, trying to get her to do something she wasn't supposed to so he could punish her for it. She knew how much men like him liked to punish girls. He had told her over and over again that she was free to go down to the stables and ride his horses any time she wanted, but when she steadfastly refused to go, knowing that her pleasure meant nothing, her sole job was to serve violent men, he had marched her down to the stables, saddled up one of his horses, and ordered her to go riding. For good measure, he had added that he'd be furious with her if she didn't, and afraid of being punished, she had gotten on the horse and ridden it around the arena for an hour before taking it back to the stable, removing the saddle and putting it away in the tack room, and tidying everything up. Then unsure if she should return to the house on her own or wait for him, she had settled on waiting, and eventually he had found her hovering uncertainly in the stable door.

Every day for a month, Noah had taken her down to the stables to ride, sometimes he'd go with her, flying along on his black stallion Thunder, some days he'd stand and watch, and some days he would leave her to spend time on her own, and bit by bit she came to realize that he meant her no harm. That beating her and raping her and making her do disgusting things wasn't what turned him on.

Still, it had taken a lot longer for him to earn her trust. It took more than a year for her to even look him in the eye, closer to eighteen months before she would speak without being given permission, and almost two years before she finally started to relax in his presence.

Now he was her life.

Emerald knew that she didn't fit in in the real world anymore. She was too damaged, even though she had fought hard to get to where she was, there were definitely pieces of herself that she hadn't been able to recover. Out in the real world she was nothing, but here, in her safe place, on Noah's estate, she was something.

She was his.

She knew how that sounded. It sounded like she was right back where she had been before, someone else's possession, but it wasn't like that. Noah treated her like she was the most special thing he had, he had shown her more love and patience than was necessary for someone who had no biological ties to her, and no responsibility to be there for her and support her.

Noah was her savior, and she loved him more than she had ever loved another person.

He was her life.

He was the only reason that she got up in the morning.

He was the only reason she slept relatively soundly at night.

He was the only reason that she hadn't completely fallen apart.

He was the only reason that she had been able to glue most of the pieces of her heart and her mind back together.

He was the only reason that she was alive.

There was no way, even if she lived to be a million years old, that she could ever repay him for everything he had done for her. There had been times—lots of them in fact—where he'd had to be tough with her, harsh even, where he'd had to use the brainwashing that had been done to her against her in an effort to break its hold on her, but she knew that it had all been for her own good.

Storm whinnied again, and Emerald realized that she hadn't given the horse her carrot yet. "Sorry, girl, here you go." She held out the carrot, and the horse crunched it down in three seconds flat. "You ready to go for a run?"

As though she could understand what she was saying, the horse snorted and stepped over to the side where she always stood when Emerald was getting her ready to go riding.

"You're such a smart girl," Emerald told Storm, giving her a rub behind the ears, before heading to the tack room. She got the horse ready quickly and with practiced ease, then she took the reins and led her out of the stable. They stopped by the stable door, and Emerald used a small wooden step to get up onto Storm's back.

There was nothing like sitting on the back of a horse. They were such strong animals, she could feel the power flowing through Storm's body, and when she was sitting up here she felt like that power flowed all the way into her.

Emerald kicked her feet and Storm started to walk, then as they approached the large field that separated the stables and the arena from the woods that covered most of the fifty acres that Noah owned, she kicked her feet again, and Storm broke into a gallop.

The wind ruffled her hair which hung free beneath the riding helmet, and a little bit of sunlight streamed through the clouds, making the lingering dew on the grass sparkle like little drops of diamonds that had fallen from the heavens.

It felt like she was flying.

That was what she loved the most about riding a horse, it was the closest you could get to flying while still being on the earth.

It was the most amazing feeling.

Even Noah couldn't give her this feeling. It was the only time she felt truly free. Her past didn't matter, the damage it had done to her didn't matter, she was just a girl on a horse, flying across the ground at what felt like the speed of light.

Storm slowed a little as they reached the woods, and began to weave her way between the trees at a fast trot. It wouldn't be long now until there was snow on the ground instead of muddy dirt, and then rides like this would be on hold until spring was back.

Sometimes she and Noah would take their horses out even in the winter, but with all the snow, it made riding through the dense woods treacherous. She knew that because the first year when she had been finally starting to learn to be a human being again, she had come riding out here because back then, it was the only time she felt safe. She'd fallen off the horse, hit her head, knocked herself out, broken her arm, and been hypothermic by the time Noah realized something was wrong and came looking for her.

He'd been so sweet those weeks where she had been mostly confined to bed as she recovered from a concussion and the badly broken limb. He had fussed over her, read to her, sat and talked with her for hours, he'd helped her eat, and given her a bath each day, before tucking her in and sleeping in an armchair beside her bed.

That had been when she'd first started to see him differently.

See him as someone that she could share her life with.

It was when she had first started to fall in love with him.

When she had been well enough to return to the horses, he had forbidden her from riding alone in the winter. Well, he hadn't actually *forbidden* her, but he had been very stern with her, and since that desire to please was still strong, she had acquiesced.

Emerald lost track of time as she and Strom wove through the woods. It was so beautiful out here, so quiet, if she could, she would stay out here all the time. Maybe those years she'd spent living in the yard with the dogs had made houses feel a little odd to her now. She rode most days unless it was raining, Noah didn't like her to be out in the rain, he was always worried she would get pneumonia or something, but so long as there was no precipitation falling from the sky then you could find her out here, on Storm, being a part of nature.

Eventually, it was a rumbling in her stomach that said it was lunchtime and had her heading back toward the stables. As she broke through the tree line and urged Storm back into a gallop, she saw Noah standing waiting for her. He had a picnic basket in his hands, and her heart did that little pitter-patter that it always did when she saw him.

He was perfection.

He was her hero.

He was the man she loved, and when he did sweet things for her like pack her a picnic because he knew she had been unsettled lately, her love for him grew.

Noah was the light in the darkness that had been her life, and she felt so lucky that fate had brought him to her.

~

3:15 P.M.

Sapphire pressed the buzzer again.

"Give him more than five seconds to answer," Elijah told her with a wry smile.

"I gave him at least ten," she shot back, then pressed the buzzer to apartment four hundred and twenty-four again. The apartment belonged to a Bobby Tompson, a thirty-year-old executive at a computer company that did everything from home and business security systems, to video games, and software for businesses.

After visiting the Pickle family this morning and speaking with the older couple, they'd looked into the car they had seen parked out by the woods and found who the registered owner was. Before coming here to speak with the man they'd done a bit of research into him, hoping to find something that might indicate whether this could be the man they were looking for, or just someone who happened to be out there at the same time as the Pickles.

They had found nothing useful at all on Bobby Tompson.

The man had a clean record. A couple of speeding tickets from when he was in his teens, and that was it. Could someone with no criminal record really be someone who could abduct a person, hurt them, and then keep them prisoner while the cuts healed and scarred, then beat a woman to death?

Sapphire wasn't sure.

And the man did live in an apartment building, there was no way he could have kept their Jane Doe here while he waited for those cuts to scar over, there were over five hundred apartments in this building, over one thousand residents, someone would have seen or heard something.

"His car is here, he should be in there, why isn't he answering?" she said, getting frustrated. Maybe Bobby knew that it was the cops buzzing his apartment and he was avoiding them because he did have something to hide. Just because the man didn't have a criminal record didn't exclude him from being the killer. Maybe he had committed other crimes, and he just hadn't gotten caught for them.

"Sapphire, we've been standing here less than thirty seconds, maybe he was in the bathroom, or the shower, or right in the middle of something," Elijah said in that irritating calm voice of his. Gideon had the same ability to remain calm when she was flustered, and it never failed to drive her crazy, which she suspected was half the reason he did it, he loved to tease her.

"I'm pressing the buzzer once more, and if he doesn't answer, then I'm buzzing a neighbor and getting them to let us in," she warned, pressing the button again.

She waited as patiently as she could for another thirty seconds and just when she was about to give up a voice floated through the intercom. "Hello?"

"Mr. Tompson?" she asked.

"Yes, who is this?"

"I'm Detective Hatcher-Barlow," she said, holding up her badge at the camera mounted above them for him to see. "And this is my partner Detective Newton. We need to speak with you."

"About what?"

"We'd rather not discuss this out here, may we come up to your apartment?"

"Umm," the man waffled.

"We can always do this down at the station," Elijah said.

"No, no, you can come up, it's fine," the man relented. "I'll buzz you in."

The door to the building clicked open, and they walked inside. It was a modern building all plain white walls, brightly colored pieces of art, and lots of large glass windows. There was a row of four elevators on the far wall, and they walked over to them, pressing the number four, they waited for the lift to reach them.

"I don't like him," she said while they waited.

"And you're basing that on what? The fact that it took him a full minute to answer the intercom?" Elijah asked.

"No. I'm basing it on a feeling I have."

"Sapphire, you know that usually I'm all for listening to your instincts, they've been right more times than I can count, but this time your gut is just telling you that because you want it to be true. I get it, I do, because this is about your sister. I want this case closed just as much as you do because you and Diamond and Emerald are all sisters, but you have to treat this as we would any other case."

"I am," she countered as the lift beeped and then the doors slid open. "And my gut is telling me that Bobby Tompson is not as good a guy as his clean record would imply."

"Well, we'll see," Elijah replied non-committedly.

She didn't care if her partner believed her or not, he was right, her instincts were almost always spot on, and if her gut was telling her that Bobby Tompson wasn't as innocent as he seemed, then she was proceeding under that assumption.

They walked out of the lift and down the hall, then knocked on the door of apartment four hundred and twenty-four. "Mr. Tompson, it's the detectives," she called out, wondering whether he was still in there or if he had split as soon as he buzzed them into the building.

"Coming," he called out, and they could hear him walking down toward the door.

Okay, so he hadn't split right away, didn't mean he wasn't guilty. When the door opened an attractive man the same age as she was stood there smiling at them. He had white teeth, tanned skin, golden-brown hair, and long-lashed light brown eyes. When he smiled at them his dimples came out, and he ran a hand through his thick hair as though they were a prospective date instead of the cops.

"What's this about, detectives?" he asked as he opened the door wider for them to enter. The apartment was more like a hotel room than a home. The furniture was all new and looked expensive, the artwork on the wall also looked expensive, but there were no family photos, no books or magazines, nothing that added any personal touches to the space.

"Your car was seen at a crime scene," she said, being deliberately vague because she wanted to see what the man's reaction was going to be.

"A crime scene?" he repeated as he gestured for them to take seats on one of his white leather sofas. "You mean like a car accident or something? Or while my car was parked in the garage at work? A mugging or something?"

"A murder," she informed him.

"A murder?" he echoed, his eyes growing wide. "I don't remember hearing anything about a murder at work. And I'm sure that I would have noticed a crime scene while at the grocery store or the gym or something."

"No, it wasn't at your office, or the grocery store or gym. The body was found out by the woods, over near the waterfall."

"The waterfall? I haven't been there in years."

"Well, your car has," Elijah said.

"My car has?" Bobby scrunched his brow in confusion, but she couldn't tell if he was being sincere or hamming things up for their benefit.

"It was seen parked out there on more than one occasion by the same couple who found the body. How do you explain that?" she asked.

"I can't," he said simply, adding in a shrug for good measure. "I haven't been out there in years, we had a work Fourth of July picnic out there about three years ago, but that's it. Why would I be out there? I'm not really an outdoorsy sort of guy, I don't go hiking or running in the woods. I don't have a dog or anything, and I work out at the gym, there's no need for me to be out there. Whoever thinks they saw my car there is mistaken."

"I don't believe they are," she countered. "They saw it on several occasions and made a point of looking closer at the car because they thought it might be a homeless person living in their car and wanted to see if there was anything they could do to help. They wrote down the license plate and the make and model of the car. Your car."

"Well, I don't know what to tell you," Bobby said with another shrug. "I haven't been out there, they must have made a mistake."

Sapphire knew that wasn't true. She knew that there was no way the Pickles had made a mistake. What were the chances that they had written down a license plate and the make and model of a car, the car that matched the license plate, and they'd made a mistake?

None.

The chances were none.

"Does anyone else have access to your car, Mr. Tompson?" she asked.

"No. I'm single and don't have any relatives that don't have their own car. The only one who uses it is me."

"Is there anyone who has a copy of the keys, or who might have been able to get a copy made?" Elijah asked.

"No one that I can think of. I can't tell you why these people thought they saw my car there because it hasn't been there."

Bobby sounded sure of himself, but she didn't believe him.

His car had been there, and by his own admission, no one else had access to the car which meant that he had been there too.

And he had lied about it.

If he'd been there for some innocent reason then there would have been no reason to lie about it.

He had lied because he had something to hide.

Something she was determined to find out.

～

7:28 P.M.

Noah strode through his house.

He'd gotten preoccupied with work and lost track of time, usually he liked to set work aside by early evening so he could spend time with Emerald.

His Emerald.

The woman was as gorgeous as her name implied. Huge, shimmering green eyes, soft, silky brown locks, and the sweetest temperament he had ever seen in a woman. It was a testament to the kind of person she was deep down inside that despite the hell she had endured it hadn't ruined her.

He often wished that he had known Emerald before she had been damaged. Not just her body, but her mind, touched by despicable men that he had made sure paid the price for what they had done. Although that essence of sweetness that existed inside her hadn't been extinguished, it had been broken. She was so quiet, so restrained all the time, and he knew there wasn't a day that went by that she didn't feel fear.

Noah had tried his best to give her a safe place so she could let go of that fear, but so far nothing had worked. He let her spend her days out with the horses, or wandering the grounds, he never made her leave because he knew that she wasn't ready yet to leave this safe haven he had created for her. He treated her like the queen she was, showering her with gifts, with jewels, with gorgeous clothes, and anything else her heart desired.

Except for the one thing it desired the most.

Her old life back.

Or more accurately, the life she had dreamed about having.

While he knew that she was happy here and that she loved him, he also knew that part of her wanted her family back. She wanted her sisters back in her life, and she wanted to do all the things she had dreamed about as a teenager. Sometimes, he wondered whether one day she *would* leave him and create a new life that didn't include him, but Emerald insisted that it was better for all of them if her sisters believed she was gone forever.

He couldn't say that was any sort of hardship.

If it were up to him, he would keep her here forever, his precious queen, his and his alone, because he didn't want to share her with anyone else. Not even with her sisters. He had nothing against them, he was sure they loved Emerald, but they had families, and all he had in the world was his sweet jewel.

His life hadn't been full of rainbows and roses, and Emerald was so much more than he deserved. He'd done things he wasn't proud of—a lot of things he wasn't proud of—bad things that should land him in prison, and he knew that he could never deserve something as good and sweet and pure as Emerald even if he spent a million years trying.

Noah walked into their bedroom and found it empty, the doors to the balcony were open and he sighed, he was sure she was standing out there dressed in her nightgown with no consideration of the dropping nighttime temperatures as winter approached. Grabbing a shawl from the back of the rocking chair in the corner, a chair he often woke in the middle of the night to find Emerald curled up in when nightmares prevented her from sleeping, he headed out to join her.

Despite the chill in the air, it was nice out. The sky had cleared up a little, and while he could see dark puffs floating across the inky black expanse, the moon shone brightly, and the stars twinkled merrily. Noah knew from experience that Emerald could stare at the sky for hours. He knew why, it had taken a lot of work, but he had managed to pry out of her what had happened to her between the time she was sold, and when she landed on his doorstep, and he knew all about the man who had thrown her outdoors to live with his dogs.

That man was no longer among the living.

He had seen to that.

There was no way he was allowing anyone who had hurt his sweet Emerald to go unpunished. He could have just turned the man into the cops, but that would have led to questions he didn't want to answer, so having him killed was just the easier option.

Anyone who presented themselves as a threat to Emerald would be eliminated. He wouldn't hesitate to take them out of the equation, because no one hurt his woman, and no one was going to come between them and take her away from him. She was his, he had been the one who brought her back from the brink when she had been all but the shell of a human being, he was the one who had tended to her, caring for her when she couldn't care for herself, and helping her to learn to live again.

"Don't you feel the cold?" he asked as he walked up behind her and draped the shawl around her shoulders. More evenings than not, he found her out here, it was so often that it was almost part of their nightly routine. He'd check on a few things after dinner then come up here, ready to make love to his woman before they turned in for the night only to find her not in bed but out daydreaming on the balcony.

"I was too busy watching the stars," she said, leaning back into him.

Her body rubbed against him as she snuggled closer, her innocent little mind having no idea how she turned him on with such a simple action. "Did you eat dinner?" he asked. She had a bad habit sometimes of forgetting that she was no longer someone's toy, that she was a person who mattered, and as such, it was perfectly acceptable to go to the kitchen and ask the cook to make her something to eat.

"I ..." the way she trailed off gave him his answer.

"You're the lady of the manor," he reminded her sternly, turning her around to face him. "You should have gone and asked for something to eat if I was working late."

"I'm sorry," she murmured, dropping her gaze to the floor.

Sometimes he wanted to shake some sense into her. Why couldn't she accept that she wasn't his possession? He'd told her more times than he could count, and it frustrated him that she didn't believe it.

"What are the rules about apologizing in this house?" he demanded, lowering his voice so she knew he was serious.

"Unless you have done something rude or nasty there is no need to apologize," she parroted.

Her obvious fear abated his anger, and he scooped her up into his arms, kissing her because he knew it would soothe her.

It did.

As his lips touched hers, he felt her relax into his arms, she gave a small sigh, then her fingers lifted to curl into his hair.

Carrying her into the bedroom, he closed the door behind them, then laid Emerald down on the bed. Last night he had forgone sex because Emerald had been distracted and upset and hadn't been in the mood, but tonight he was going to have his way with the woman he loved, then go to sleep holding her in his arms.

Noah balanced himself on one arm so his weight didn't crush Emerald's small frame, and without tearing his mouth away from hers, he pushed her white silk nightgown up around her hips, and since she never wore underwear because she knew he didn't like it, his hand immediately began to touch her. He inserted a finger, then a second, and a third, stretching her, stroking her, teasing her with his thumb as he plunged deep.

Emerald whimpered beneath him, her hips moving restlessly, wordlessly begging him for more.

But he didn't like wordless begging.

He wanted to hear her beg before he gave her what she wanted.

He increased the pressure, enough to have her squirming but not enough to give her any relief, he knew how to get her to say what he wanted without outright ordering her to.

"Noah, please," she whispered against his mouth.

"Please what?" he asked.

"Please, I need you ..."

"You need me to do what?"

"Inside me," she said with a shudder. "I need you inside me. Now."

"There's my girl," he said, pleased that she had given in so quickly tonight. Maybe she was coming to realize that there was nothing sexier than begging your partner to give you what you were both burning for.

Freeing himself, he entered her in one swift move, plunging deep and filling her up. She was hot and tight, and everything that he needed. Noah began to thrust faster, deeper, perhaps a little rougher than he should have given Emerald's history, but he knew that she wanted this as much as he did.

Reaching between them as he thrust in and out, he squeezed her between his thumb and forefinger, and she came with a strangled scream. He came a split second later, growling out his own pleasure as it rippled over him in wave after wave.

Pulling out of her, he lay down at her side and spooned her against him, nibbling on her shoulder. "See, a girl who begs always gets her reward."

She gave a small—but embarrassed—laugh, and her fingers curled around his forearm. This sweet, shy girl was everything to him. She thought that he had saved her, but she was wrong. She was the one who had saved him, stopped him from going down a dangerous path from which he would never have been able to return. She needed to eat some dinner, and then she needed her rest, but before he wrapped her in a sheet and took her down to the kitchen, he wanted a moment to just hold her.

His precious Emerald.

The light of his life.

The only good thing he had ever done.

~

8:47 P.M.

"Nothing," she muttered, annoyed.

Sapphire had been going over and over the information they had on Bobby Tompson, hoping that something would jump out at her, but so far it hadn't.

He was involved, she was sure of it, which meant there was something, somewhere, that would incriminate him, she just had to find it.

It was all she could think about.

She barely remembered driving home from work, she had no idea what they'd eaten for dinner, she couldn't remember what story she had read to Leo when she put him to bed, she had no idea if she and Gideon had made conversation since she'd been home, her brain had been consumed with this case.

Emerald was counting on her.

How could she let her sister down?

Again.

Images of the night she and her sisters had been sold flashed through her mind. She had been an impetuous teenager, boisterous, outgoing, confident, and a little too sure of her own abilities. She had tried to run from the men who had come into the bedroom she shared with Emerald in the middle of the night, planning to tie them up and take them away. When they had caught her before she made it out the window, intending to run to a neighbor's house for help, she'd tried to fight them off.

It had been a ridiculously mismatched fight.

Talk about a David and Goliath situation.

Only this time, it hadn't been David who had won, it was Goliath who was victorious, and those men had taken away her and her sisters.

She had been the first to be saved and that had eaten away at her for the last fourteen years.

Survivor's guilt.

That's what Gideon told her she was suffering from. Survivor's guilt was when someone felt like in surviving something that others hadn't, they had done something wrong. She wasn't sure that she would describe herself quite that way, but she couldn't deny the fact that she had been spared some of what her sisters had gone through still affected her.

A hand landed on her arm, and she startled, knocking her chair over and landing with a loud crash on the hardwood floor.

"Mama," a concerned little voice called out, and her son scrambled to climb over the chair to get to her.

As she struggled to right herself, Sapphire heard smothered laughing and looked up to find her husband standing in the doorway trying to hide the fact that he was snickering, but doing a poor job of it.

"Mama hurt?" Leo asked, his green eyes, just like her own—just like Emerald's—stared at her, full of concern. Their son had inherited her desire to save people and his father's desire to help people, but he had definitely not gotten his daddy's light-hearted nature, calm, and sense of humor. Leo was more like her, serious, a little neurotic at times, intense, and sometimes a little too focused on work and not on having fun. For a two-year-old Leo was very smart, he loved to learn things, read books, ask Siri questions, and try new things, but playing and being a carefree toddler, not so much.

"No, Mama is okay," she assured her son. "What are you doing up? It's way past your bedtime," she said with a glance at the clock. "We tucked you in over an hour ago."

"I woke up," Leo explained with a shrug like he didn't have a better explanation.

"Well, you need to go right back into bed, mister, you need your sleep," she said, picking him up and carrying him toward the door. "I can't believe you laughed at me." She swatted at Gideon as she walked past him.

"You looked funny all twisted up in the chair," Gideon said with a smirk.

Sapphire rolled her eyes at her husband. In the four years they had been together, he had helped her loosen up a lot. She might not ever be a free-spirited, giggly, relaxed person, but she had learned that while her job was important there were other things in her life that should be important too.

"Back into bed you go," she said in Leo's room as she laid him in his race car bed and tucked him in.

"Story?" he asked hopefully.

"Nope, you get two stories a night," she reminded him, smoothing his soft brown hair. It was getting long, he had been mostly bald up until his first birthday, and even now it continued to grow slowly, but he might be nearly ready for his very first haircut.

"Please," he begged, batting his big green eyes.

"No way." She shook her head firmly. She was definitely a strict parent, Gideon might be lenient every now and then, but she knew the kind of man she wanted Leo to be when he grew up, and she was determined to do whatever it took to get him there. "You want to listen to some music as you go back to sleep?"

"Okay." He nodded enthusiastically. Leo loved music, and she wouldn't be surprised if they had a little musician on their hands. In another year or two they'd have him start learning an instrument.

She stood up, scrolled through the playlist on Leo's iPad, choosing one, she started it playing, then leaned over to kiss his little forehead. "Love you, sweetheart, sweet dreams."

"Love you, Mama," he said, kissing her cheek.

"Say night-night to daddy," she told him.

"Night, Daddy," Leo called out.

"Night, Leo." Gideon came over and kissed their son.

Switching the nightlight on and the main light off, Sapphire closed Leo's bedroom door and immediately headed back toward her study.

"Uh-uh." Gideon caught her arm and stopped her. "You've worked enough for tonight."

"I have more I want to do before I go to bed," she protested.

"Like last night? I know that this case is eating you up, but you need rest," he reminded her. "I know you think that you're superwoman and you can do things us mere mortals can't, but I love you, and Leo and I need you, you have to take care of yourself. Especially now," he added.

She was wavering, her instincts were telling her that she had to keep working. How could she find who had her sister if she didn't dedicate every single second she had to working the case? And yet, the sensible side of her brain was telling her that her husband was right. What if she missed that one important piece of information because she was too tired?

"I suppose you're right," she relented with a sigh.

"Of course I'm right. I'm *always* right." He grinned at her, dragging her closer for a kiss.

"You have such an ego," she said, resting her head on his sturdy chest. She didn't mind that Gideon liked to push her buttons, and tease her, and that he always thought he was right. She knew it was because he loved her and he wanted to remind her that having fun just to have fun was an important part of life too.

"And you love it." One of his large hands trailed up and down her spine, making her shiver. She knew that he wanted a little grown up time before they went to bed, but she was so tired. Now that she had made the decision to stop work for the night, all she wanted to do was curl up under the covers, lay her head on her pillow, and go to sleep.

"Can we pass on making love tonight? I know we haven't done it in a while, but I'm so tired."

"Of course." Gideon kissed the top of her head. "What about a massage before you go to sleep."

"I never say no to a massage," she said with another sigh, a delighted one this time.

Gathering her into his arms, Gideon carried her down the hall to their room, and set her down on the bed. She removed her sweater and jeans, putting them away in the hamper in the ensuite, then wearing nothing but her white cotton panties with the little ribbon bow on the front, she returned to the bed and sank down into the soft, comfortable mattress.

Gideon joined her a moment later, dressed in only his boxers, looking irresistibly sexy, and she almost relented and decided that they could make love quickly before going to sleep, but then her husband gently turned her over onto her stomach, and straddled her thighs. The second his hands touched her shoulders and began to work their magic, all thoughts of sex fled her mind.

This was heaven.

His hands kneaded her tense muscles, bit by bit, working away the stress and the anxiety of the last few days.

This was the closest she had ever been to finding Emerald, and that had to be a good thing. Who knows, maybe by Christmas there would be another member of the family sitting around the table, and not another baby. It seemed almost too good to be true, but finding her little sister finally seemed to be within her grasp.

Gideon's magic hands were relaxing her mind as well as her body, and by the time he had worked his way halfway down her back, she was fast asleep.

CHAPTER
Seven

November 27th
10:01 A.M.

Sapphire couldn't help but imagine what Alice Lincoln's final days must have been like.

Well, actually she kind of could, and that made it worse.

Early this morning, they had finally got a hit on the DNA samples taken from the woman found in the woods in the database of missing people. The woman was twenty-nine-year-old Alice Lincoln, she had worked as a manager of a high-end clothing store, she'd been single, never married and no children, but a large extended family with seven siblings, some of whom had their own families, and her elderly parents who were both in shaky health but alive.

Alice had been missing for nearly a year and a half.

Plenty of time for whoever had abducted her to cut her stomach open to simulate the appendectomy scar, and to cut her foot to simulate the scar Emerald had there, and for both of those wounds to heal and begin to form scars.

Eighteen months.

That was a long time for Alice to be held prisoner, and although she hadn't been gone anywhere close to that long when she and her sisters were sold, she could empathize closely with the fear and terror the woman would have been feeling. There were no other wounds—healed or otherwise—on Alice's body besides the missing hands, the beaten face, and the marks from where she had been strangled, so they knew that Alice hadn't been tortured during the time she was held captive. That meant that the entire point of abducting and killing the woman was to make them believe that it was Emerald's body found in the woods.

Whoever had killed Alice had obviously been hoping they were convinced enough that the body was Emerald's, that they wouldn't run DNA tests, if it hadn't been for Elijah believing the scars were too fresh they might not have.

Then what would have become of Emerald?

This was the closest she'd ever been to actually finding her sister, and she had invested literally thousands of hours into the case since she became a cop, there was no way she was letting this opportunity slip through her fingers.

"What are you thinking about?" Elijah asked as they parked the car outside a nice ranch with a slightly overgrown garden.

"Alice, Emerald, this case. What Alice's last days must have been like, where my sister is right this second." She listed off the things weighing on her mind. Last night she had dreamt about Emerald, her sister was scared and alone and in pain, and every time she thought she had found Emerald, her sister disappeared like smoke. Apparently, she had been thrashing and moaning in her sleep to the point that Gideon had eventually woken her up to break the nightmares.

"Hopefully, when we find who killed Alice, we'll find who has your sister."

"And then we can finally bring her home." That had been her dream ever since she had been rescued. Back then, she hadn't had a home waiting for her, she had gone briefly into the foster care system before an aunt had stepped up and taken her in. But now there was a whole big family of sisters, and brothers-in-law, and nieces and nephews waiting for Emerald.

"That's what Diamond is hoping for," Elijah said as they both got out of the car.

"Then let's make it happen," she said, full of determination as they headed up the garden path.

The couple was obviously waiting for them, watching out the window because the second they stepped onto the porch, the front door was flung open, and a pretty brunette who looked to be in her mid-thirties looked at them expectantly. "Detectives?" she asked.

"Detective Hatcher-Barlow and this is Detective Newton, you are?" Sapphire asked.

"I'm Alice's older sister, Margot," the woman replied. Alice was the fifth child of eight, three boys, then a sister, then Alice, and another three boys after Alice, Sapphire guessed that with six brothers the sisters had been close. She knew what it was like to have a sister gone and not know what had happened to them, and while she knew Alice's death would leave a huge hole that could never be filled, at least Margot and her family had closure now.

"May we come in?" Elijah asked when the woman made no move to show them inside.

"Oh, yes, of course, I'm sorry, I just can't believe that it's finally ended this way. We kept hoping that ..." Margot trailed off, but they knew how her sentence ended. The family had been hoping that this would end with Alice being returned to them alive. Unfortunately, they hadn't gotten their happy ending, and Sapphire prayed her family would be luckier.

"Do you live here with your parents?" Sapphire asked as Margot led them through the house.

"No, I actually live next door with my husband and our four kids. It's nice to be close to Mom and Dad, especially as they get older and aren't able to get about as easily as they used to," Margot explained. "Mom, Dad, these are the detectives," she said as they walked into the kitchen.

An elderly couple rose from their seats. "Good morning, detectives," Mrs. Lincoln greeted them.

"Please sit down," Mr. Lincoln said, his voice heavy with sadness.

"We're very sorry for your loss," Sapphire said as she and Elijah took seats at the table. Those words never felt like enough, but what this couple needed wasn't condolences, it was for her to find the person who had stolen their daughter from them.

"Can you tell us a little about Alice?" Elijah asked.

"She was such a sweet girl," Mrs. Lincoln told them, her eyes going all dreamy. "She was such a kind soul, if helping someone was within her power then she'd do it, sometimes even when she shouldn't she did. There were times when she wouldn't have any food in her apartment because she'd used her last few dollars to buy something for a homeless person or to pay a friend's bill. She loved animals, her dream job was to work with horses."

The woman might as well be speaking about Emerald. Alice sounded just like her little sister, was that why the killer had chosen her?

"Was Alice involved with anyone?" she asked.

"She had been up until about a month before she disappeared," Mr. Lincoln told them.

"Was the ex looked into by the cops when she went missing?" Elijah asked.

"He was, but he'd already moved out of state, so they thought it was unlikely he had anything to do with it," Mrs. Lincoln replied.

"Margot, was there any other man in her life, maybe someone that she told you about that she didn't tell anyone else?" Sapphire asked. If anyone would know, then it would be Alice's sister.

"Not that she ever told me," Margot replied. "After she broke up with Ted, she was thinking about making other changes in her life. She wanted to finally live her dream instead of just working a job to pay the bills."

That Alice had never had a chance to fulfill those dreams was just one of the many unfairnesses of life. "What can you tell us about the abduction? Who reported her missing?"

"I did," Margot told them. "I had plans to go out to dinner with Alice the Friday before she went missing, but I had to cancel last minute because two of my kids came down with the flu. She said it was fine and that she was going to have a bubble bath, watch her favorite movie, and then go to bed early. I remember she was excited because she'd just moved into this new place and it had a bathtub, the apartment she had shared with her ex only had a walk-in shower. I texted her a couple of times over the weekend, but she never replied, and I got distracted because then the other two kids got sick, and then my husband as well, and I was busy running around taking care of everyone. By Monday morning everyone was on the mend, and I realized that she had never gotten back to me so I went around to her place. The backdoor was broken, and there was blood inside but no Alice. I called 911, and that was how this all started."

"Were there any suspects?" Elijah asked.

"Not really, they ruled out her ex pretty quickly and there never really was any others," Margot replied.

"You said that Alice had recently moved, how recently?" Sapphire asked.

"Only about a week before she disappeared," Mr. Lincoln told them.

"Where was she living before that?" A week in a new place meant it was unlikely that the killer had seen her there. Since the point was to make them think Emerald was dead, they had no doubt been scouting for the perfect decoy woman for at least a few weeks before the abduction.

"Apartment four hundred and twenty-six, eighty-two Grove Street," Mrs. Lincoln answered.

Sapphire felt her mouth drop open in surprise.

That apartment was right next to where Bobby Tompson lived.

There was no way that Bobby could deny knowing Alice Lincoln.

So many questions flew through her mind.

Was Bobby Tompson involved in human trafficking?

Was Alice also a human trafficking victim, perhaps pimped out while they waited for her scars to heal?

Was Bobby Tompson the one who had Emerald right now?

He was the same age as she was so he wasn't involved in the initial buying of her and her sisters, but he could have become involved at a later date.

As soon as they finished up they were going straight to Bobby's work to bring him down to the station. Once again her gut was correct, Bobby Tompson was in this up to his eyeballs.

∽

12:24 P.M.

Emerald wandered the halls of the large house.

When she had first come here, she had been overwhelmed by the size of it and the grandeur of each room. Everywhere you turned there was a gorgeous painting, or a sculpture, or a vase, or something else that caught your eye and drew you in for a closer look. Despite the size of the mansion, there wasn't a very large staff, Noah was a private person, and he didn't like to let a lot of people inside his world, there were a couple of maids, a couple of gardeners, two cooks, and Noah's personal assistant, and that was it.

That was just the way she liked it.

She didn't want to see people, she didn't want to have them look at her, talk about her behind her back. She knew that her past was never going to go away, the scars—both physical and psychological—just went too deep, the impact would be lifelong, but she didn't want to be defined by it. If she left this safe haven Noah had created for her, then she would forever be the girl who had been sold to human traffickers, the sex trafficking victim, the woman who had been raped and tortured so many times she had lost count.

But here she could just be Emerald.

She no longer thought of herself as Emerald Hatcher. Emerald Hatcher was a girl with emotionally detached, distant parents. She had four older sisters who she loved. She had friends and boys that she liked. She wanted to live on a farm and help animals when she grew up. She had hopes and dreams for the future. She was a free spirit, she loved to laugh, she loved to help people, she had a big, warm heart and wanted to make the whole world smile.

That Emerald was gone.

She didn't exist any longer.

She had been beaten down until she just evaporated.

Now she was Emerald.

Just Emerald.

This Emerald was quiet and reserved, she wasn't comfortable speaking unless she was spoken to, she didn't like to see people, and if she could live the rest of her life in solitude, she would be happy. This Emerald still loved animals, and still wanted to help them, but her dreams for the future were just to live quietly and peacefully. She didn't have parents or sisters, because having a family was just harder than she could handle.

This Emerald had one reason for living.

Noah.

As if by thinking his name she brought him into being, he appeared at the end of the hallway. Looking irresistibly sexy in the black pants and white shirt, rolled up to the elbows, and with the top few buttons undone, that were his usual attire. He smiled when he saw her and walked toward her, making her heart flutter.

He always knew what she needed, and he was never afraid to take control of the situation, because in reality, if he didn't she never would. When he reached her, he pulled her in and planted a kiss on her lips. When he kissed her it was like she was transported out of this world, into another, better, world.

If it was possible, this was how she would always stay, cocooned in Noah's arms, his heart beating against her, his lips on hers, easing away the pain and suffering she had experienced that still haunted her.

That was the thing about trauma, it was forever.

It didn't go away.

Ever.

It was always there, kind of like your shadow. Sometimes you couldn't see it, sometimes it appeared to be hidden away, but it was still there, all it needed was for someone or something to shine a light on it, and it reared its ugly head.

"What did you do this morning, darling?" Noah asked, stroking her hair.

"Nothing much, I read a little, wrote a little," she replied, knowing that he wanted an answer but not having much of one to give him.

Besides spending time out in the stables with the horses, she spent the majority of her time reading or writing poems, or occasionally she would draw or paint a little, maybe play a little music. Although she knew Noah would be angry with her for it, she often felt like she was a burden. What would Noah's life look like if she wasn't in it?

She knew the answer to that.

He would go into work every day instead of spending most days working from home. He would go out to parties and dinners with friends, he would get married, have kids, spend a lot less time at home.

But because of her, he was basically a recluse.

What did she contribute to their lives?

Nothing.

She didn't work, she didn't bring in any money, she just took, and took, and took some more.

Noah should be annoyed with her for that.

If she was him, she wasn't sure that she would be able to tolerate someone like herself.

"What are you thinking?" Noah asked, his shrewd blue eyes bored into hers as though he possessed the ability to read her mind. "Something upset you."

She could lie, but Noah didn't like her to lie, and she wasn't very good at it anyway. He always knew when she was hiding something from him. "I was just thinking that I didn't really do much this morning. You work hard so we can live in this beautiful house and I just read and wrote a new poem," she murmured in a rush before she lost her nerve.

"Don't you think that if I wanted you to work that I would request that you get a job?" Noah asked, taking her chin between his thumb and forefinger and holding it tightly enough that it gave a small pinch of pain.

"Y-yes," she stammered.

"And don't you think that I love treating you like the queen I believe you to be?"

"Y-yes," she stammered again. She knew that Noah thought of her as his queen, it was why he bought her beautiful dresses even though they never went out anywhere, it was why she had enough pieces of jewelry that she could open her own store. But she didn't see herself as a queen, she'd had it drilled into her for years that she was nothing, and queens weren't nothings, and nothings couldn't be queens.

"Then let's not have any more talk about you not contributing, you give me everything that I want," Noah said firmly, like his say so was all that was needed to change her thinking, even though they both knew from experience it didn't work that way.

"Okay," she agreed obediently. Obedience was a hard vice to break, she was so used to deferring to someone else that she wasn't sure she could ever stop doing it.

"I asked Paul to pack us a picnic, it's cold out, but I thought we could go down by the waterfall, there's that little rocky alcove that would make a perfect sheltered place for us to sit. How does that sound?"

"Delightful," she beamed, and clapped her hands, she loved it when Noah took time out of his day to spend with her. He worked long hours, and she often didn't see him until dinnertime or later, so she cherished these special moments because they were little treasures. She knew how lucky she was to have a man like Noah even look at her given what had happened to her, and that he not only gave her a place to live, and beautiful clothes, and the freedom to do what she wanted all day every day, but he also gave her himself.

"Why don't you go and put on something warmer, and I'll meet you down in the kitchen," he suggested.

"Okay," she agreed. "I won't be long."

"Wear the green coat," he told her. "The one that matches those stunning eyes of yours."

"Okay," she agreed again. Emerald turned and headed back down the hall toward their bedroom, but went only a couple of steps before she stopped and returned to Noah's side, wrapping her arms around his waist and pressing her cheek to his rock hard chest. As much as she knew that she couldn't face people it sometimes got lonely locked away here. She was like the bird in the gilded cage, she had been trained to find safety in the cage, and freedom was a scary thing, but wandering these empty halls day after day sometimes the loneliness was crushing.

"Thank you for taking the time out of your day to spend time with me. It means so much to me."

"It's not a chore," he said with a chuckle.

"I know, but you do so much for me, and you're so busy, yet you always look for ways to make me feel special. Not many men would do that."

"I'm not most men."

"No, you're not," she said, snuggling closer. "I love you so much, Noah."

～

4:33 P.M.

"Do you think he packed up and ran?" Sapphire asked Elijah as they sat in their car outside Bobby Tompson's apartment building. They had been sitting here most of the day, after speaking with Alice Lincoln's family they had gone over to Bobby's work where they'd been told that he hadn't been in yet today, so they'd come here. They'd tried his buzzer several times, but he hadn't replied, so they'd buzzed a neighbor who let them into the building, and they'd tried knocking on Bobby's door, but there was still no response.

At least they had irrefutable proof that Bobby knew Alice.

While speaking with the neighbor, they'd asked him if Bobby knew Alice and he said that he did and that he had been friends with her and her ex-boyfriend. He hadn't known that she'd been missing, saying he had been friends more with Alice's ex than with her, but he remembered several occasions when he, Alice and her boyfriend, Bobby, and several other neighbors had gotten together for dinners or parties.

Bobby knew Alice.

Bobby's car had been seen on several occasions in the same vicinity that Alice's body had been found.

Bobby was involved in Alice's murder.

In her mind, it was as simple as that, but in order to prove it in a court of law they would need something more than circumstantial evidence. There had been no fibers, no fingerprints, no DNA found on Alice's body, so using forensics to prove Bobby was the killer was out of the question. They needed to find a motive and go from there, or they needed to get a confession.

Her money was *not* on getting a confession.

"I don't think he'd run, not yet at least," Elijah answered her question. "I think he knows we don't have anything concrete on him, and he's probably cocky enough to believe that we never will find anything. Running makes him look guilty, I think he's going to stay and continue to deny everything."

"We know that Emerald was sold to human traffickers. If someone wants us to believe that she's dead then it has to be someone involved in trafficking that ordered Alice's death, either someone who wants to sell Emerald or someone who bought her. The logical next step is that Bobby is also involved in trafficking, and if he is involved in trafficking, then he likely has access to a lot of money."

"Or whoever ordered her death does."

"You think that it wasn't Bobby?"

"I believe that Bobby is involved somehow, but we don't know exactly how yet."

"We need warrants to go through his financials and everything," she said. They knew Bobby didn't own any other properties, but they would need a warrant to get access to his bank statements and any investments and such like. She was sure they would find the answers they needed there, but first they had to convince a judge to give them a warrant. She was about to say more when she saw a car turn into the street up ahead of where they were parked. "Elijah, look. It's Bobby's car."

"Told you he wouldn't run," her partner teased.

Sapphire rolled her eyes. "Let's go wait for him at the door, I want to see his face when he sees us there," she said, opening her car door. They knew that there were only two ways into the building, and neither of those was from the parking garage. Once he parked his car, he would have to come around to either the front or the back entrance, and since the front was closer she suspected this would be where he came.

She and Elijah crossed the street, and just as they were walking up to the front door she saw Bobby coming out of the garage. He had his phone in his hand, and he was typing away furiously, he was dressed in a nice suit—an expensive-looking suit—and he looked like he had been at work even though they knew he hadn't, perhaps he was meeting with someone else, maybe whoever was associated with what happened to Alice.

All of a sudden Bobby looked up.

His eyes met hers.

For a second he froze, staring back at her, a blank expression on his face.

Then he turned and ran.

"I hate it when they do that," she muttered, taking off after him.

"I'll go round the back," Elijah called out, dashing off in the other direction.

Sapphire had no idea whether Bobby intended to get back to his car and try to drive off, or whether he might carjack someone to make his getaway, or if he was simply going to try to lose her in the maze of cars in the parking garage and then escape on foot, but she was determined that the only way he was leaving here was in handcuffs.

She was a fast runner, and although she didn't work out as obsessively as her sister Amethyst did, she was in great shape, and she started to gain on Bobby.

It seemed he didn't intend to go for a car, either his own or someone else's because he headed straight toward the staircase. That seemed counter-productive, to head up when someone was chasing you, but she'd take it, it certainly increased the odds in her favor.

"Bobby, stop," she called out to him as he took off up the stairs.

He ignored her.

Her legs were shorter than his, and he was taking the steps two at a time, so the distance between them grew a little as they ran up flight after flight. She kept expecting him to veer off at any second and go through one of the doors to a different level of the garage, try to lose her that way, but he didn't. He knew that she was following him, and he had to know that she wasn't going to stop, so she didn't know why he didn't just surrender.

She was starting to get a little breathless by the time she heard the door to the roof slam closed. He'd gone all the way up to the roof, and she still had no idea what he hoped to achieve by doing that. Maybe he thought he could hide, then when she came up and started looking for him, he would sneak back inside. It didn't seem like the smartest plan, but then again, most criminals weren't smart. If there had been any doubt about whether or not Bobby was involved in Alice's death, it had been erased by the fact that he had run from them.

As she burst through the door and out into the bright fall sunshine, she saw Bobby running straight toward the edge of the building.

Her stomach dropped as she realized what he intended to do.

He was going to jump.

He was ahead of her, and there was no way she could reach him before he threw himself over the edge.

There was only one thing she could think of that would stop him.

She pulled out her weapon. "Bobby, stop or I'm going to shoot you," she called out.

He didn't slow down.

Aiming for the man's leg, she fired.

Bobby screamed and dropped to the ground, clutching at his leg.

Putting her gun back in its holster, she started running again. Her chest was heaving from the exertion of running up ten flights of stairs, but she barely noticed that she was gasping for air as excitement pulsed through her. She had him, and that meant she was one step closer to finding Emerald.

As she approached Bobby, he kicked his good leg at her, she dodged to the side, and pulled out her handcuffs, intending to get him cuffed and under her control. He swung a fist at her, but she ducked and reached for his shoulder to flip him over. The second fist he swung at her connected, getting her right in the center of the chest and making her see stars as her already oxygen-deprived body took another hit.

"I didn't like that," she muttered, managing to flip the man who was twice her size onto his stomach and slap on handcuffs. Pulling out her phone with hands that were beginning to tremble, she dialed her partner's number.

"Where are you?" Elijah demanded as soon as he answered.

"Roof," she wheezed. "He was going to jump, I had to shoot him, he's going to be fine, but we need an ambulance."

"I'll call one, I'm coming up."

Disconnecting the call, she put her phone away then looked down at the man who had twisted so he was staring up at her belligerently.

"I didn't do anything," he said sullenly.

"Then why did you run?"

"Because you were chasing me."

"I was chasing you *because* you ran. You did it, you killed that woman, we found out who she was. Alice Lincoln, your neighbor. We know that you knew her, and we know your car was seen in the area where she was found. You killed her, Bobby."

"I didn't kill anyone," he said, but his gaze dropped. "My car was never out by the waterfall, and I didn't kill Alice Lincoln."

"Then why were you going to jump off a ten-story building? You killed Alice, and you wanted us to think it was Emerald. Do you know where she is?" Sapphire leaned down, grabbed the man's lapels and shook him. "Do you know where my sister is? Do you know who has her? Do you know if she's still alive?"

Slowly the man's eyes met hers, and this time there was something sinister about him. "I. Don't. Know. Anything. I. Didn't. Do. Anything."

He could deny it all he wanted, but there was only one reason a thirty-year-old man would run from the cops with plans of throwing himself off a building. He was guilty, and more than that, he was afraid of whoever he was working with.

~

10:51 P.M.

There was nothing in the world she loved to do more than watch her daughter sleep.

Ruby Hatcher-Willow stood beside two-year-old Chloe's crib and watched as her little girl's chest rose and fell with each breath she took.

Chloe had her blonde locks and blue eyes just like her own and her husband's. She had Judah's smile, and her laugh, and the sweetest little voice.

Every time Chloe called her Mama her heart swelled a little bit bigger, some days it felt so full of love that it was going to burst.

She still had to pinch herself sometimes to make sure she wasn't dreaming, that this really was her life. She was such a lucky woman, after her parents sold her and her sisters, she had thought that her life was over. Even after she had managed to escape she had been plagued with post-traumatic stress disorder and suicidal thoughts, to the point where she hadn't even been able to comprehend the idea that one day she might be happy.

But she was.

A crime spree in her neighborhood had led her to stop pretending that she didn't have feelings for one of her sister Sapphire's colleagues, and take that leap of faith that led her to find true love.

It all sounded so fairytale-like.

Okay, so a dark, twisted fairytale, not the kind you would read to small children, but a fairytale nonetheless. Sometimes it was out of the darkness that the most beautiful things grew. And it was definitely out of darkness that her relationship with Judah had begun. But now it was a thing of beauty, a happy marriage, a beautiful child, the prospect of so many more years of joy to come.

How could that be anything but a fairytale?

The best thing to grow out of her life with Judah was this precious little girl. It was hard to believe that her sweet, sassy, little ball of energy had been in the pediatric intensive care unit fighting for her life just six months ago. Chloe had contracted bacterial meningitis and gone from fever and vomiting to barely conscious in less than twenty-four hours.

Ruby didn't think she would ever forget the feeling of clutching her tiny daughter in her arms as Judah sped to the hospital well and truly smashing the speed limit.

Nor would she forget the feeling of having her little girl snatched from her arms by doctors who spirited her away, or seeing her lying in a bed with a tube down her throat to breathe for her. Or being told by doctors that although they would do everything they could, they didn't think her daughter was going to survive.

The whole thing had been the worst kind of nightmare.

There was no waking up and realizing it had all been a dream. It was like life had decided to taunt her with happiness, dangled a husband and child in front of her, teased her with the idea of a happy ending, only to snatch it back when she reached out and took it.

Judah had been her tower of strength. He hadn't left her side once during those dark days, he hadn't urged her to leave the hospital to get some rest, or told her she had to take care of herself. He had known that she couldn't leave her daughter to fight for her life alone. Although the best she could do was sit at her daughter's bedside and hold her tiny little hand, it was enough to make her feel like she was doing something. Should the worst happen and Chloe's small toddler body couldn't fight off the disease, then she didn't want her daughter dying alone.

By some miracle, Chloe *had* managed to fight off the disease and come back to them. Slowly at first, her strength had begun to return, until now, six months later, she was back to her old self.

While Chloe would never remember those terrifying weeks, neither she nor Judah would ever forget them.

Her daughter was a miracle, and a reminder that even when life was at its darkest point, light could be just around the corner.

She had learned that when Judah had come into her life, and again when she got Chloe back from the brink of the grave, and she was determined she wasn't going to waste a second of her life not living it to the fullest. She still battled suicidal thoughts, although much less regularly than she had a couple of years ago, but she was done beating herself up about it. She had nothing to be ashamed about and a lot to live for. She was a survivor, Judah was a survivor, and they had passed that trait along to their daughter.

Carefully she reached down into the crib, intending to pick up Chloe's sleeping form when a voice in the doorway spoke.

"You sure you want to risk waking her?"

"Perfectly positive." She shot a smile over her shoulder. There was always time to sleep, but moments like these, when she could pick up her sleeping daughter and hold her in her arms, they were short-lived.

Before she knew it, Chloe would be too big to carry around, then she would be more interested in friends than spending time at home with them, then there would be boyfriends, and before she knew it, her baby would be a grown-up with babies of her own.

One blink and a lifetime seemed to pass by.

One blink and things could forever be changed.

One blink could take you from the light to the dark, or the dark to the light.

Scooping Chloe off the mattress and into her arms, her daughter stirred a little but didn't wake, and Ruby carried her to the rocking chair in the corner of the room. Soon they would be saying goodbye to the nursery décor as their baby moved from being a toddler to being a little girl. They had already been shopping for a bed, and Chloe had been talking about wanting unicorns on her walls instead of the sweet Noah's Ark scene that she and Judah had chosen when they started preparing the room for the upcoming birth of their first baby.

Judah came and squatted beside her, resting one hand on her shoulder while his other stroked Chloe's soft blond locks. She loved this man so much. He had given her more than she could ever have asked for, understanding, unconditional love, the baring of his own dark secrets so she didn't feel alone, and a precious child.

Every time she looked at him she felt blessed.

Judah was one in a million, and she was so glad that their lives had cross paths and they had both found the happiness they thought would never be theirs.

Their lives were already complete, there wasn't a single thing more she would ask for even if she was granted a wish, but there was one more thing that she would like.

Another baby.

She wanted Chloe to grow up the way she had, with siblings who became your best friends once they no longer drove you crazy fighting over clothes and time in the bathroom.

"You want to put this little poppet back in her crib and go try to make another?" Judah asked, his mind obviously wandering to the same thing hers had.

"Do you really have to ask?"

Judah took Chloe from her arms and laid her back in her crib, then took her hand and guided her to her feet. They barely made it out of the nursery before they were ripping each other's clothes off. They had been together for three years now, but none of the heat, the passion, that bubbled between them had dulled. She was just as attracted to him as she had been when she was busy avoiding him so he didn't ask her out, and she hoped that it never faded.

Her lips found his, and her hand closed around him, squeezing tightly. Judah's hands found her breasts, kneading and teasing her nipples, and she knew that there was no way they were making it to the bedroom.

His hands circled her hips, and he lifted her, bracing her against the wall as he shoved the sweatpants he slept in down enough to free himself, then he plunged deep inside her. As he began to move, the friction made her tingle both inside and out, and little fuzzy dots appeared before her.

The dots grew as Judah moved faster, and she clawed at his back, dragging him closer.

The pressure inside her grew and grew and then burst, making the dots before her explode into stars as she tipped over the edge and fell into a pit of ecstasy.

Sagging against Judah, as she slowly floated down from the high, she trailed a lazy line of kisses along his jawline.

Had they conceived a new little baby tonight?

If they had, it was hardly the most romantic of conception stories, there had been no flowers or rose petals, not even a bed, but it had been raw, and real, and full of heat and passion.

It had been perfect.

Just like the new life she hoped was about to grow inside her.

CHAPTER *Eight*

November 28th
8:50 A.M.

"I hope Noah is on time today," Sapphire said as they waited in his office. She knew Noah, although not well. Among other things, his computer company made and installed custom home and business security systems. After a break-in at the house she used to share with her sisters—where Amethyst, Zeb, and Lucy now lived—that had almost ended in one of her sisters being killed, she had hired Noah to install the best security system money would buy, because nothing was too much to spend when it came to her family's safety.

"Is Noah ever late?" Elijah asked.

"No," she replied. She couldn't remember a time when Noah had ever been anything but punctual, usually down to the second. "But I particularly want him to be on time this morning, and you know how CEOs are, they always think that whatever they have on their plate is the most pressing thing."

She liked Noah, he was reserved and quietly confident, smart and paid attention to the smallest of details, which no doubt helped to make him a powerhouse in the computer world, but his world was about money and business decisions. She was sure that he could be ruthless when it came to his company, and she suspected the most important thing in the world to him was money and power.

Her world was about as far away from that as possible.

Growing up, her family hadn't been poor, but thanks to her mom's shopping addiction and her father's gambling addiction, money was tight. They always had what they needed but not much more. She had been a cop for most of her adult life, and while her pay wasn't bad, it certainly wasn't extravagant, Gideon made more than she did, and they lived comfortably, but nothing like the kind of money Noah had. To her, life wasn't about money, she had been saved, and she felt it was her duty to save others, so to be honest, she would be a cop even if she was paid nothing and had to live in a box under a bridge. Although having enough money to pay the bills and hire a good nanny for Leo was nice.

To her, family and her job were the most important things, and she wouldn't trade them for all the money in the world.

"I don't think he'll be late," Elijah said. "When we called and spoke with his secretary she made it sound like he rearranged his entire schedule so that he could be here to speak with us first thing this morning."

"That's true." From what she understood, Noah usually worked from his country estate, only coming into his offices when he had meetings.

Voices sounded outside the office where Noah's secretary had told them to wait, and from the deep timber of one of the voices she knew that Noah had arrived. She really was grateful that he had taken time out of his busy day to speak with them about Bobby Tompson. Bobby worked for Noah, and while she was sure Noah didn't personally know all of his employees, she was also sure that he had a say in every single person who was hired here so he had to know something about the man.

Right now something—however small—was better than nothing, and Bobby was giving them nothing. He was still insisting that he didn't know anything, that his car had never been out by the waterfall near where Alice was found, that he didn't remember the woman, and that he had no idea why they thought he was a killer.

She knew he was lying, she had seen that sinister look on his face yesterday when they had been alone up on the roof, and besides that, she didn't believe in coincidences.

"Good morning, Sapphire," Noah said as he breezed into the room. He was a good looking guy, had a great body, a smooth voice, billions of dollars, and an air of smug confidence that she knew a lot of women found attractive, she wondered why he was still single.

"Morning, Noah, thanks so much for meeting with us this morning," she said, standing to shake his hand as he came over to sit behind his desk.

"Of course, anything to help. How is the system running at your place? Did that bug get sorted out?"

"Yes, thank you, everything is running perfectly." Although she was a cop and confident that she could protect her family from any intruders, she wasn't there all the time. She worked unusual hours, and some days the nanny was there with Leo and her nephews and nieces, and she wanted to make sure her home was secure. Call her paranoid, and with a past like hers she knew she could be, but she had also made sure that the homes where her sisters lived were similarly well protected. When she and Gideon had bought their place, she'd had Noah's company install the security system, then done the same when Ruby moved in with Judah, and Diamond moved in with Elijah. You could never be too careful.

"So, what is all this about?" Noah asked, studying them with serious blue eyes. "Something about a murder my secretary said when she called me yesterday evening."

"Yes." She nodded her head for added emphasis. "We believe that one of your employees killed a woman whose body was found out by the waterfall," she explained, wondering if he ever had time to listen to the news, she suspected that the majority of Noah's time went into running his very successful business.

"Oh, I heard about that," Noah said, his face turning sad. "And you think that one of *my* employees had something to do with it?"

"We know he did. But he denies everything. When we went to pick him up yesterday to take him down to the station to be questioned, he ran from us, would have thrown himself off the top of a ten-story building if I hadn't shot him."

"You shot him?" Noah asked with a bemused smile. "Why am I not surprised to hear that?"

"Because you know how seriously I take my job," she replied.

"That I do." He nodded. "Which employee are you talking about? I know you know how large my business is, and that I have thousands of employees across multiple sites in several states, so I can't guarantee that I can give you much about the one you're looking into," he warned.

"Right now, we'll take whatever you can give us," she assured him. "It's Bobby Tompson. He's one of your executives here in these offices."

"Bobby Tompson?" Noah echoed. "You think he's a killer?"

"We do, why do you sound surprised about that?" Elijah asked.

"I guess I just wasn't expecting you to say Bobby's name."

Since they knew there was a possibility that Bobby was working with at least one other person, Sapphire asked, "Is there a name we could have given you that wouldn't have surprised you?"

"No, I guess not," Noah said thoughtfully. "I don't hire killers, if I suspected someone was unstable or involved in criminal activities, then they would never make it through the first round of interviews."

"What can you tell us about Bobby Tompson?" Elijah asked.

"Well, he's smart, he graduated top of his class, he's been with me for going on five years now, he works well as part of a team, he performs all assignments he's tasked with promptly and professionally. He has a good management style, he listens to people, makes sure everyone feels like their opinions are valued, and yet at the same time he's not afraid to be the one in charge and make tough decisions if the occasion calls for it."

"You seem to know quite a bit about him," Elijah noted.

"I guess it's because he's one of my hardest working executives," Noah replied.

"Have you had any problems with him?" she asked.

"None."

"Does he have any financial problems that you know of? Does he take inordinate amounts of time off? Has he had any problems with anyone in the office, any complaints about him, any issues of sexual misconduct or the likes?" Sapphire rattled off more questions. Bobby Tompson had abducted and held a woman prisoner for eighteen months before brutally strangling and beating her, she found it unlikely that no one had noticed anything unusual about the man.

"I know that you want me to answer yes to one or all of those questions, but I can't," Noah said, shooting her a sympathetic smile. "He's a model employee, clean record, he shows up every day, he works long hours, often weekends, without a complaint. And while I don't know about his personal finances, I know I pay him a small fortune, so unless he has an addiction of some sort, then I doubt he's struggling financially."

That wasn't what she wanted to hear.

What she wanted was for Noah to give them something that would help them crack this case wide open.

Emerald was counting on her.

"Do you mind if we spend some time here today, speak with some people who work with Bobby?" she asked.

"No, of course not," Noah answered. "You do what you have to do to find the man who killed that poor woman."

She would do exactly that.

The answers were here in this building, she could feel it, and she was determined to find them.

～

10:48 A.M.

To tell her or not to tell her.

Noah hadn't decided yet.

There were certain things that happened that Emerald didn't need to know. Not everything that he did was a concern of hers. Although he tried to live his life on the right side of the law, there were times when he had to cross over to the wrong side. It was what it was, and while it didn't really concern him, he knew that it would concern Emerald.

It was fair to say that Emerald should know to expect anything when it came to him, she knew who he was and what he had done, but she seemed to have perfected the art of living in denial.

Who was he to take that away from her?

Living in denial was her way of coping with the hell that she had been through, and there was no way he was going to burst her bubble. If she needed to believe that he was her knight in shining armor, who had ridden in on a white horse to save her then she could believe that.

Even though they both knew it couldn't be further from the truth.

But from the moment Emerald had become his, claiming his heart and his soul with her sweet innocence and pure heart, his protective instincts had been thrown into overdrive. There literally wasn't anything that he wouldn't do for her, not excluding lie, cheat, steal ... or kill.

If Emerald was in danger, then he would take action.

When Emerald was in danger he *had* taken action.

Now it was time to find out if it had worked or not.

His driver pulled the limousine to a stop in front of his house, and he opened his own door and climbed out. Striding up the steps, he crossed the porch and walked through the front door.

The first thing he heard when he stepped inside was the sound of music.

Emerald was creative, she loved to write poetry, she loved to draw and paint, and she loved to play music. She played the piano, the harp, the flute, the saxophone, and the cello, right now it sounded like she was playing the harp.

She played beautifully, and he stood in the foyer, listening to the music float through the house. When Emerald played—like everything else she did—she played with her heart. He could hear her pain, her fears, and also her joy with every note she played.

He almost hated to disturb her.

Heading toward the music room, he'd had set up for her, Noah paused again in the doorway. Emerald sat by the window light streamed through, making the reddish hints in her hair sparkle and shimmer. She was wearing a white dress, a gold necklace with a large emerald set in a nest of diamonds hung between her breasts, and gold bracelets caught the light with every movement of her hands.

She was a vision.

Noah often thought of her as an angel sent from heaven to stop him before he completely crossed over to join the devil in Hell. It was why most of the clothes he bought for her were white, white was fitting for an angel, and he liked to see her wearing it.

As much as he would love to stand and watch her play forever, he had left work as soon as the detectives had for a reason. A reason that couldn't be brushed aside and hidden away.

He stepped into the room, and as soon as he took a step toward her, she noticed his presence and immediately stopped playing, her hands falling down to rest in her lap.

"Noah," she beamed at him, standing and rushing over to throw her arms around his waist and cling to him in the way she always did. Sometimes her devotion and unconditional love reminded him of a puppy. A poor, abused puppy that kept circling back to a cruel master because it didn't know what else to do. He didn't abuse Emerald, but he could hardly be described as the hero she thought him to be.

"You play so beautifully," he said, stroking her long brown locks.

"Thank you," she murmured in that sweet, shy way she did. He could tell her cheeks had tinted pink with embarrassment without even needing to see her face. Emerald's self-esteem had been decimated because of what those men had done to her, training her to be their perfect little sex slave, and as hard as he had tried, she had some bad habits she couldn't break.

"Walk with me," he said, reaching for her small hand and enclosing it in his large one.

"Is something wrong?" she asked meekly, another of her bad habits was worrying about talking without being given permission. But permission to speak wasn't needed in his house. "You're home so early, I wasn't expecting you until at least lunchtime."

"There was a ... development at work this morning," he told her.

"What was it?" There was a hint of inquisitiveness in her tone, and he smiled, she might have lost her confidence, but her curiosity was still there.

"The cops believe that one of my employees committed a murder, and they wanted to speak with me about it, hoping I might be able to tell them something about the man that would help them build their case."

"What does that have to do with us?"

"One of the detectives was Sapphire."

Emerald gasped, her hand flew to her mouth, her green eyes grew almost impossibly wide, and she swayed. Noah knew that despite the fact she consistently denied that she wanted to reconnect with her sisters, that she missed them.

As far as he was concerned, Sapphire and the other Hatcher sisters would never know that Emerald was alive and that she lived with him. He had been shocked when Sapphire had reached out to him about having a security system installed, and he had realized that she was Emerald's sister.

"H-how did she look?" Emerald asked. After he had met Sapphire, he had looked into her, wanting to know what her life was like, and what she and her sisters had been up to, and he had shared that information with Emerald. She knew that all four of her sisters were now married and that they all had children of their own, but she didn't know that he had actually spent time in person with Sapphire.

Until now at least.

"She looked fine, content with her job, enthusiastic to prove this man was a killer so she could get him behind bars."

"Do you think Sapphire is going to want to talk with you again?"

"I think it's a fairly strong possibility," he replied. If Emerald only knew the extent he had gone to to protect her, then she would understand just how much Sapphire sticking her nose into this case might become a problem for them.

A problem he didn't have a solution for.

He would do anything to keep Emerald safe, but would he go so far as to eliminate her own sister?

That was something he wasn't sure of yet.

"But she doesn't know about me, does she?" Emerald looked up at him, stricken.

"She doesn't know about you," he assured her, drawing her into his arms and stroking her back to soothe her.

"But if she spends too much time around you at your offices then she could find out." Emerald was starting to sound panicked.

"Calm down," he said firmly, he wasn't in the mood for a meltdown. He had a lot to think about, a lot of decisions to make, and before he made up his mind to do something from which there would be no coming back, Emerald needed to see something.

"Sapphire can be determined," Emerald continued as though she hadn't heard him. "What if she starts digging? What if she finds something that makes her suspicious of you? What if she comes out here for some reason and she sees me? What if—"

"Stop," he raised his voice to just shy of a shout and Emerald winced, fear flashed across her face, and she cowered as though worried he might lash out at her physically. That only irritated him more. "You know better than to be thinking that," he growled. "I've never hit you before, and I don't intend to start now. Come here, I have to show you something."

Snatching her hand again he began to drag her through the house, her legs—much shorter than his own—scurrying to keep up with him.

Noah stopped outside his office and dragged in a breath.

Although he had never outright forbidden her from coming in here, he had discouraged it, and meek little thing that she was, Emerald had taken the hint and stayed away.

But today he was going to show her what was in here.

Something he hadn't ever intended her to see—but things had changed.

∾

3:14 P.M.

"Finally," Sapphire said when the doctor nodded at them. They had been sitting in the hospital corridor for over an hour waiting to be given the all clear to speak with Bobby Tompson. She was done listening to his excuses and denials, she was done being left hanging, she was done not making any meaningful progress.

She wanted answers.

Right this second.

"Let's go," she said, standing up.

Elijah stood as well, and they walked down the corridor toward the room where Bobby was recovering from the bullet wound she had given him the day before. She was glad that she'd done it, not because she wanted to hurt him, even if he had killed Alice Lincoln, and even if he had something to do with her sister, but because she didn't want him dead. If he died, then everything he knew died right along with him.

They'd spent the morning at Noah's offices, speaking with everyone who worked with Bobby, and she was sick to death of hearing the same thing over and over again.

Bobby was great.

Bobby was such a hard worker.

Bobby was such a fabulous leader.

Bobby listened.

Bobby made them feel respected and valued.

Bobby helped them become more successful.

Bobby was so attractive he couldn't possibly do anything wrong.

Bobby was thoughtful.

Bobby was kind.

Every single person they had spoken with had said the same things, they made Bobby Tompson sound like a god.

But no matter how many times she heard someone say how much they loved Bobby and what a fantastic human being he was, Sapphire knew differently. She knew that he wasn't, she knew that he was involved in this, and she knew that he was an evil man.

He was a monster, but one who knew how to hide in plain sight. How to blend into humanity so that no one noticed him. That made him all the more dangerous. Alice, no doubt, went willingly with him, or willingly allowed him into her home, when he came for her because she believed his act. Bobby wore a mask each day, but that mask was cracking, and she was hoping that with just a little push it would shatter completely, and then the true Bobby would come out.

"I know how badly you want answers, but don't push too hard," Elijah warned as they stopped outside Bobby's door. "If you're right about him, then we need to be careful. We know that someone paid him a large sum of money right before Alice went missing. And we know that he has been receiving payments every month since. Someone else is involved in this, but if it's someone that Bobby is afraid of then he might not open up."

They had finally gotten a warrant to search Bobby's financials, and thankfully, there had been something there that they could use to try to get him to start talking. But Elijah was right, someone else was involved, someone that had enough money to convince Bobby—a man with no prior criminal record—to commit abduction, imprisonment, and murder, someone like that was not to be trifled with.

"We also need to make sure that whoever paid Bobby doesn't decide that we're a threat and try to take us out," Elijah added.

Sapphire waved off that idea. "There would be no point. Eliminating us doesn't eliminate this investigation. I doubt that whoever paid Bobby to kidnap and kill Alice would be stupid enough to try anything with either of us. But I am worried that they might send someone to try to kill Bobby. We should make sure that there is a cop here twenty-four-seven so no unauthorized personnel comes in here." Bobby had been charged with Alice's abduction and murder, but he would remain in the hospital—handcuffed to the bed—until a doctor cleared him and he was taken down to the jail.

"I'm not as confident as you are that the mastermind behind this will steer clear of us," Elijah told her. "Yes, this case will remain open even if something did happen to us, but if this is about Emerald, and she seems to be at the center of it, then this guy has to know that no one is going to work this case harder than you are. Emerald is your sister, you're emotionally invested, if you disappear then whoever takes this case over isn't going to work it to the same extent that you are."

While she couldn't disagree with what her partner was saying, she felt he was completely overreacting. "Did Diamond tell you to tell me that?" she asked suspiciously.

From the sheepish smile he shot her, she knew she was right. "She's worried about you, she doesn't want to lose another sister."

"And she won't. If this works out the way I hope it will then she'll get a sister back. We all will." Maybe if she was able to find Emerald and bring her home, then she could finally let go of some of the guilt she had for not saving her little sister that night, and for being rescued first, and move on with her life.

"No one can ever say you lack in confidence." Elijah rolled his eyes at her.

Sapphire shrugged. She wouldn't really call it confidence, it was more like she had to believe it to function. She wanted her sister back, not just for herself, but for her whole family, and her best bet of doing that was lying in a hospital bed on the other side of the closed door. "Let's do this."

When she opened the door, and they walked in, they found Bobby lying in bed, his leg bandaged, staring at the ceiling, a contemplative look on his face. She wondered what he was thinking about. Was he trying to figure out what he was going to tell them? Was he thinking that he was too smart and that he would never spend a day in prison? Was he worried that whoever had paid him off was going to come after him? Or did he think his friend would send help?

"Good afternoon, Bobby," Sapphire said as she walked across to the bed.

"Afternoon, Detective Sapphire Hatcher-Barlow," Bobby returned, still staring at the ceiling.

"How's the leg?"

"Healing nicely." Slowly he turned his head, and his eyes met hers, she saw fear pass quickly through them before the smugness was back.

She wasn't here to play games. Bobby had the answers she wanted, and she intended to get them the easy way or the hard way. "We know that you killed Alice Lincoln, continuing to deny it is ridiculous. Your car was at the scene, we know you knew her, and you wouldn't have run from us yesterday if you didn't have something to hide. We also know that someone paid you a huge sum of money the week before Alice went missing and has been depositing money into your account every month since. I'm guessing since you would have jumped off the building and killed yourself if I hadn't stopped you, that this person who's been paying you is someone that you're afraid of. The way I see it is we have two options moving forward. Number one, you can tell us what we want to know, and we'll make sure that this man doesn't get to you. Or, number two, we can broadcast it all over the place that you were very helpful and then send you off and let your little friend deal with you."

Bobby said nothing, just returned his gaze to the ceiling.

Which she supposed was an answer.

"I'm going to find out anyway. You don't know me, you don't know that I'm someone who doesn't ever give up on anything, especially this. I know that you know where my sister is, we know that this is about Emerald, and I will find out who your friend is, because I know he's the one holding my sister prisoner. You were prepared to die yesterday, you still prepared for that today?" she demanded.

Stubbornly the man ignored her.

It was like he thought that if he waited long enough she would just give up.

He wasn't going to be that lucky.

She had never given up on a case in her life, and she wasn't going to start with one so personal.

"Fine," she said when Bobby wouldn't speak or even look at her. "You want to play this the hard way, then that's what we'll do. When we walk out of this room, we're going to start spreading the word about what a helpful suspect you've been. We were going to keep a cop on your door to make sure your friend didn't come after you, but I think we'll tell our boss not to bother. This friend of yours is rich, I'm sure he already knows where you are, I hope he won't be *too* angry with you for talking to us."

With that, she stood and stalked out the door praying that this worked. They'd let Bobby stew overnight, wondering what his wealthy friend was going to do to him if he believed that he had turned him in, then they'd come back tomorrow, and hopefully, he'd realize by then that playing along with them was the only way to stay alive. Jumping off a building was one thing, but she doubted that the man who had paid Bobby to abduct and kill Alice would give him a quick death if he thought that he had snitched.

Although they weren't moving as quickly as she would have liked, they were getting closer and closer to Emerald with each passing day.

~

7:06 P.M.

"Snap," Archie said, beaming up at them. "I have all the cards, that means I win again."

"You have the fastest little hands this side of the Atlantic," Elijah said.

"What's the Atlantic?" Archie asked.

"It's the name of an ocean," Diamond explained to her four-year-old son. Archie was at an age where he wanted to learn everything about everything. He was so full of questions that she felt like she needed a degree in every subject on the planet just to answer them all. Some days they spent more time on Google looking up things than she did doing anything else.

"The ocean? You mean the beach?" Archie asked, his gray eyes full of innocent curiosity.

"Well, the beach has sand and ocean," she reminded him. "And I seem to remember a certain someone who was afraid of the waves last time we went to the beach."

"That was *ages* ago," Archie said. "I was just a little kid then."

Diamond tried to hold back a laugh. She loved that Archie thought being four made him practically an adult. He was growing up so quickly. When she had first become part of Archie's life, he had been only twenty-two months old, now he was four and had started preschool this fall. Next year he'd be off to kindergarten, and in just a couple of years their baby would follow him.

"I go swim," Oscar demanded in that toddler way. They were sitting around the kitchen table playing snap, since two-year-old Oscar was a little young to play, he was sitting on her lap, and she was holding his little hands in hers, helping him snap when there were two matching dinosaurs.

"Not today, Ozzy," she told him. "But next summer I'm sure we'll take a few trips to the beach."

"I want swim *now*," Oscar insisted, his face setting into that determined expression she was so used to seeing. While Archie was laid back, easy-going, loved to laugh and learn, Ozzy was a much more serious little boy. He was fiercely independent, liked to have his own way, and didn't always take kindly to the word no. Despite how different her sons were, she loved them both the same, and couldn't be more thrilled that after so many years believing that since she couldn't get pregnant due to injuries sustained while she had been kept prisoner, she would never get to be a mother, she finally *was* one.

"No," she said firmly. "It's too cold, and too late."

"Ozzy, you know where you can go swimming?" Brooke asked her little brother.

"Swim?" he asked hopefully, turning his bright brown eyes onto his sister.

"In the bathtub," Brooke said, setting the last dish in the dishwasher. The sixteen-year-old had been living with them for two years now, since before they had adopted Oscar, and although she was still technically their foster daughter, she was every bit as much one of their children as the boys were. Things had been a bit rocky at first, but Brooke had settled in here, and she particularly loved being a big sister. "We can splash about, and pretend there are waves, and sea animals, it'll be a lot of fun," Brooke continued.

"Fun," Ozzy squealed, excited about the idea now, the ocean forgotten.

"I don't mind giving him his bath," Brooke offered.

"Thanks," Diamond said, handing over the toddler. Although Brooke had chores around the house and sometimes babysat not just her brothers, but her cousins too, they made sure that she never felt like they only had her around to be their maid. She was their daughter, and while all three of their kids had chores, even Ozzy, Brooke was also a kid, and they wanted her to focus on her schoolwork, and spend time with her friends, and do all those normal teenage things.

"Can we play snap again?" Archie asked once Brooke had taken Oscar upstairs.

"No, that's enough for tonight. You can have thirty minutes of TV or iPad time, then it's time for your bath and into bed," Elijah answered his son.

"iPad," Archie said.

"Set the timer, and are you playing games or watching videos?"

"Watching videos," Archie replied as he headed off to grab the iPad from the writing desk in the family room where they kept it. Since he had a list of approved videos he could watch, and he was so good at following the rules, Diamond didn't worry about him viewing things he shouldn't. Now when Oscar was a little older, and he had his own iPad that would be a very different story. She suspected that Ozzy was going to be a much more difficult child than either Brooke or Archie, or the two of them combined.

"I don't want Brooke staying up too late doing homework tonight," she said as she stood and began to pack away the leftovers into the fridge. "She was up late every night this week studying for that test."

"How did she say she thinks she went?" Elijah asked, straightening up the pile of snap cards so they would fit back in the box. Since he worked such unpredictable hours, and while her hours as an art teacher were predictable, they were long—since she worked both in a school and at the community center—and time with the kids was limited, they tried to do something together, usually a board game or a card game, together each night after dinner.

"She said she thought she did really well, and that the studying paid off, she thinks she might even get a B or higher." Brooke had struggled in algebra all through her sophomore year, now she was a junior, and she had been so worried she was going to fail, but she'd been working hard, and it looked like it was starting to pay off. "I thought as a treat I might take her out on Saturday, we'll get massages, and facials, maybe a manicure or pedicure, kind of have a girls' day. If you have to work then maybe your mom can watch the boys, do you know if she has plans for the weekend?"

Elijah's mom hadn't liked her when they first started dating, but over the last few years, they'd grown close. Now that she wasn't Archie's full-time carer and just grandma again, she had taken up some hobbies and even had a boyfriend. "I don't think she has plans, I'm sure she'd love to hang out with Archie and Oscar, she's been wanting to go to the zoo again before the real winter weather hits."

"Great, you can go along with them if you don't have to work. And then maybe Brooke can have a friend over for a sleepover Saturday night, she's been asking to for a couple of weeks now, but we've been so busy."

"Sounds like a plan," Elijah agreed.

Wiping down the counter, not because it was dirty, Brooke had already cleaned it when she was loading the dishwasher, but because she needed something to do with her hands while she asked her husband this question. "Elijah?"

"Yeah?" he asked, coming up behind her and wrapping his arms around her waist, drawing her back to rest against his chest.

"I know we agreed that we weren't going to talk about it, but ..."

"But you want to know about the case," he finished for her.

"I do," Diamond nodded, wiggling around so she was facing her husband. "I need to know how it's going. Do you know anything about Emerald yet?" Although last night they had decided that until he had anything meaningful to tell her he was going to keep the case at work, and their home life focused on family, she had to know. Emerald was her baby sister, and she had never given up hope that one day she would return to them. Hope had saved her life, keeping her alive when the desire to give in and die had been strong, and hope had led her to Elijah and the life they now shared, maybe hope could bring her sister home as well.

"We know who killed the woman in the woods, and we know that he's working with someone. He's been receiving money every month since the woman he killed disappeared. But so far he isn't talking, and we haven't been able to trace where the money is coming from," Elijah told her.

"Do you think whoever has been sending him money is the one who has Emerald?"

"Sapphire does."

"And do you?" she asked. She knew her sister couldn't help but be emotionally invested, and she was worried that would cloud Sapphire's judgment and make her take unnecessary risks, or miss something important, she'd asked Elijah to watch over her sister, make sure Sapphire didn't do anything crazy.

"I think that it makes sense, but for now, it's just conjecture, we need to find who paid this man to kidnap this woman and kill her, setting it up to make us think it was Emerald, and then we'll know more."

"Do you think you can get this man to talk? Tell you what he knows?"

"I believe that we will close this case, whether or not it means we find Emerald, I can't tell you that. All I can tell you is that I will do everything within my power to find your sister and bring her home to you," he told her.

She knew that he would.

Elijah loved her, and he was a good cop, she believed that he would not only solve this case but also find Emerald in the process.

Hope had been her mantra for almost half her life, and it had made everything work out, even if it had been a rocky road getting here.

Resting her head on her husband's shoulder, she held onto him. Hope had led her to safety when she'd been a prisoner, it had led her to Elijah, it had led her to their children, and it would lead her to her sister, too.

CHAPTER Nine

November 29th
9:31 A.M.

"I was hoping we would have heard from Bobby by now," Sapphire said as she glanced in the rear vision mirror before changing lanes. It had been eighteen hours since she'd told Bobby Tompson what was going to happen if he didn't start talking, and he hadn't made any move to contact them.

He was still in the hospital, still with a plainclothes cop watching his door, and according to the doctors, they would be releasing him by the end of the day which meant that she and Elijah had to decide what their next move was going to be. If they had him taken down to the jail, then chances were this mystery money man wouldn't be able to get to him, which meant Bobby would probably feel safe enough to keep quiet. However, if they let him go, even if it was to try to use him as bait, then there was a chance he could run, and then not only would they not get justice for Alice Lincoln, but they would also lose their best chance of getting information about Emerald.

It felt like a no win situation.

"That might be the best way we have of getting information, but it isn't the only way," Elijah reminded her. "Bobby won't speak, but we know he's involved, and we have other people we can speak with."

The other people he was referring to was a man who had gone home supposedly sick when they had been at Noah's office building yesterday. It was someone who worked with Bobby, and in leaving when he heard the cops were there, he had painted a bright red target on himself.

"I hope this leads somewhere," she said, taking the exit and heading off toward a quieter part of town where one, Dean Winters lived. The man was independently wealthy, having inherited a small fortune when his widowed mother married a rich businessman, then both his mom and step-father were killed in a helicopter crash. The older man had left everything to his new wife, who had left everything to her only son.

That this man had access to a large sum of money meant it was possible he was the one paying Bobby Tompson. That this man lived in a quieter part of the city where the houses had larger blocks of land, meant this could be where Alice Lincoln had been held for the eighteen months she had been missing.

It also meant that Dean Winters could be the one who had Emerald right now.

"I hope it leads somewhere too," Elijah agreed. "Take this next left, then it's a right, another left, and another, then we should be there."

Following her partner's directions, Sapphire wondered whether this could be it. If this could be the moment that she came face to face with her sister. If she got even the slightest of indications that Emerald was on this property, then she wasn't leaving it until the entire place was searched.

"Let's play this calmly," Elijah said as she parked the car outside a three-story white colonial.

"I will." She had no intention of doing anything to mess up this case. She wanted her sister back, and she wouldn't do anything to jeopardize that, she was just prepared to take some—but nothing major—risks to get there. "You can tell that wife of yours that she doesn't have to worry."

"Somehow, I don't think Diamond would believe me," Elijah said with a smile.

"She's a worrywart," Sapphire said. Even before their parents had sold them and their lives had spiraled into hell, Diamond had been the kind of older sister who wanted to mother them. They were all close in age, only four years between youngest Emerald and oldest Diamond, but for some reason, Diamond always seemed to think that she was so much older than the rest of them.

"She loves you."

She did.

Sapphire had never doubted that she was loved. Maybe not by her parents, but definitely by her sisters, and they had rallied around each other and helped each other through the struggle of rebuilding their lives. She loved them so much, and she owed it to them to bring Emerald home to them.

"It's not true you know," Elijah said as they walked toward the front door.

"What isn't?"

"You think that you have something to make up for, which implies that you did something wrong, and you didn't. You were a sixteen-year-old kid, I know that you fought back that night, that was brave, and that you weren't successful in getting away and getting help is only indicative of the fact that a teenage girl can't take on half a dozen armed men and win. Your sisters don't expect you to bring Emerald home for any other reason than because they love her."

Sapphire wanted to believe that, but old patterns of thought were hard to break, and although she had come a long way in dealing with her survivor's guilt since she met Gideon, she still had a way to go.

"All the blinds are drawn," she noted, wanting to move on from the mushy stuff. Having these kinds of talks with her partner, who she respected and trusted, made her uncomfortable because she knew they wouldn't be having them if it wasn't for the fact that he was married to her sister. "You think he's here, or do you think he packed up and ran yesterday?"

"I think that you're avoiding what I said, but I also think there's a chance he might have run yesterday. It depends on whether or not he's involved."

"The only way to find out if he's involved is to speak with him," she said, frustrated. Not about Elijah and Diamond, she knew they only worried because they cared, she was frustrated because it was like answers kept being dangled in front of her and then snatched away when she reached for them.

Elijah hammered on the door, and they both waited.

And waited.

And waited.

She knocked as loudly as she could on the door, and then for good measure she walked over to the nearest window and knocked on that too.

There was no answer.

"He's not here," she said, her frustration growing. Why couldn't something, for once, just go easy in her life?

"I agree," Elijah said. "We may as well leave, we can go and see Bobby Tompson, then we can speak with family, colleagues, friends of Dean Winters, see if anyone knows anything."

It was as good a plan as any.

They trailed back down to the car and got in, some days it felt like all she did was drive around from one place to another. It wasn't that she minded, but today she just wanted to get helpful information, not drive around the city.

Just as they were buckling their seatbelts, Elijah's phone rang. He pulled it out, and she turned the engine on but didn't start driving.

"Detective Newton," Elijah said into his cell phone. "Uh-huh. Uh-huh. And you got a match? You're sure? That's great. Thanks, bye."

"Who was that?"

"It was crime scene. They got something for us."

"They did?" she asked, hopeful.

"A hair in Bobby Tompson's car, in the trunk, it's a match for Alice Lincoln, we now have irrefutable proof that Bobby is involved, maybe that will get him talking."

"I hope so," she said, but it felt like a weight had been lifted off her shoulders. Finally, they had something that Bobby couldn't try to wiggle out of, although she wouldn't put it past him to try. Releasing the brake, she started off down the street. "I can't wait to get to the hospital and tell Bobby what we found. Do you think this will finally get him talking?"

"I don't know. He's been stubborn so far, but I think it's more out of fear than anything else. I think we need to convince him that we can protect him and keep him safe before we're going to get anything out of him."

"We can offer to put him in protective cus—"

She broke off as something slammed into the side of the car.

Not something.

Another car.

She was flung forward, hitting the steering wheel hard.

Pain shafted through her, centering in her head.

"Sapphire."

She heard Elijah call her name, but he suddenly sounded a long way away instead of in the passenger seat of the same car.

Voices.

She heard voices.

Help.

Someone must have seen the car accident and were coming to check on them.

Her door was opened, and rough hands grabbed her, undoing her seatbelt and dragging her from the vehicle.

All of a sudden it hit her.

This wasn't a car accident, it was an abduction.

Sapphire tried to reach for her gun, but her hand didn't want to co-operate.

The world grayed, her vision dimmed, and then despite her best efforts to cling to consciousness, she faded away.

∽

11:28 A.M.

. . .

Emerald lay in the field down past the stables.

She was lying on her back in the grass. It was long, overgrown, no one cut the grass out here, there was no need to, the field was beautiful and wild, full of flowers in the spring and summer. The grass tickled the back of her neck and her cheeks, but she didn't bat it away, she was too preoccupied with her thoughts.

Ever since yesterday when Noah had taken her into his office, she hadn't been able to stop thinking about her old life.

Back before they were sold, she and Sapphire used to love to lie on the grass in their backyard and stare up at the sky. They'd watch the clouds float above their heads, making different shapes, trying to see if they could find animals or vehicles or anything else recognizable. At night, they would always try to see who could find the first star so they could play the 'Star light star bright' game, and make a wish.

Sapphire usually won.

There was no one more determined when they set their mind to something than Sapphire. If her sister knew for sure that she was alive, then there wasn't anything she wouldn't do to find her. And if she found out that she was living here with Noah, then Emerald knew that Sapphire would go to any length she had to to make her leave.

She didn't want to leave here.

She didn't want to go back to her sisters because that would mean trying to make her old life a reality.

That was impossible.

When she and Sapphire used to race to see who saw the first star and who got to make a wish, she never cared if Sapphire won. While her sister would gloat and make a big deal about winning and making her wish, Emerald would just choose a star and make her own wish.

It was always the same one.

She would wish that one day she would have a beautiful place in the country where she could be surrounded by animals.

In a way, that wish had come true. She did live in a beautiful place in the country, and she was surrounded by animals. There were the horses, which she spent most of her time with, but there were also a couple of cows, a goat or two, chickens, cats, and dogs. This place was basically straight out of her dreams, and yet it wasn't right. It wasn't the way she had imagined it.

She was what was different.

She'd had such dreams of rescuing abused animals and helping them recover and move on to live with a family who would love and cherish them. And yet, in a way, *she* was the abused animal that Noah had taken in and helped recover. Only instead of sending her away to a family who would love and cherish her, he had kept her for himself.

Not kept in the sense that she was his property, but he had made her his, and she had no desire to be anyone else's.

This was her life, her home, where she wanted to be, but she knew that Sapphire wouldn't understand. None of her sisters would. Although they had all gone through similar things they had all reacted differently. While her sisters might be happy with the lives they had now, she was happy too.

Tears welled in her eyes, but she fought them back.

It was hard being away from the sisters she loved. Just because she chose to stay here with Noah didn't mean that her feelings for them had gone, and it hurt her to know that they wouldn't support her choices. She supported theirs, she was happy for them, she was glad that they had moved on with their lives as best as they could, and she wished them all the best.

"Why are you crying?"

The voice came out of nowhere, and a shadow blocked out the watery late fall sunshine. Emerald shrieked and launched to her feet before she realized who it was. "You just about gave me a heart attack," she said, her hand flying to her chest where she pressed it to her wildly hammering heart.

"Sorry," Noah said, although he didn't sound particularly apologetic. "I assumed you heard me coming, I didn't try to hide it."

"Lost in thought," she said, quickly gathering her control because she sensed that Noah was not quite her Noah at the moment. He was angry, he was preoccupied, he was teetering on the edge.

She'd seen him there before.

She loved Noah, but she hadn't forgotten how they had met.

Sometimes she thought that he believed she had wiped all of that from her memory and started over with a clean slate.

But she hadn't.

She would never forget.

It might not change the fact that she loved him, but it did make sure that she never completely let her guard down around him. She was always careful to read him, to adjust her behaviors and her actions in accordance with what kind of mood he was in at any given time.

Right now, his mood was volatile, which meant she needed to be careful. She knew that this edginess had nothing to do with her, and yet also everything to do with her.

Keeping still, like a mouse trying to hide from a predator, she slowed her breathing and kept her gaze fixed on the grass, which was blowing in the gentle breeze. If she possessed the ability to make herself invisible, now would be the time she would invoke that power.

"What were you thinking about?" Noah demanded, stepping closer so he was just inches away. He towered above her, he was so much bigger and stronger than she was, he could crush her in a single second if that was what he wanted to do.

"N-nothing," she murmured.

Noah reached out, took her chin in a grip that almost hurt, and forced her head back. With nowhere else to go, her gaze met his. Fire and ice blazed from those blue eyes of his, and they seemed to slice right through her skull, delving deep into her brain and reading her thoughts.

She didn't know what to do.

She couldn't hide her thoughts if she tried, she wanted to look away, break the connection, but she didn't. It wasn't just because she was afraid to do anything that might make him angrier it was also because his eyes were magnets. They gripped hers and refused to let them go.

"You know that everything I've done is because I love you," he said, a statement not a question even though he had phrased it as one.

"I know," she assured him. And she really did know. She knew that Noah loved her and that he would do anything to protect her and keep her safe.

"You're upset about what I showed you yesterday," he said. Again not a question even though he phrased it as one.

"Not upset," she corrected. Not *really* anyway. She was more shocked than angry about what he'd shown her. He had made it clear without coming right out and saying it, that she wasn't allowed to go into his office. She had followed his wishes, because she really had no interest in going in there anyway, but had she known what he did in there then she might have rethought that. Even now, it was hard to stay away, but they hadn't discussed if she was allowed to go in there any time she wanted.

"Don't lie to me," he said, tightening his grip on her chin.

Emerald trembled, she knew he would feel it, but she couldn't help it. "I'm not upset, I promise. I ... I ... I don't know how I feel, but I'm glad that you showed me."

He searched her eyes for a moment longer then nodded and released her chin, his hand threading through her hair instead, before settling on her cheek. He stroked her cheekbone with the pad of his thumb, it was smooth, and the motion soothed her jangled nerves. "You may go into my office any time you want to."

That surprised her, but maybe it shouldn't. Noah really *did* always have her best interests at heart, even if he did go about things in an unorthodox manner. "Thank you," she said, and she meant those words from the bottom of her heart.

"You're welcome." Noah touched a tender kiss to her forehead, then took her hand. "It's time."

As Noah led her back toward the house, her stomach churned. How could she be ready for this?

She was nervous, she was excited, she almost couldn't believe this was real.

But it was.

It was real, and she was about to come face to face with something that she wasn't sure she could ever have.

～

12:09 P.M.

. . .

"Ugh," Sapphire groaned as she swam back to consciousness.

Her head ached.

And felt like it had been stuffed with cotton wool.

She'd been drugged.

And there had been a ...

Her mind searched for an answer, knowing it was there, knowing it was important but unable to recall it.

Accident.

A car accident.

She and Elijah had been run off the road, and then they'd been dragged out by men and then ...

Then her memories ended.

"Elijah?" she called out.

There was no answer.

Was he badly hurt?

Dead?

Ignoring the headache, Sapphire opened her eyes and pushed herself into a sitting position. She was in a bedroom, a beautiful bedroom, it was large, and the furniture looked like it was genuine antiques. She had been put on a canopy bed, there was a small stain of blood on the pillowcase, and when she touched her fingertips to her temple they came away sticky with blood.

That she had been abducted was obvious.

That it was related to Alice Lincoln's murder was a given as far as she was concerned.

Right now, she felt more angry than scared, and she pushed herself to the edge of the bed and stood slowly. A wave of dizziness washed over her, but she pushed through it because she didn't really have time for that right now.

On her feet, Sapphire headed straight for the window, throwing back the lacy white curtains, her heart dropped when she saw what was there.

Metal bars.

Going out the window was not an option.

Her next move was the door, she was halfway across the large room when the door opened all on its own.

Sapphire felt for her gun, but it was gone. "Of course it is," she muttered under her breath. Who went to all the trouble of kidnapping a cop and then let them remain armed?

A woman stepped into the room, followed by a man.

Her mouth dropped open.

"Emmy," she gasped. Without even thinking about what she was doing, or any of the ramifications of the fact that her missing sister was standing before her, she ran across the room and threw her arms around her Emerald. "You're alive."

"I'm alive," Emerald said, hugging her back.

"I missed you so much." Tears streamed down her face, the headache forgotten, *everything* forgotten, but the fact that her sister was really and truly alive and in one piece.

Emerald didn't say anything.

Slowly her euphoria began to dim.

Emerald hadn't said anything.

Not that she missed her, not that she loved her, not that she was afraid for her life, not anything.

Letting her arms drop, Sapphire turned to the other person in the room and gasped again. "Noah."

Why was Noah here?

She might not know exactly where she was, but she knew that whoever owned this place was wealthy.

Noah was wealthy.

Noah worked with Bobby Tompson.

Noah was rich enough to have paid Bobby to kill Alice Lincoln.

Since Emerald was standing in the room with them Noah obviously had a reason—although she couldn't fathom what it was—for wanting them to think Emerald was dead.

"It was you," she threw the accusation at him.

Noah didn't flinch, his blue eyes met hers squarely, and he gave a single nod.

Emerald moved away from her over to Noah. She stood close to him, and he slipped an arm around her waist.

Sapphire wanted to throw up.

"You're the one who bought my sister," she growled.

"It wasn't like that," Emerald said quickly.

"So, what? You walked here yourself?"

"Well, n-no," Emerald stammered.

"You were brought here because he paid money to buy you."

"Noah didn't know. He didn't know that I didn't want this," Emerald said, her tone begging like she really wanted her to understand, but she didn't understand any of this.

"I don't know what that means," Sapphire snapped, her headache was back and worse than ever, and she pressed her fingers to her temples.

Emerald looked up at Noah, obviously seeking his permission because when he nodded, words began to tumble out of her mouth. "The man who bought me first, when he got bored with me he sold me to Noah, only Noah thought he was buying someone who wanted to be a sex slave, he thought that I had signed up voluntarily. When he realized that I was a victim he helped me."

"A lot of help he gave you, you're still here aren't you," she said, shaking her head at what she heard like in doing so she could erase it.

"I'm not Noah's prisoner, I'm here because I want to be here, I love Noah," Emerald protested.

"Stockholm Syndrome."

"No, not Stockholm Syndrome. Noah sent me away at first, he said I shouldn't be here, but I love him, and I came back of my own free will. *This* is where I want to be," Emerald said firmly.

That hurt.

If Emerald wasn't a prisoner, then that meant she had stayed away on purpose.

"So you let us think that you were still in trouble, you let us worry about you, wonder if you were dead or alive, grieve your loss," she yelled at her sister. She didn't even know the woman standing before her. While Emerald hadn't changed much from the fifteen-year-old girl she had been when they'd all been sold, she wasn't the same sweet, innocent, kind girl who cared more about others than she did herself.

"I-I'm sorry," Emerald stammered.

"You threw away four sisters who love you for this man?" she waved her hand at Noah who was standing watching the exchange. "Do you know what he did? He paid someone who works at his company to kidnap some innocent woman. He had her hurt in the exact same places where you have scars, then he kept her prisoner while those wounds healed. Then he had this man kill her. Do you know what it was like when I found her? I thought it was you, Emerald. He even gave her your necklace. I thought you were dead."

Emerald dropped her gaze to the floor.

Sapphire felt her stomach drop. "You know." Just what had her little sister become? She was okay with this? With an innocent woman being killed?

"There was nothing else we could do," Emerald said desperately.

"Nothing else you could do?" she echoed incredulously.

Emerald looked to Noah again, and when he nodded, she said, "Noah had a friend, back when I first came here. They bought me together, they thought it would be fun to buy a sex slave. But when Noah found out that I wasn't in this willingly he wanted to stop, he didn't want a helpless victim, he wanted someone who was enjoying it as much as he was. Alfie wouldn't have cared if I was into it or not, so Noah faked my death, so his partner would leave me alone. But somehow he found out I was still alive, we just wanted him to believe that I was dead for real this time."

She just stared at her sister in shock.

This whole thing was surreal.

"Maybe if you didn't decide to let your sisters think you were dead too, then I could have helped you. I'm married now you know, my husband is a criminal psychiatrist. Diamond, Ruby, and Amethyst are all married to cops too. We would have found a way to keep you safe and find this man."

"We couldn't go to you," Emerald said softly. "Because when you learned what Noah did you would have wanted to arrest him."

"So you two and what you want is more important than anything else. A woman died, Emerald. She was *tortured* and then *murdered*. I can't believe you're okay with this. And I can't believe I trusted you with my family's safety." She turned disgusted eyes on Noah. This man had been in her home, the house she shared with her husband and her two-year-old son. And he had been in the homes of her sisters and their families. Knowing that made her ill. Knowing how her disappearance was going to affect Gideon and Leo made her feel worse. "So what are you going to do with me? I'm here because I was getting too close, right? You can't let me prove that you're alive and that Noah was involved in Alice's death, so you brought me here. Are you going to kill me?"

"What? No! Of course not." Emerald looked horrified by the suggestion. "You're my sister, and I love you. Plus, I would never do that to your little boy. He has your eyes."

Sapphire staggered back.

How did Emerald know that?

Had Noah told her all about them or had she seen them for herself?

"Have you been watching us?" she demanded. "Do you use the cameras Noah put in our homes as part of the security system to spy on us?"

~

12:37 P.M.

"Have you been watching us?" Sapphire demanded again.

Emerald froze beside him, unsure how she should answer that question.

Emerald hadn't been watching Sapphire and her family, and the families of her sisters for the last few years, but *he* had been. Ever since Sapphire reached out to him because he was the best in the business of security systems and she wanted the best, he had been watching her. He had set up the systems so that he had access to the cameras, and that enabled him to keep track of the family, but he had only told Emerald about it yesterday when he realized he was going to have to do something about Sapphire. He'd thought that Emerald might be more amenable to the idea of bringing Sapphire here if she had actually seen her sister.

Sapphire was dangerous.

He had always known that.

She was like a dog with a bone, there was no way she would let things go if she got even an inkling that Emerald was still alive, as evidenced by her presence here in his home.

This wasn't how he had wanted things to turn out.

But he had been backed into a corner. Protecting Emerald was his only goal, and there was no way he was going to let his ex-friend hurt her. If Sapphire and her partner had just believed that the body they'd set up to mimic Emerald's was indeed Emerald, then they wouldn't be in this mess.

Unfortunately, things hadn't gone the way he'd planned.

They had figured out the ruse and started investigating who might want to make them believe that Emerald was dead. That had led them to Bobby Tompson and would sooner or later lead them right to his doorstep. The only option he had was to take Sapphire out of the equation.

"I ... we ... it wasn't like that," Emerald stammered.

Sapphire already knew more than he was comfortable with her knowing, he didn't want her learning anything else. "It's time for us to leave, Emerald," he said, taking her elbow and guiding her toward the door.

"So you're just going to leave me here? You're quite okay with this man keeping me a prisoner, leaving my husband to raise our son alone, leaving my little boy to grow up without a mother? That's your plan? Keep me here forever?"

"Not forever," Emerald quickly countered.

"Then how long? Days? Weeks? Months? Years? I don't know what happened to you, Emerald, but you're not the same sister that I remember. The Emerald that I know would never even think of kidnapping her own sister and holding her captive. I hit my head when Noah had me run off the road, I'm bleeding," Sapphire said, holding out her hand which was smeared with blood.

"Noah had a doctor look at you, you don't have a concussion," Emerald said.

"Oh well, that makes everything better then," Sapphire huffed.

Emerald was getting upset, and that was unacceptable. Sapphire may be Emerald's sister, but that didn't mean he wouldn't eliminate her if she hurt his precious Emerald.

"Let's go," he said firmly, unlocking the door, and walking through it, bringing Emerald with him.

"You won't get away with this, Noah," Sapphire screamed after him. "You think this will stop the investigation? It won't, it will only make them more determined to find out who wanted us to believe Emerald was dead. They'll find you, and then both of you will be going to prison."

As he closed the door behind him, he heard something crash into it, Sapphire had obviously thrown something at it. He understood her frustration, if someone had taken him away from the people he loved he would be just as angry, but for him, this was about protecting that person he loved.

Emerald looked up at him, she was trembling, and teardrops sat on her eyelashes, he caught them with his lips, and then kissed her.

Nobody made his woman cry.

Nobody.

Not even her sister.

"We can't let her go," he said when he broke the kiss.

"We can't keep her here," Emerald immediately countered.

"She knows too much now," he reminded her. "She knows that you're alive, and she knows that we're responsible for that woman's death. If we let her go the first thing she is going to do is go straight to her colleagues and come back here with a team of cops and arrest us." There was no way he was going to allow his beautiful, sweet woman to go back to being a prisoner. Emerald behind bars was such a repulsive prospect to him that it made him feel physically ill.

That this mess was all his fault made him angry.

He should have done things differently, so many choices along the way where he should have picked option B instead of option A.

Starting with never going on that website.

Now Noah couldn't even remember what had possessed him and his friend to even think of the idea of looking into buying a sex slave. They were both good looking young men, neither of them struggled to find women, but it had gotten boring. He wanted more, he wanted excitement, he wanted the power rush that nothing else could give him. And when Alfie had suggested it, he had gone along with it.

The website they had bought Emerald from said that the women had all voluntarily signed up for this, and they had signed contracts giving the company permission to sell them to someone in the market for a slave.

They had believed it.

There was no reason to think that the website was a scam, run by human traffickers selling girls who had been stolen, girls who had been so badly traumatized that they were never going to speak up and tell whoever bought them that they were victims, not willing participants.

It wasn't until he realized that Emerald never became aroused by the sexual games that they played that he knew something was wrong. Sending Alfie away so that he could have time alone with her, it took him months to coax her into admitting that she was, in fact, a victim.

The anger and self-loathing that had hit him like a baseball bat that day had never fully faded.

The things he had done to her when he believed that she wanted this every bit as much as they did still haunted him. He'd hurt her, he'd traumatized her, he deserved anything and everything the cops threw at him.

But Emerald didn't deserve any of this.

She was such an innocent woman, even with everything she had been through, she was just a good person, and even now, knowing that her freedom hung in the balance, she was more worried about her sister than she was about herself.

"Whatever happens, we can't keep Sapphire a prisoner," Emerald said. "I know what that's like, and she does too, I won't ever make anyone else go through that. I can't."

"It won't be like that," he protested. "She'll be safe here, she'll have her own room, a bathroom, no one is going to hurt her, anything she wants she can have."

"Anything except her little boy and her husband," Emerald said with so much pain in those big, green eyes of hers that it almost broke his heart in two.

He might not be a good man, but he had a heart.

It wasn't his heart that was the problem, it was just life had dealt him a hand that made him into the man he was today.

"Then we'll bring the husband and boy here," he said like it was that simple.

"You're going to kidnap her husband and her two-year-old son?" Emerald asked incredulously. "That sounds like a recipe for disaster. And then where would it stop? If you brought her family here, then what about my other sisters? Then they'd be grieving too, are you going to kidnap them and their families as well?"

While he knew that Emerald was being facetious that was an idea he would consider. If he could bring her whole family here—well not here, he would sell this place and disappear with Emerald and her family—then maybe Emerald would finally be happy.

He knew that she liked her life here with him, but there was still a piece of her missing, a piece that could never be restored until she was back with the family that she loved.

"And how could we live with ourselves if we made Sapphire's sweet little boy grow up here as someone's prisoner? I love Sapphire, and I don't want to keep her here against her will. We have to let her go, if she goes straight to the cops and tells them about us then we'll deal with whatever happens, but I won't keep her captive. And I know you can't do it either," she said, circling her arms around his waist and resting her head against his chest.

She had such faith in him.

Such faith that he was a good person.

But she was wrong.

He wasn't a good person, and her faith was misplaced, she thought that he couldn't go through with keeping Sapphire here as a prisoner, but he could.

He could do anything to keep Emerald safe.

Anything.

∼

5:34 P.M.

. . .

Amethyst checked the pot of potatoes boiling on the stove, they were soft but not quite ready for mashing. She set the lid back on the pot and then checked on the vegetables, they were steaming away, and the fish was in the frying pan, dinner would be ready in around ten minutes, she hoped Zeb was home by then. He was supposed to have been home at five, but she knew his schedule was unpredictable and there were plenty of times that she ate on her own.

Lucy was babbling away as she sat on the floor of the kitchen, blocks scattered around her, and she was throwing them about and banging them together, a huge smile on her little face, and giving gurgly baby laughs every time she managed to get the two blocks in her chubby little hands to connect.

She loved evenings like this. Cooking dinner, folding laundry, watching her daughter play, what could be better than that?

Sometimes, it was the simple things in life that gave you the most pleasure.

There were days when her job kept her away all night, and days when Zeb's job did the same, those were the days when she had to rely on one of her sisters to step in and watch Lucy, so she treasured these moments because she didn't get to enjoy them every day. Given what her past had been like, she knew how quickly things could change, and she didn't ever want life to pass her by again. She wanted to enjoy every second of the time she got with her husband and her daughter.

The back door swung open, and she heard the sounds of Zeb dropping his keys and wallet on the table by the door. "Honey, I'm home," he called out as he walked through into the family room.

"Do you have to say that every single night?" she asked, adding an eye roll for good measure.

"Sure do," he said, coming up behind her and nibbling on the side of her neck. "How was your day?"

"Quiet. Yours?"

"I wish it had been quiet."

"Dada, Dada, Dada," Lucy squealed when she caught sight of him.

"How's my princess?" Zeb asked, laying down on the floor in front of Lucy and grabbing her feet, pulling her closer so she could wrap her little arms around his neck. He tickled her tummy, and she shrieked in delight. "You like that, don't you? You want to fly?"

"Fy," she agreed with a giggle.

Zeb rolled over onto his back and lifted Lucy up, holding her at arms-length and swinging her around like she was flying. Lucy laughed, and Zeb laughed, and a huge smile filled her face as she watched her husband play with their daughter.

Nothing touched her heart more than that.

All those years she has wasted, trying to convince herself that all she needed in life was her next adrenalin rush felt like years she couldn't get back. She would have felt like they were years she had lost, but in reality, if she had realized earlier that she wanted more out of life then she might not have ended up with Zeb, and she couldn't imagine anyone else making her happier than he did.

"Water's boiling over."

"What?" She blinked and saw that Zeb had stood up and was standing in front of her, Lucy on his hip.

"The water in the pot is boiling over," he repeated, pointing to the stove behind her.

"Oh, no." She spun around and saw that water had indeed bubbled up, pushing the lid up and cascading down the sides. "What a mess."

"Want some help cleaning it up?"

"No, you play with Lucy, she missed you today, and dinner should be ready anyway, once I clean up this mess I'll dish it up."

Amethyst turned the gas on the stove off, carried the pot to the sink, drained the water out then left it there while she cleaned up her mess. She mashed the potatoes, dished up the steamed vegetables and the fish, prepared Lucy's meal, she ate the same thing they did, but she needed her fish cut into little pieces. She was looking forward to the days when her daughter was more independent and could do more things for herself. She was also looking forward to the days when Lucy had more teeth so they didn't have to cook the vegetables until they were almost mush.

Just as she was about to call out to Zeb—who was down on the floor laughing and giggling with Lucy—that dinner was ready, and it was time to wrangle Lucy into her highchair, a near-impossible feat that usually took a good five minutes, her phone rang.

Leaving the plates on the counter, she picked it up, seeing Diamond's name on the screen. "Hey, Diamond, what's up?"

"Uh, nothing much," her sister said, but she could hear in her tone that there really was something up.

"It doesn't sound like nothing, what's wrong?" A million scenarios ran through her head. Had something happened to Elijah? To one of the kids? One of their sisters?

"Well, I, uh, I don't actually know that anything is wrong, it's just that, have you heard from Elijah?"

"Heard from Elijah? No, why?" It wasn't that she wasn't close to her brothers-in-law because she was, she got along well with all of them, but she usually spoke with her sisters not any of their husbands.

"I haven't heard from him, not since this morning, and I was getting a little worried."

"He's probably just working late," she said, but she could tell that Diamond had already dismissed that possibility.

"If he's not going to be home by five he always calls or texts."

"Maybe he's just right in the middle of things, and you know what Sapphire is like, particularly on this case, they probably just got caught up in something, I'm sure he'll contact you soon."

"That's just it," Diamond said, a small waver in her voice, "Gideon hasn't heard from Sapphire either. He called me around fifteen minutes ago asking if I had heard from her. He said that she was supposed to call him at lunch because they had to set up a time to take Leo to the doctors, he keeps getting ear infections, and they wanted to know if there was anything they could do to stop them."

"I know," she said, she knew how much Sapphire had wanted to get something done because poor little Leo would be screaming in pain for days on end when he got an ear infection.

"Well, she didn't call him about it, and that isn't Sapphire, there is nothing work-related that would come before her son, not even this case."

She agreed. "And Gideon hasn't heard from her?"

"She hasn't come home, and she hasn't called, and neither has

Elijah. We know they were together this morning, and now they've both disappeared. You haven't heard from either of them?"

"No, I haven't heard from Sapphire since yesterday, and the last time I specifically texted or called Elijah was back in February when we were planning your birthday."

"Is Zeb there?"

"Yes."

"Can you ask him if he's heard from either of them?"

"Of course." Lowering the phone from her ear, she called out, "Zeb?"

"Yeah? Who's on the phone?"

"It's Diamond, she and Gideon haven't heard from Sapphire or Elijah, and neither has come home, do you know anything? Have you heard from either of them?"

"Not since this morning, I saw them both at the station before they went off to work their case, and Judah and I went off to work ours." He had stood up, crossed over to her, and his face had gone all cop-like. "Have either of them answered phone calls?"

"Diamond, did you try calling Elijah?" she asked into the phone.

"Of course, it goes straight to voicemail, same with Sapphire's phone."

"She said both phones are going straight to voicemail," she relayed to her husband.

"I'm going to go back down to the station, do you mind?" Zeb asked.

"No way, if something has happened to my sister and Elijah then I want to know what it is," she said, real worry beginning to form in her stomach. Had something happened to them? Were they okay?

"I'll keep you updated, sorry I'll miss dinner."

"There'll be others," she assured him. He gave her a quick kiss, picked up Lucy, set her in her highchair, then kissed her and disappeared out the back door to the garage. "Zeb is going to go down to the station," she told Diamond. "Do you want to pack up the kids and come over? I have plenty of food if you guys haven't eaten." She didn't want to sit here alone and worry all night. "Gideon and Leo can come too, and I'm sure Zeb will call Judah to meet him there, so we may as well ask Ruby and Chloe to come as well."

"All right, we'll be over soon."

As she disconnected the call, Amethyst prayed that nothing was wrong and there was a simple explanation for Sapphire and Elijah not answering their phones, their family had been through enough, they didn't deserve more suffering.

~

6:47 P.M.

It felt like she was back in that same nightmare she knew so well.

Just last night, Diamond had been so happy, spending time with her husband and their children, hopeful that soon her youngest sister might come back to them, and now her life had fallen apart.

Elijah was gone.

Sapphire was gone.

No trace of either of them.

It was like the two of them had arrived at work and then just disappeared into oblivion, being swallowed up by a black hole, and ceasing to exist.

Only she prayed that they hadn't really ceased to exist.

Even the possibility that she wasn't going to get her husband back left her so petrified she could barely draw in her next breath. How would she raise a teenage girl and two little boys on her own? How would she cope on her own without her husband by her side? What would happen to her? To her children? To her family?

And Sapphire's family too. She had a two-year-old son, how would Gideon cope raising him alone?

Why was this happening to them?

Hadn't she and her sisters been through enough?

Why were they suffering all over again?

It wasn't fair.

Diamond knew more than most the raw reality of the fact that life was often not fair, but there was unfair, and there was *unfair*, and this was definitely going beyond normal unfairness and taking it to a whole other level.

All she wanted was to raise her kids with her husband, go to work, paint, and enjoy a simple life. Was that too much to ask?

"We don't know anything yet, don't go thinking worst-case scenario."

Diamond looked up to see Ruby standing above her. "I'm trying," she said. "But it's hard. Elijah isn't answering his phone, and he hasn't called or texted me since this morning. Same thing with Gideon and Sapphire. We know they're together and both of them are AWOL. What else could it be other than something's happened to them?"

"Neither of them has been dropped off at a hospital," Amethyst reminded her. "Zeb texted to say that they contacted all major hospitals and there were no Jane Does or John Does admitted today."

While that was true, and she was happy that her husband and sister hadn't been so badly injured that they had been admitted to a hospital in such a state that they couldn't identify themselves, it didn't mean that they hadn't been hurt. "What if they crashed their car or something? They could be trapped and dying."

"If they crashed somewhere that no one saw the car then they would have had to be way outside the city, were they going out there today?" Ruby asked.

"Who knows? I suppose they were going wherever the case took them," she replied.

The case.

That was what had been nagging at her brain, refusing to be ignored. Diamond knew that the main case Elijah and Sapphire had been working was the one related to Emerald. Emerald was a human trafficking victim which meant that this case somehow involved traffickers. They were people not to be messed with. They were dangerous, and she knew they would go to any lengths to protect themselves and their business.

If Sapphire and Elijah got in their way they would eliminate them.

"Diamond?" Brooke called out, walking over to the kitchen where she, Ruby, and Amethyst were sitting. The teenager had offered to keep an eye on all the kids so that they could talk, or really, worry.

"Yes, honey?"

"The kids want ice cream, is that okay?" Brooke asked.

"Sure. Amethyst, do you have any?" she asked her sister.

"Is that a trick question?" Amethyst asked, mustering a smile. "Zeb is a huge ice cream addict, we probably have half a dozen flavors in the freezer. The kids can have whatever they want, Brooke."

"Are we staying here for a while? It's nearly seven, do you want me to put the boys, Leo, and Chloe all down to sleep in Lucy's room?"

"You don't have to worry about that, honey, I'll put the kids to bed," Ruby offered.

"No, it's okay, I don't mind," Brooke said. "You guys have enough on your minds. Is Lucy's room okay for all of them? I can put Chloe in the crib with her, and I can put Leo and Oscar in the fold-out crib, Archie can go in the spare bedroom, I'll sit in there with him and do my homework if he's scared on his own."

Diamond smiled at the girl, she had really matured and become so responsible these last few months. "That would be great, honey. Thanks."

"No problem." Brooke smiled back and went to grab bowls, spoons, and ice cream from the freezer.

Brooke was such a great kid, and Diamond knew that she would help out with the boys if something had happened to Elijah, but she wanted the girl to enjoy her teenage years not have to step up and take on responsibilities she was too young for.

If the same people who had bought Emerald had something to do with Elijah and Sapphire's disappearances, then instead of getting Emerald back she might lose another sister and her husband.

She was about to ask whether Ruby and Amethyst thought that the human traffickers might be involved too when she heard the front door open.

This could be it.

Zeb, Judah, and Gideon might be back, ready to sit her down and tell her that her husband's body had been found.

Diamond steeled her spine and tried to prepare herself as best as she could.

"Diamond."

She gasped and spun around.

Elijah.

Her husband was standing there looking at her. There was blood on his face, but he was standing on his own, and he looked okay.

She flew across the room and threw herself into his arms. He held her tight, his hand cradling the back of her head, and he buried his face in her hair.

"You're alive," she whispered into his chest, tears blurred her vision, but she held them back because she didn't want to worry the boys.

"I'm alive," he echoed.

"I'm so glad you're okay," Brooke said, rushing over to hug Elijah.

"I'm okay, kiddo," he said, hugging her tightly.

"Arch, Ozzy, come say hi to Daddy," she called out.

"Mo-om, we're watching TV, and the ice cream will melt," Archie whined.

"Now, Arch," she said, her tone firm. The boys came over, and Elijah snatched them up, holding both in his arms, while still keeping a hold on her and Brooke. She hadn't seen her husband this rattled before, and she wondered what had happened and where he had been.

"Can we go watch TV now?" Archie asked.

"Sure," she agreed.

Elijah set the boys on their feet, and they ran off to join their cousins, Brooke followed them, and Elijah took Diamond's hand and led her to the kitchen where Ruby and Judah, and Amethyst and Zeb, and Gideon were waiting for them.

But no Sapphire.

Her sister wasn't here, but her husband was, she had no idea what that meant.

"Where's Sapphire? What happened? You're hurt, who hurt you? And how? Where have you been all day? You didn't call or text, and I was worried, are you really okay?" Questions tumbled out in a rush, and a shiver washed over her.

"I'm really okay," he answered that question first, then guided her onto a stool at the breakfast bar and wrapped an arm around her shoulder, holding her close. "Zeb and Judah found me tied up in the trunk of my car."

"In the trunk? Is that where you've been all day?" she asked, horrified.

"At least since around ten this morning anyway," he said. "Sapphire and I were going out to interview someone, but they weren't home, we got a call about a hair found in the car of our suspect, and we were going there to speak with him when our car was hit. There were men—I'm not sure how many—they dragged us out and injected me with something that knocked me out. I don't know how long I was out, but when I woke up I was tied up in the trunk, I couldn't get free enough to unlatch the lid and get out. Whoever hit our car must have driven it down to a local shopping mall parking lot, luckily someone heard me banging, called 911, and when they reported the license plate, and they realized whose car it was, they called Zeb and Judah who found me."

That was lucky.

A string of luck, had it been the middle of winter her husband probably would have died of hypothermia, summer and it would have been heatstroke, if the car hadn't been left in a populated area he could have died from dehydration.

Thankfully, she had Elijah back, and he was okay, but that didn't mean this was over.

"Where's Sapphire?" Diamond asked, looking at Gideon who was standing stiffly, his face a blank mask but his brown eyes a violent mess of emotions. Unfortunately, she didn't have to imagine what he was going through because she knew. She knew every thought, every fear, every imagining that would be running through his head right now.

Elijah tightened his grip on her, his voice stark when he uttered the words she was both expecting and dreading, "I don't know."

∾

8:23 P.M.

. . .

"Ugh," Sapphire groaned as she swam back to consciousness for the second time in ... well in however long it had been since she and Elijah had left Dean Winters' house and been run off the road.

They'd drugged her again.

The 'they' being Noah Landry and her *sister*.

She still couldn't believe that her own sister had participated in orchestrating Alice Lincoln's abduction, torture, imprisonment, and murder. *And* been a willing participant in her own abduction.

She was so angry she could hardly think straight.

So angry that the fuzziness in her head from whatever they'd given her to knock her out faded away.

How could Emerald do this?

What had happened to her that she thought nothing of using other people as pawns to get what she wanted?

No matter what Emerald thought of Noah, he wasn't a good guy, and he didn't love her. Anyone that would have people kidnapped and killed was an evil monster, and it seemed that her own sister was now an evil monster too.

With a groan that said the fuzziness in her head wasn't completely gone yet, she opened her eyes and was surprised to find that she was in a different room, not the same one that she had woken in earlier, where she had learned that her sister was indeed alive but that she wasn't the same person she remembered.

They'd moved her, but why?

Her instincts were to believe that it was Noah who had her taken to a different location. She wanted so badly to believe that Emerald hadn't been able to go through with keeping her a prisoner and wanted to let her go, only Noah hadn't been on board. Maybe he had told Emerald that he had set her free, but in reality, he had whisked her away some-place where no one would ever find her.

She wanted to believe that but ...

But she wasn't sure that Emerald really cared about what happened to her. Just because she had said that they didn't plan on keeping her captive forever, didn't mean that Noah was on the same page. Or that Emerald wasn't going to change her mind. They had to know that if they let her go the first thing she was going to do was go straight to the precinct and report the fact that Emerald was alive, and that she and Noah were responsible for Alice's death.

Well, that wasn't the *first* thing she was going to do. The first thing she would do when—if—she got out of here was go straight home and hug her husband and her son.

Tears brimmed in her eyes as she thought of the possibility that she would never see them again. She loved them so much, Gideon was the best thing that had ever happened to her, and she wished she had told him more often just how much she loved him. And Leo was the light of her life, she wished she had spent less time at work and more time with him just building with blocks, and playing trains, going to the park, and just laughing and having fun. She didn't want her little boy to grow up without her, she had wanted to give him the warm, loving home that her parents had never given her and her sisters, and while she hadn't done as good a job as she had planned, she loved him more than she could ever express.

Sapphire chewed on her bottom lip to keep from crying, she didn't have time for tears right now. She had to figure out a plan. The last room she had been kept in had bars on the window and the door had been locked, but she hadn't had a chance to check out this room yet.

Swinging her legs over the side of the bed, she stood up, the pain in her head was still there, but it wasn't as bad as it had been before. At least she knew she didn't have a concussion since Noah had had a doctor look her over.

Quickly, she shoved away all thoughts of Noah and Emerald, if she thought about them too much she was going to get so angry that she couldn't function. And functioning and keeping a clear head was her only hope of getting home to the family she adored.

This room was a bedroom, but it wasn't quite as fancy as the other one, the floor was hardwood, the walls were papered in a dark maroon flower print, the bed was a four-poster, and there was also a closet, a bureau, two armchairs and a small table by the window.

The window was her best bet of getting out of here. She would scale the wall or jump if she had to, she was doing anything it took to get out of this room. Crossing over to it, she threw back the drapes—which matched the wallpaper and the quilt on the bed—and then growled in frustration when she saw more bars. Whoever had put her in here, and she had no reason to believe it wasn't Noah, obviously intended on keeping her here.

Permanently.

The door would be locked, she knew that it would be, and yet she still had to check. Hurrying over to it, she grabbed the door handle and yanked as hard as she could, but it didn't budge. The door was oak and felt thick, she didn't think she stood a chance at breaking it down, and yet she would certainly try as soon as she had finished checking out her new prison.

There was another door on the far wall, and she headed for it expecting to find a bathroom, and when she opened the door she saw she was correct. It looked like it had been prepared for her arrival, there were towels hanging on a rack on the back of the door, and there was a stack of toiletries on the counter, every single thing was exactly the brand that she had at home.

A bad feeling brewing in her stomach, she ran to the closet, opening the door to find it full of clothes, the bureau was also packed with clothes, and she picked up a neatly folded sweater and found that it was exactly her size. Quickly, she grabbed another and another, they were her size too, and when she ran back to the closet and checked the jeans and dresses hanging in there she found the same thing.

Her favorite toiletries, clothes that were in her size, none of this was an accident, whoever had stashed her here knew enough about her to know these intimate things. No one but her sisters knew what size clothes she wore, and that was only because they sometimes borrowed her things, but even Gideon couldn't pick out her size, because guys didn't notice things like that.

But her abductor did.

She knew that Noah and Emerald had been watching her and her family so it made sense that they could have found out what size clothing she wore and what shampoo she used and her favorite body wash.

They were diabolical.

The chances of her finding a way out of here seemed to be getting slimmer by the second. If someone had gone to enough trouble to buy her clothes and collect toiletries, then they weren't going to leave her a way to get out.

Talking her way out wasn't an option either. There was no way that Emerald and Noah were going to be persuaded to let her go, they were in full on self-preservation mode and didn't care about what they did to her. Maybe she could play along for a day or two, and then make her move when Emerald or Noah came in to see her, she could knock them out, grab the key, and run.

Other than that it was down to Elijah.

Her partner wasn't here, and she prayed that that was because they had left him behind when they abducted her. If he was okay then he could tell everyone what had happened and maybe, just maybe, they would be able to track her down.

Only Noah hadn't been on their radar.

So how would anyone know to look into him?

As far as she and Elijah had been concerned, Noah was nothing more than Bobby's boss, he wasn't a suspect, and if he hadn't had her kidnapped then she didn't think he ever would have been.

There was only so much Elijah, and her family and colleagues could do, and she wasn't sure it was enough to get her home.

Unless ...

No, she didn't think it would happen.

But maybe ...

What if Emerald grew a conscience and realized that this was wrong and talked Noah into letting her go.

Of course, that only worked if Emerald knew that she was still a prisoner. If she had stood her ground and insisted that they let her go, and believed that they had only Noah had spirited her away behind her back, then there was no way that Emerald would find out that she wasn't home with her family. She obviously wanted nothing to do with them, so how would she find out that Noah hadn't done what she wanted?

She wouldn't.

Drained, Sapphire walked over to the bed and dropped down onto it, she missed her family more than she could say, and the thought of never getting to see them again drained all the fight out of her.

∼

11:11 P.M.

"Starlight, star bright, first star I see tonight," Emerald murmured.

She was out on the balcony, the place she spent time every single night, thinking about her sisters.

Just because she hadn't wanted to go back to that time in her life when she had a family, didn't mean that she had stopped loving them. Her decisions had been based on self-preservation. She needed to disconnect herself from the girl she had been when she was sold, and being sold was too closely linked to her sisters, being with them would be like going backward instead of forward.

But now ...

Now she was second-guessing herself.

Her doubts had started when Noah had shown her the cameras in his office. It wasn't just seeing her sisters for the first time in almost fifteen years, it was seeing how happy they were. Watching them with their husbands and their children, watching them together, how they seemed to draw strength from one another. Was she missing out by giving that up?

What would her life have been like if she had left when Noah sent her away?

She had been just days away from eighteen when she was first brought to this house, and for the first six months, her life had been hell. She had been tortured, humiliated, raped, beaten. It was like living in a never-ending nightmare.

Then everything had changed.

One day it had been just Noah who entered her room, he had taken her out, and she had let her mind go blank, the only way she could cope with what they did to her. But he hadn't done anything awful, he had just taken her hand and led her through the house and out to the stables. He'd let her pat the horses, feed them carrots, and then he'd asked her why she signed up for this. He had told her that she was never aroused, and he was wondering if either she had never willingly signed up for this or if she was in over her head, and it wasn't what she thought it would be.

She'd said nothing.

It had taken him months to coax her into admitting the truth and so much longer to convince her that she could trust him.

Once he had earned her trust, he had spent months helping her overcome what she had been through, and then when she finally started making progress he had given her a suitcase full of clothes, thousands of dollars in cash, and had his driver take her to the police station.

The same station where Sapphire would later get a job.

Left on her own, she had debated going in, telling them who she was and what had happened to her, but she hadn't.

She didn't want to.

She didn't want to go backward, she wanted to go forward, and going forward meant being with Noah.

It wasn't Stockholm Syndrome like Sapphire had suggested, it was love. Real love, built through months of trust and support that had grown into something more. She was only twenty back then, and the world had been a big and scary place, but believing Noah didn't want her she had tried to build a new life, she had gotten a job as a waitress and lived in an apartment all by herself.

Those couple of months on her own had been terrifying.

She was afraid of everyone she met, she was terrible at her job mostly because she jumped at every little sound, which usually caused her to drop cups of coffee or plates of sandwiches, sometimes onto the customers. She didn't sleep, she barely ate, several times she almost got hit by a car when she was sure that she saw one of the men who had trained her in the basement and forgotten she was crossing a road.

In the end, she had accepted there was only one place where she could find peace.

Noah's.

So she had returned, begged him to let her stay, told him she couldn't live without him, and while he had at first been reluctant, he had finally relented and let her stay.

Emerald was happy with her life, she loved Noah, and she loved living here with him, but what if she had walked into that police station that day? What would she be like? What would her life be like? She wouldn't have Noah, but she would have had her sisters, it was hard to believe that that would have made her life any better.

And yet the more she had watched her sisters, the more she missed them, then seeing Sapphire face to face, being in the same room as her, hugging her, it had made her sisters seem so much more real. They stopped being the almost mythical beings of a life that hardly seemed to have anything to do with her, and became real live people again.

Sapphire had looked so much older, and even though she knew she did too it was weird to see her sister as a cop and not a teenage girl, but she had been the exact same Sapphire she remembered. A little angrier maybe, but still the same passionate, confident person she had always been.

The hurt and pain in her sister's eyes when Sapphire learned that she had stayed away on purpose had been a punch to the gut. And when she had accused them of kidnapping her so they could kill her it had been like a knife through her heart.

She should never have let Noah talk her into kidnapping her sister. It was crazy, and now looking back, it was never going to achieve anything good. But when he had suggested it, the need to see one of her sisters had temporarily overridden her common sense, and she hadn't tried to talk him out of it. She hadn't really thought any further ahead than seeing Sapphire, but of course letting her sister know she was alive would only make her more determined to figure out everything that had led to this point in their lives.

Now the fact that she wanted to keep herself a secret might become a moot point. She doubted that once her other sisters learned the truth, that she had deliberately kept the fact that she was alive and safe a secret, that they would be any less angry with her than Sapphire had been.

She might have lost her family for real now.

And that made her doubt everything that she had done and every choice she had made.

Why was it that you didn't realize what you had until it was gone?

"Emerald, come in to bed." Noah came up behind her and drew her into his arms, holding her close and letting her body absorb his heat.

"We did the right thing, letting Sapphire go," she said, curling her fingers into his shirt. "Thank you for everything you've done for me. Thank you for protecting me and thank you for respecting my wishes and letting my sister go back to her family. It really was the right thing to do." Emerald was surprised that cops hadn't already come knocking on their door. She was sure that within an hour or so of setting Sapphire free she would be back here with her colleagues, ready to drag both her and Noah away in handcuffs, but it had been hours now and nothing. Maybe Sapphire hadn't been able to do it, maybe despite the anger, she loved her enough to not be able to watch her be thrown into prison.

"Come inside," Noah said, leading her indoors.

"You think you're such a tough guy, but inside you're hiding a big heart," she said, kissing his neck. Usually, Noah was the one that instigated sex. While he had taught her not to fear it, she couldn't say that very often she enjoyed it in the way normal people did, but tonight her heart was swelling with so much love for him that she needed to express it.

With barely shaking fingers she began to unbutton his shirt, running her hands over his abs, she loved that he was so muscled because it made her feel safe, Alfie was never getting through Noah to get to her. Her fingers moved to his belt buckle, and she undid it then his pants and shoved them down, leaving him half undressed and her still in the white nightgown Noah liked her to wear. It wasn't often he was more undressed than she was.

With what she knew was extreme restraint, Noah stood still and let her remove his clothes, stepping out of each side of his pants as she pushed them down his legs. When her hands reached for the waist of his boxers they started to tremble, sometimes her feelings for Noah scared her. He had quite literally saved her life, and that kind of connection never went away.

Emerald pushed his boxers down and sucked in a breath at the size of him. Sometimes she wondered how he fit inside her, but like they had been made for each other, he always slipped in and perfectly filled her up.

With a gentleness he didn't usually show, Noah scooped her up into his arms and carried her to the bed, she expected him to lay her down and enter her body, but instead, he laid down and set her on top of him so she was straddling him.

She was never the one in control.

Never.

But tonight was different.

Tonight something had shifted between them.

Today she had gotten what she wanted when it came to Sapphire, Noah had conceded to her wishes instead of the other way around.

Lifting her hips, she brought them down slowly, taking him inside her inch by inch until he filled her completely. She began to move, up so just his tip was inside her body, and then back down until all of him was in her. With each movement, that feeling inside her grew. It filled her up, all over, her body, her heart, her mind, her soul, it was like a mix between rainbows and butterflies fluttering, that kind of magical feeling that was almost too good to be true.

Noah's hands gripped her hips holding her in place as he thrust up, once, twice, and then the world exploded into a mass of starlight.

Stars.

For some reason her life always led back to stars.

From the wishes she and Sapphire used to make as kids, to lying out in that cage with the dogs and watching them twinkle above her feeling a connection to the family she had lost, to the stars she looked at every night on the balcony outside the bedroom she shared with the man she loved.

Today those stars had brought her closer to Noah, and maybe in some weird way closer to the family she had left behind as well.

CHAPTER
Ten

November 30th
8:40 A.M.

He hadn't slept a wink all night.

Every time he had closed his eyes he was back in the trunk of the car, tied up, annoyed, and trying to get free but failing, wondering what had happened to his partner and how he was going to get out of that trunk and do something about it.

Elijah was wired this morning. He knew that his body needed sleep, that he needed time to decompress, but he didn't have time. Sapphire was missing, and he had to find her before she became another statistic. So instead of sleep, he had to satisfy himself with kissing his wife, hugging his three kids, and hoping it was enough to keep him going through the day.

"Why don't you catch us up on the Alice Lincoln case and we can go from there," Zeb said.

"Then we should go through your other cases as well, there's no way to know for sure that Sapphire's abduction is related to this case," Judah added.

"We were just leaving a person of interest's house on our way to interview our prime suspect, who we had just gotten forensic proof that he was our guy, what are the chances it isn't related to that case?" he said. As far as he was concerned, his partner's kidnapping was because of this case, because they'd gotten too close to the people who had Emerald.

What was weighing most on his mind was whether or not she was still alive.

If Sapphire was a threat, then the simplest way to take care of her was just to kill her and bury her body someplace where no one would ever find her. Having them run around, chasing their tails, looking for her gave these people plenty of time to move out, disappear, and never be heard from again.

Or there was another option.

Sapphire was a beautiful woman, and as a cop she could be highly attractive to the right buyer. If these were human traffickers who had Emerald and who had paid Bobby Tompson to abduct and kill Alice Lincoln, making them think it was Emerald, then they might decide instead of killing Sapphire they could get a bonus, eliminate her as a threat *and* get a tidy sum of cash by selling her. In the end it did the same thing, getting her out of the way and making sure she would never be in a position to threaten them again.

With a tired sigh, he scrubbed his hands down his face. "It's about this case, but just to be safe we can run through our other cases and see if there's anyone else who might want to hurt her." As much as he didn't want to waste time, he couldn't gamble with Sapphire's life if there was even the slimmest of possibilities that someone else had kidnapped her.

"All right, run down what you know so far," Zeb said.

"Alice Lincoln was abducted eighteen months ago, there were no suspects, and the case went cold until we found the body in the woods a couple of days ago. Because of the scars, we initially thought it was Emerald, but you know all of this already. The couple who found the body mentioned seeing a car around there several times in the few weeks before the murder, that led us to Bobby Tompson. He denied being there, but when a neighbor informed us that Bobby knew Alice who used to live next door to him, we knew he was lying. When we went to pick him up, he ran and would have jumped off the building had Sapphire not shot him. We were speaking with people at Bobby's work, and when we realized that someone had left to avoid us, we went there to speak with him, that's where we were when it happened."

"Who is this person you were looking into?" Judah asked.

"His name is Dean Winters. He inherited a small fortune when his widowed mother married a rich businessman, they both died, and he was left with everything."

"What else do you know about him?" Zeb asked.

"Not much, we looked up a few basics on the way to his house, but we intended to learn what we could about him when we interviewed him. We knew that Bobby was paid by someone, and Dean had the money to pay him, but beyond that, we didn't have anything else to point to him as a suspect. If he hadn't of run when he heard we were there we probably never would have looked at him."

"You would have if you saw this," Judah said, turning his laptop around so they could see the screen. "This," he tapped at a photo, "isn't Dean Winters. This is," he said, tapping at another photo on the screen.

"What?" Elijah asked, confused, and wishing they had looked into Dean a whole lot more closely before heading to his house.

"This is Dean Winters' driver's license, and this is the photo of Dean Winters on the company website, it's not the same guy," Judah replied.

"So there are two Dean Winters," he said, not catching the point.

"They have the same date of birth, and the address on Dean Winters' driver's license is the same address as the house you and Sapphire went to yesterday. It looks like someone might be impersonating him," Judah explained.

"Who? Why?" he asked, knowing that his friend didn't have those answers.

"Why?" Zeb echoed. "You know for sure that Bobby was involved, right?"

"Yes, forensics found a hair with Alice's DNA on it in the trunk of Bobby's car. He's involved, and we know he's not the mastermind, someone paid him to do it, with what we know now it really could have been Dean Winters. He started working at Noah Landry's company around two years ago, is that a coincidence or something more?"

"My guess would be something more, I don't like that timing. He starts working there and then six months later he pays someone to abduct a woman, I don't like that. We need to find out if he has any connections to Bobby Tompson beyond working for the same company. Does he have a criminal record?" Zeb asked.

"None. But that doesn't mean he doesn't have a connection to human trafficking," Elijah said.

"Human trafficking," Judah said slowly, "it all seems to circle back to that, but really, we don't have anything to conclusively prove that this has anything to do with it."

"It's a safe assumption given they wanted us to believe that Emerald was dead and we do know for a fact that she was sold to human traffickers," he reminded Judah.

"But I don't get why," Judah said, his blue eyes perplexed. "*Why* would they go to all this trouble to make us think she's dead? It's been fifteen years since Emerald and her sisters were sold, so why now? Why all of a sudden is it important for the cops to believe that she's dead? I know that Sapphire works the case every chance she gets, but as far as I know, she hasn't made any progress. So why do this? They planned this well in advance, it wasn't a spur of the moment thing, and they put a lot of effort into it, paid a lot of money to get it done. But why all this fuss over a human trafficking victim? They're usually throw away victims because as far as their owners are concerned, they can be easily replaced. I think if we want to find Sapphire, and maybe Emerald too, we have to start focusing on the motive. If we can find the motive, then we'll find the who."

"I agree, but that's easier said than done," Elijah said. "We haven't been able to trace the money, so unless something shows up there, then we're not going to find this other man through that. And I don't think Bobby is going to flip on him, he's too afraid of what will happen to him if he speaks. We tried to spook him into confessing, but so far he's standing firm. I don't know how we're going to figure out a motive. We know Emerald was sold, but we have no idea to whom. They never found the original people who bought the girls so there is no way to know who she was sold to. If we don't know who bought her, then we don't know what their motive might be to want the world to think she's dead."

This case was feeling more hopeless by the second.

The revelation that someone was impersonating Dean Winters raised a million questions but didn't answer any of them. Dean was still in the wind, and Bobby wasn't talking, there was no one to give them the answers they needed.

So how could they get Sapphire back?

And if they didn't get her back, how was he going to live with himself? She was his partner, it was his job to watch her back, and he had failed. Now she might be gone forever.

∾

10:54 A.M.

She paced the room like a caged animal.

Another day or two in here and Sapphire was going to lose her mind.

How long had she been here already? She wasn't sure, but it couldn't be more than forty-eight hours or so.

Forty-eight hours was a long time when you were away from your family, being held prisoner, with no idea what the future held.

So Noah was going to keep her alive for now, no doubt because Emerald wanted him to, but that was no guarantee he would keep her alive indefinitely. Sooner or later she was bound to become more trouble than she was worth and then he'd just eliminate her. Sapphire wasn't even sure that Emerald knew she was here, her heart wanted to believe that her sister had stuck to her guns and insisted that they let her go home, but her head wasn't convinced. She was wary of putting too much faith in the sister who was now unrecognizable to her. If Emerald thought that she was at home with her family now, and decided to keep her distance, then she would never know that Noah had gone behind her back.

Or her sister knew she was here and just didn't care.

It was clear that Emerald didn't care about any of them anymore, if she did, there was no way she would keep the fact that she was alive and no longer someone's prisoner from them. The Emerald that she knew would never let them suffer, believing that she was still hurting, or worse, dead.

But Emerald had changed.

Sapphire understood that enduring what she had would change her, it had changed all of them, but the rest of them had pulled together, sought comfort and support from one another.

With a frustrated growl, she stopped her pacing to drop down onto the bed, where she snatched up a pillow and curled her hands around it trying to let go of her anger. If she couldn't stop being angry then she was never going to be able to figure out something she could do to get out of here.

Although she knew the chances of her finding a way to escape were slim, she couldn't give up. If she gave up then she was guaranteeing that she would never see Gideon and Leo again, and that was something she couldn't accept. No matter the odds, she had to keep a clear head because her husband and her son needed her and she was determined to be there for them.

The sound of a lock turning caught her attention and she turned toward the door. A maid accompanied by an armed guard had already been by several times with food, good food, *real* food, in fact some of her favorite foods. It was so unnerving that Noah had gone to such lengths to make sure she was comfortable here, the food, the clothes, the toiletries, there was even a TV that had been programmed with all her favorite shows. It certainly indicated that this was a long term thing as far as he was concerned.

But what exactly was long term?

Months?

Years?

Decades?

There was no way that she was sitting in some room for decades while her little boy grew up without her.

There was no clock in here but from the position of the sun outside her barred up window, she suspected it was approaching the middle of the day but not quite there. Too early for lunch, maybe a morning snack?

The door swung open, but it wasn't the skittish maid who refused to make eye contact and just passed over the tray without a word who walked into the room. Nor was it one of the armed men. This time it was a man dressed in a black suit, white shirt, and red silk tie. He strolled in like he was here for a pleasant chat, and immediately her cop instincts kicked into overdrive.

"Good morning, Ms. Hatcher," the man said, shooting her a smarmy smile that made the hairs on the back of her neck stand up.

"Actually," she said, standing and staring the man down, "it's *Detective* Hatcher-Barlow. I took on my husband's name after we were married. And you are?"

He just smiled back at her, taking his time turning around, closing the door, locking it, and then leaning against it. "There are two armed men out there, if I don't walk out of here in ten minutes, then they come in, shoot first ask questions later, so I wouldn't bother trying anything stupid."

The man was relaxed, calm, almost joyful and she wondered what his purpose was here. Why would Noah send someone into her room to do … what she wasn't sure yet, but why was he here? If Noah didn't want anything else to do with her and was planning on just leaving her here, then there was no need to send anyone to her room.

Unless …

Unless he was planning on pimping her out.

Despite the rose-colored—or Stockholm Syndrome colored—glasses Emerald seemed to be wearing, Noah wasn't a good guy, and by her own admission, he had bought her intending to use her as a sex slave, maybe he saw this as an opportunity to make a little extra cash.

Although she was no longer the helpless sixteen-year-old girl she had been back then, she couldn't help a cold shiver shaking through her.

Faking an easy smile that she certainly didn't feel, she took a step closer to the man, feigning bravado. "Now, why would I cause you any trouble? I'm a prisoner here, aren't I? Your boss' prisoner. You one of Noah's goons? How much is he paying you?"

"Paying me?" The man looked amused. "I think you're a little confused."

"Sure." She rolled her eyes. "You're just another one of his puppets. If he's not paying you maybe he just used his apparent mind control powers on you, talked you into doing this for free. He seems pretty good at convincing people to do things that they otherwise wouldn't do."

"Noah didn't talk me into doing anything, and he didn't pay me," the man told her.

"Then you must be some sick pervert like he is."

Her words obviously struck a nerve because the man lunged at her and shoved her up against the wall. "I'm not a pervert," he hissed, the smug smile gone, now fury burned in his dark eyes.

"If you say so," she said with another eye roll.

His fingers curled around her neck, and he squeezed just hard enough to make it hard for her to breathe without completely cutting off her air supply. "I'm not a pervert," he repeated.

"So you just like to beat up women for fun?" she snarled. She couldn't believe that Emerald was okay with this. Okay with having her kidnapped and kept here against her will, okay with Noah sending some man in to rough her up. Maybe this was supposed to scare her into keeping quiet if they eventually let her go, but if that was the goal it was never going to work.

"No." He curled a lip up, the anger gone, something sinister brewing in his face now. "I do this to women for fun." His hand grabbed her breast, and he squeezed it hard enough to make her wince. "I also do this for fun," he said, keeping one hand around her neck, his other went between her legs and rubbed her, making her extremely glad she had put on jeans this morning.

Since she wasn't some helpless kid anymore, she kneed the man right in the groin and gave him a smug smile of her own when he groaned in pain.

"I *don't* like that," he said, his fist slamming into her face.

"Well I don't like you," she spat back, she wasn't letting any man push her around, Noah may as well learn that now, either he killed her, he let her go, or he just kept her in here alone, but sending men in to try to grope her was unacceptable.

"Irrelevant," he said with a smirk. He leaned in close, his mouth just a millimeter away from her ear, his breath hot against her skin. "Next time I'll show you *exactly* what I like to do to women."

His hand around her neck tightened, and although she wanted to keep her cool, the lack of oxygen was enough to have her nails clawing at him. He smiled, pleased to know he had rattled her, then he released her, and swung his fist at her again. This blow was harder and without his hand to hold her up, she fell to the ground.

The man walked to the door and left her alone again. Sapphire lifted a hand to her cheek, it came away sticky with blood. For the last almost fifteen years she had beaten herself up because she had been rescued so soon after their parents sold them and now it seemed she had found herself in the exact same position her sisters had when they were all teenagers.

~

7:17 P.M.

Gideon felt like his life had been ripped apart.

The hole left by Sapphire's disappearance was huge and gaping.

It was like the very center of his world, his heart, his soul, everything that was bright and interesting about his life was gone.

Life with Sapphire was anything but dull. She was a spitfire of a personality, she was confident and self-assured, or at least that was the persona that she liked others to see, but inside she was full of doubt and uncertainty. He knew that he provided her the grounding that she so desperately craved. He gave her something to focus on besides the recrimination she constantly heaped on herself because she didn't possess superhuman powers to save everyone in the world who was suffering.

Especially her own sister.

Knowing that Emerald was out there and that she couldn't do anything to bring her home was something that he knew Sapphire thought about on a daily basis. Survivor's guilt was a hard thing to overcome because, in the end, nothing could change it, you had still been spared when others hadn't.

Not that in reality Sapphire had been spared. She had been sold to human traffickers right alongside her sisters, she had been sexually assaulted, and even though she had been rescued within days, she had been the one who had to turn her parents into the cops and then testify against them.

He wouldn't call that being spared anything.

But in her mind, she had gotten off easier than her sisters, and that continued to be a sticking point for her.

He tried hard to be there for her, support her, give her a different opinion than the one she had clung to for over a decade, and while he knew it had made a difference, he hadn't been able to erase those thoughts from her mind. As a psychiatrist, that he couldn't take away his own wife's pain bothered him. He loved Sapphire more than he thought it was possible to love another person. He'd shown her how to have fun, that life didn't have to be always about work, he teased her because he knew she needed that in her life, but it wasn't enough, she was still hurting, and he couldn't stop it.

That made him feel like a failure.

What kind of psychiatrist was he—what kind of *husband* was he—if he couldn't take away his wife's pain?

"Daddy."

Pulled out of his thoughts, Gideon looked down to see Leo looking up at him with his mother's eyes. His son was missing his mother, all day he had asked about her. Where was she? Why hadn't she come home? What was she doing? All questions he had no answers for.

Whoever had taken Sapphire hadn't just hurt her, but their son as well and that was unacceptable. The idea of someone messing with his family filled him with a deep protective rage that only came when someone messed with what was yours. Sapphire and Leo were his world and no one messed with them and got away with it. When he found who had kidnapped her, he was going to make sure they suffered the full extent of the law. As much as he wanted to pummel that person into oblivion, it wasn't worth spending the rest of his life in prison, or even a few days in jail, his wife was going to need him.

"Daddy," Leo said again, his mouth full of toothpaste as they stood at the sink in the bathroom, getting him ready for bed.

"Did you brush up and down?" he asked, as much as he wanted to focus all his energy in helping the cops find who had abducted his wife, his son needed him, he was going to have to do a better job at focusing on Leo because ...

Well, he wasn't ready to entertain that possibility just yet.

"Yes," Leo answered, toothpaste dribbling down his chin.

"Side to side?"

"Yes."

"Okay, here you go." He handed Leo a cup of water, and he swished it and spat out his toothpaste into the sink. "Clean your face," he said, passing him a towel, and once Leo had wiped his face, he lifted him down off the stepstool. "Time for bed."

"No," Leo said firmly, adding in a shake of his head for good measure.

"No?" he echoed, surprised by Leo's sudden disobedience, his son was a good boy who rarely threw tantrums and who almost always did as he was asked without complaining. He was a serious child, just like his mother, and every time he looked at Leo he saw Sapphire, he might be a boy, but he was definitely his mother's mini-me.

"Mama," Leo said. "I want Mama to read me stories."

"I know you do, buddy," he said, picking Leo up and hugging him tightly. "But Mama isn't here right now."

"Why?"

How did you answer that question in a way a two-year-old understood?

Leo was too young to know that his mother had been kidnapped and even if he told him that didn't mean he would understand, it was too abstract a concept.

But at the same time, he didn't want Leo to think that his mother wasn't here because she didn't want to be here with him. Gideon knew that Sapphire had grown up in a home with emotionally detached parents and her fears were that she wouldn't be able to give Leo the loving, warm home that she had wanted as a child. Her fears had been misplaced, she was an excellent mother, and Leo adored her, but he knew it was something Sapphire still struggled with.

Knowing he needed to settle on an answer, Gideon said, "Because she can't be."

"Why?"

"She just can't, but I bet she misses you so much, she misses hugging you and kissing you, and hearing you tell her that you love her," he said, giving Leo a tight hug and a kiss on the cheek. He knew Sapphire would do anything she could to try to get home to them, but that scared him more than reassured him because he was worried that she would wind up getting herself killed in the process.

Carrying Leo down the hall, he took him into his bedroom and tucked him into his bed, they read one of Leo's favorite books, and then he kissed him goodnight, turned on the nightlight, and closed the door.

Then he sunk down against it.

The anger was back.

Burning so brightly he half expected steam to come pouring out his ears.

He shouldn't be tucking their son in alone, Sapphire should be with him, she should be home with the people who loved her.

With a sigh, he pushed himself up and headed back downstairs where the rest of the family were gathered. They had all spent the previous night at Amethyst and Zeb's house because that's where they had gathered when they realized Sapphire and Elijah were missing, but today he had wanted to bring Leo home, he was already confused and missing his mother, he needed to be in a familiar environment. The rest of the family had insisted on coming, adamant that they weren't going to leave him and Leo alone. The house had five bedrooms, Amethyst and Zeb and Lucy were staying in one of the spare rooms, Ruby and Judah and Chloe in another, and Diamond and Elijah and their three kids in the fifth. As nice as it was to not be alone and to have his family rally around him, he knew this couldn't last. If Sapphire didn't come home, then eventually they would all go back to their homes, and their lives, and it would just be him and Leo.

"How's Leo doing?" Ruby asked when she spotted him.

"As you'd expect, he misses his mom and doesn't understand why she's not here."

"We're doing everything we can to find her," Elijah assured him.

"I know." He knew that every cop in the city was looking for Sapphire, but that didn't mean she would be found, especially when there were wealthy people involved. Even if she wasn't dead, she could already be out of the country for all he knew.

As hard as it was not to, and as hard as he was trying to stop such thoughts from sneaking in, it was inevitable that thoughts of what might be happening to her at this moment kept getting past his defenses.

What *was* happening to her at the moment?

Had she been hurt?

Raped?

Or worst of all, had she been sold?

If this was to do with whoever had Emerald, then there was a good chance they might decide to sell Sapphire, it would eliminate her as a threat, and it would earn them a little extra cash.

If they found out that Sapphire ...

No.

There was no reason for them to figure that out, and he knew his wife wouldn't tell them, but if somehow they did find out then it would make her extra appealing to keep and then sell.

11:03 P.M.

"You're not out on the balcony," Noah said, sounding surprised as he joined her by the fireplace in their bedroom.

Despite the large house, she rarely used many of the rooms, their bedroom, the dining room where they ate meals, the music room, and one of the sitting rooms, that was it. She didn't like all the big empty rooms that sat unused, there were so many places for someone to hide.

Even though she was nearly thirty, and it had been almost fifteen years since she had been sold, over a decade since she and Noah had become a couple, those fears hadn't left. They hadn't really even dimmed. Monsters were everywhere, and they were smart and cunning and determined. If someone really wanted to get to her, even here at Noah's well-secured estate, then they could.

Emerald knew that besides the state of the art security system there were also several armed guards here. Armed guards that had been trained to shoot before asking questions.

But still ...

Noah's ex-partner wanted her.

Badly.

And she knew that if he learned that the body in the woods wasn't her, then he wouldn't stop until he got his hands on her.

And unfortunately, she already knew from firsthand experience what those hands were capable of.

From the very beginning, she had known that Alfie and Noah weren't the same. She had been able to feel it. Noah, while he might not be the most innocent guy around, he wasn't evil. But Alfie was.

Alfie was evil personified.

Noah had noticed the fact that she never got aroused by the things they did to her. Things that according to the website they had bought her from—the website that claimed she had willingly trained to be the perfect sex slave and wanted to live in a twenty-four-seven slave environment—she loved and enjoyed.

Of course it was a lie, she had never signed up to be a sex slave, and the things they did to her terrified her, but Alfie had never noticed. He hadn't cared. Yes, he might have thought that she was a willing participant in their games, but it wouldn't have bothered him if she wasn't. If he had known that she had been sold by her parents, and then again by her first owner, he still would have wanted her, it wouldn't have changed anything for him.

But it had for Noah.

He had been aghast when he finally coaxed her into answering his questions, and he had his suspicions confirmed.

She still remembered the look of horror and self-recrimination in his eyes.

A piece of him had died that day. He had learned that he had beaten, whipped, raped, tortured, and humiliated someone who hadn't gotten the rush he had expected out of any of those things.

As soon as he learned the truth, he immediately promised her that no one would ever lay a hand on her again.

And he had been true to his word.

He'd told Alfie that he had taken a game with her too far and she had died. He'd reimbursed the man the money he had put in to purchase her, but then because he was afraid that Alfie would use it to buy someone else, he had secretly gone into the man's bank account and drained it.

But that wasn't all he had done.

He had gotten into the computer system of the people who ran the website selling trafficked girls as trained and willing slaves and managed to tip off the cops to their existence. The website had been shut down, and the men had been arrested and imprisoned.

It gave her some small comfort to know that they weren't able to do that to anyone else, and she tried not to think too much about the fact that there was probably another site set up by the same sorts of people. But what gave her more comfort was knowing the lengths Noah had gone to to protect her and to punish those who had hurt her. She was safe with him, and as much as some of those lengths were things they probably never should have done, what other choice had they had?

Alfie had somehow found out that she was alive, Noah had received an email from him telling him that he was coming for her. She knew what that meant, they both did, he would kill Noah and take her away some place where he would resume torturing her until he got bored, then he would kill her too.

They couldn't go to the cops, men like Noah and Alfie never went to the cops, they handled things themselves, and she had gone along with it. Emerald was ashamed of letting fear rule her, and she prayed daily for forgiveness for putting her own life above others.

Fear.

It always came down to fear.

But for the first time, she was done bowing down to it.

It had been wrong what they did to Alice, it had been wrong to let her sisters believe she was dead, and it had been wrong to have Sapphire abducted just so they could try and convince her to drop the case.

Now she was ready to make the right choice for once.

She wasn't going to be selfish anymore, and she wasn't going to make decisions based on fear.

"I want to go and see my sisters," she announced, turning to meet Noah's gaze. She rarely did that because it had been drilled into her so many times that she was not to look her owner in the eye. But Noah wasn't her owner, he was her lover, and he had told her so many times that he didn't want a slave he just wanted her.

He studied her for a long moment with those probing blue eyes of his. "What changed?"

"Sapphire. Seeing her, it made me realize that I've been living here, *hiding* here, because I'm a coward."

"You are not a coward," he growled, dragging her off the couch and into his arms. "Don't ever say that again. What you lived through, what you survived, no coward could do that."

Her arms curled around his waist and her hands began to stroke his spine, soothing him. "I love you, Noah, more than words can ever express, but I *have* been a coward hiding here. I didn't want to see my sisters because I didn't want them to see what I had become. I stayed away because it was what was best for me, but I never really thought about them and how my letting them believe I was still gone was affecting them."

"There's nothing wrong with making decisions that are best for you."

"There is when it hurts someone else. We *should* have gone to the cops when Alfie came back, what we did to that woman was wrong. Not just wrong, it was evil, it made us like Alfie, and we're not. *You're* not. You didn't do anything wrong, you thought I wanted it just like you did, the cops would have understood that, and you could have told them how you shut that ring down. It would have been okay, but we let fear make our decisions for us, my fears of losing you, and your fears of losing me."

Noah's arms tightened convulsively around her.

He didn't like to admit that he was ever afraid, but she knew that he was.

"Everything is going to be okay," she promised, snuggling her head against his chest and pressing a light kiss to his bare skin. He liked to walk around the house with his shirt partially unbuttoned because he knew that she liked to see his rock hard abs, it made her feel safe, and there wasn't anything he wouldn't do for her. "You are a good man, Noah. You think you're not, but you are. I don't know what's going to happen when we go back, we did something awful, something we should be punished for, but I'd rather spend the rest of my life in prison than with Alfie, and I'm afraid that if we try to do this on our own that's what's going to happen."

Tears seeped out the corners of her eyes, there was nothing she was more afraid of then Alfie.

Even the prospect of spending her life in a jail cell was preferable.

"Sapphire might not tell them we were involved," she said.

"Even if she doesn't, they'll know. Who else would have reason to make the world think you were dead?"

"Then we could tell them the truth about Alice," she whispered. They had promised not to, but she was sure that Alice wouldn't have wanted them to go to prison for her death.

"You really want to do this?" Noah's hands closed around her shoulders, and he pulled her back so he could look at her.

"I really do," she nodded. "Let's go right now."

One side of his mouth quirked up in a smile. "It's the middle of the night. We'll go in the morning. Once you do this, things will never be the same again," he said, waving his arms around the room to indicate their lives together.

"I know, but I'll still have you. No matter what happens I'll always love you, and I'll always know that you love me."

Noah brushed his knuckles across her cheek and then trailed his fingertips along her neck until they reached her hair. He wrapped a hand around it and yanked her head back. His mouth claimed her with power and veracity and love. He snatched her off the ground and carried her toward the bed, and Emerald felt like her whole body was on fire.

She needed him.

She craved him.

She loved him.

CHAPTER
Eleven

December 1st
9:00 A.M.

"It's nine o'clock," Emerald announced. They had been sitting in a limousine outside her sister Sapphire's house for nearly an hour already. She'd woken early this morning and immediately gotten ready to come here, but Noah had insisted that they wait until nine before going to knock on the door.

It was the very first time she had left Noah's estate since he had kicked her off it back when she had been a scared teenage girl.

Ever since she had returned, that place had been her home, her safe haven, the only place where she had felt it was possible for her to live out the rest of her life.

But now she felt differently.

Now she wanted to gain strength from her sisters as well as Noah.

He would always be there for her, he would always be exactly who he had been for her these last several years, her savior. Nothing and no one was ever going to change that, but that didn't mean it always had to be just the two of them.

Noah had always been on his own, this was his chance to finally have the family that she knew deep down inside he craved.

This was both of their chances to have more than they had ever dreamed of.

If it worked out.

And that was still a pretty big if.

"Are you positive that this is what you want? Because I think you have this romanticized picture in your head of how this is all going to turn out. Once you do this there is no turning back, our lives will never be the same again, and you might not get what you're looking for from your sisters," Noah warned her.

"I'm prepared for the worst, but hoping for the best," she assured him.

"Then let's do this," Noah said, opening the limo door and reaching for her hand.

Emerald took it and held on tightly as they walked toward the front door. She had thought that since Sapphire already knew she was alive, it would be best to start at her place, but there were several cars parked in the drive, and she wondered if perhaps all her sisters were here.

There was nothing she could do to prepare them for the shock of seeing her, or to prepare herself for what might be more negative reactions, but she was ready to do this. It had taken her many years to get to this point, most of that time she had believed she never would, but now that she was actually here, nervous butterflies danced about in her stomach.

There really was no going back.

Once she did this, the entire course of her life would be changed. She really might end up in prison for the rest of her life, she really might never get to see Noah again, her sisters really might hate her as she was afraid that Sapphire did, but regardless, this had become a need. She was never going to spend another day allowing fear to rule her life, if she did, then it was like Alfie, her parents, and Richard Curtwood won. They had wanted to use her, destroy her, but they hadn't, because of Noah, and that meant she had a chance at still having the life she had dreamed of as a kid.

She lifted her hand, held it by the door, paused to draw in a deep breath, and then she knocked.

A moment later it was flung open, and she came face to face with her oldest sister.

"Diamond," she said, fighting the urge to throw her arms around her sister's neck, she might have done it, but she wasn't sure how well her arrival was going to be received.

Diamond's eyes grew wide, her mouth dropped open, and she gasped. "Emerald?"

"It's me," she acknowledged.

Diamond squealed and grabbed her, hugging her hard, then calling over her shoulder, "It's Emerald. Ruby, Amethyst, it's Emerald."

Footsteps sounded and a moment later two more of her sisters appeared. She was dragged into their arms, and for the next few minutes they hugged and cried and laughed, and she wondered why she had thought that staying away was a good idea. She loved her sisters, really loved them, and she should never have let them think that she was dead.

"Come in," Diamond finally said. "We shouldn't be standing out here on the doorstep, come and meet Elijah, and Zeb and Judah and Gideon, and all the kids."

"You're all here?" she asked, suddenly overwhelmed by the prospect of meeting so many people all at once. Her sisters were one thing, she knew them, and she loved them, but their husbands and kids were all strangers, and she had spent the last decade in virtual solitude on Noah's estate, only seeing the maids and gardeners. She wasn't sure she was ready for this.

"We're all here," Ruby said, hooking an arm through hers. "We're so glad to see you, we were so afraid that you were dead."

She was led through the house and into a large airy family room where four big, burly men stood, and a bunch of kids played with blocks on the floor. Suddenly shy and unsure of herself, wondering whether Noah had been right and this was a big mistake, she hung back, tugging herself free from her sisters' hold.

"This is Emerald," Diamond announced. "And that's Elijah,

Gideon, Zeb, and Judah." She recognized each of the men from the video footage that Noah had shown her, but she didn't know what to say to them so she just stood there. "Kids, come over here for a moment," Diamond called out and obediently a teenage girl, a preschooler, and three toddlers came over. "This is mine and Elijah's daughter Brooke, and our boys Archie and Oscar, that's Ruby's daughter Chloe, and Sapphire's little boy Leo, and the baby is Amethyst's daughter Lucy," she said, indicating the one-year-old who continued to bang blocks together. "Kids, this is your Aunt Emerald."

The kids said hello politely then went back to their blocks, the men stood and watched her, and her sisters grinned at her, but she didn't know what to do. She felt Noah's presence behind her, and she inched closer.

She shouldn't be here.

Her sister's husbands were all cops, they had to already assume that she and Noah had had something to do with the dead body, which meant they would likely be in handcuffs any minute now.

"I, uh, thought you might be putting the Christmas tree up," she said lamely, December first had always been the day she and her family had put up their decorations when she was growing up.

"Oh, we're a little preoccupied today to put up decorations," Amethyst said solemnly.

They all looked so shocked to see her and Emerald had to admit that she was a little surprised that Sapphire hadn't told them that she was alive. She had been so sure that her sister would turn her in, but it didn't look like she had. "Sapphire didn't tell you about me?" she asked.

Their faces went from puzzled to suspicious. "What do you mean?" Elijah asked, stepping forward.

She looked over her shoulder at Noah, they had come this far, and it was bound to all come out. "She, um, we, uh ..."

"*You're* the ones who kidnapped her." Gideon growled low in his throat, making him sound like an angry guard dog who had just sensed a threat. "Brooke, take the kids upstairs. Now."

Brooke didn't hesitate to do as she was asked, obviously sensing that something big was going down, she picked up Lucy and ushered the other kids toward the stairs.

"Did you kidnap my wife?" Gideon asked, Zeb held him back or she was sure the man would have been on them already.

All of a sudden, Emerald realized that someone was missing.

"Where is Sapphire?" she asked.

"What do you mean, where is she?" Judah asked. "You all but just admitted to kidnapping her."

"We let her go," she said in a rush. "It wasn't really a kidnapping, we just wanted to tell her to stop looking for me."

"Stop looking for you?" Amethyst asked.

"You're not in trouble? I mean, you got free? You're not still some-one's prisoner?" Ruby asked.

She shook her head.

"So you stayed away on purpose?" Diamond asked, hurt filling her eyes, and the eyes of her other sisters.

"I'm sorry," she said in a small voice, her head still reeling at the information she had learned. Sapphire was still missing, but they had let her go, so where was she?

"Where's my wife?" Gideon demanded, struggling to get out of Zeb's grip. "What did you do to her?"

"Nothing," she said, "I promise. We didn't do anything. She was only at our place for a couple of hours, and then we let her go, I swear."

"You swear?" Gideon repeated incredulously. "You *kidnapped* her. Let go of me," he growled in frustration.

"No. You want answers, you want us to find her, then we need them, they were the last ones to see her," Zeb told him. "You beat them up then where does that leave us? Cuff them," he said to the other two men.

"It would be a pleasure," Elijah said, pulling out handcuffs and grab-bing hold of Noah.

Judah spun her around and yanked her arms behind her back, snap-ping on a pair of handcuffs. She felt Noah's anger that they were manhandling her, and her sisters were crying, Gideon was fuming, and she knew upstairs there was a sad little boy who missed his mommy.

Pain.

There was so much pain.

And it was all because of her.

Maybe she should have stayed dead.

～

10:18 P.M.

"You shouldn't be here," Judah told his brother-in-law Gideon when the man strode through the door. There was no way that Gideon could remain in any way objective when the people who had kidnapped his wife were involved.

"I'm not leaving," he said through clenched teeth. "I'm a criminal psychiatrist, this is what I do, who's better at figuring out if they're lying than I am?"

While Judah couldn't disagree that Gideon was great at his job, and had certainly been an asset on more than one occasion when he had consulted with them, this was different. They had to interview Noah Landry and Emerald to find out if they were lying and they still had Sapphire locked away someplace. His money was on the fact that they did, but they had to keep every avenue open if they wanted to get Sapphire home alive.

Having Gideon in the room hampered their ability to do that.

"You can watch through the window." He offered a compromise.

"Fine," Gideon muttered, "I probably couldn't keep my hands off them anyway."

He knew the feeling.

They were a close family, and Ruby was hurting with Sapphire missing, as was his little girl who adored her aunt. He wanted Sapphire home where she belonged, and whether Noah and Emerald were the ones holding her now or not, they were likely facing a litany of charges. They had run two cops off the road, drugged and left one of them in the trunk of a car, and abducted the other, and they were no doubt involved in Alice Lincoln's murder since they were the only ones with something to gain.

Right now, they needed as much information as they could because he sensed there was a whole lot more to this story than there appeared to be.

"You ready?" he asked his partner. Zeb nodded, and they pushed open the door to the interview room where Emerald was waiting for them, out of the two, they believed that she was the most likely to crack and give something away.

They found Emerald pacing nervously, her hands alternating between twisting and tangling themselves in her clothing, and pressed to her chest in what appeared to be an attempt to regain control of her breathing. Judah sympathized with her, he really did, he knew that she had only been fifteen when she and her sisters had been sold, and he knew that she must have lived through hell before she came to be with Noah. However involved she was, he was sure that any defense attorney worth half his salt would have her off with some sort of severe emotional distress, Stockholm Syndrome type defense.

And he couldn't blame them.

The woman before him looked near manic like she might dissolve into a panic attack at a moment's notice.

"I was sold to a man named Richard Curtwood, he kept me in a cage in his yard with his dogs. When he wasn't abusing me. He sold me to Noah, only Noah thought that I was a willing slave, that I wanted it. When he realized I wasn't, he set me free, he helped me, he's not a bad guy. We made mistakes, but it's not what you think," Emerald rambled as soon as they walked through the door.

"Take a seat, Ms. Hatcher," he said, keeping his voice calm, the poor woman had probably been through the stuff of nightmares, it was no wonder she was a mess.

"I can't, I'm sorry, I don't like small spaces," Emerald told them.

"You know you're in a lot of trouble," Zeb said as he took a seat at the table.

"We know that it wasn't really you though," he added, taking a seat beside his partner, this couldn't be a bad cop good cop thing because he was afraid that would push the already emotionally unstable Emerald over the edge. "It was Noah."

"No," she shook her head, vehemently, "it was both of us."

"So, Noah told you he was going to kidnap your sister, and you said yes?" Judah asked.

"Well, no, not exactly, he told me, but after he already had sent men out for her," Emerald stammered.

"And he told you what he was going to do to Alice Lincoln?" Zeb asked.

"Well, not exactly, but it wasn't like that, you don't understand," she said helplessly.

"Then help us understand," he said gently.

"Noah knew Alice, she was the granddaughter of the woman who had been his nanny when he was a child. Sometimes she would bring Alice out to the estate, her brothers and sisters too, she was one of eight kids, and her parents had to work a lot, so sometimes their grandmother would look after them. Noah was quiet, he kept to himself, but he liked Alice, and she liked him, not romantically, but they were friends. Alice, she, uh, she knew that we were in trouble, that we needed help, and she wanted to help."

"She wanted you to keep her prisoner while you waited for the wounds you inflicted to scar, and then kill her?" Judah asked with a raised brow.

"Yes," Emerald replied. "Only it wasn't like that. She wasn't a prisoner, she just lived on the estate with us."

"Her parents reported her missing," Zeb said. "Why wouldn't she have let them know where she was?"

"Because she didn't want them to know. Alice's boyfriend had been abusive, he hurt her, he knew how to do it without leaving a mark, he raped her, he made her do things she didn't want to, and then when she got out, she found out that she was dying. She had an inoperable brain tumor, she was dying, and she thought it was fate that she and I had both been hurt and that she had an opportunity to help us. She didn't want her family to watch her fade away so she stayed with us, and we cared for her as she deteriorated."

That was not what he had been expecting to hear, but it should be easily confirmable if the medical examiner checked to see if she had a brain tumor. "And what about Sapphire?" he asked. "Did she voluntarily come and help you too?"

"No," Emerald said in a small voice, dropping her gaze to the floor.

"Do you know where she is?"

"We let her go," she insisted. "I would never keep my sister from her son."

"Would Noah?" Zeb asked.

"No," she said firmly. "He would never do anything to hurt me, and he would know that hurting Sapphire would hurt me. He might not have always done things the right way, but he loves me, and he just wants to protect me. Do I have to stay here?" she asked with raw fear on her face, and he wondered what she had lived through.

"No, you don't," a voice answered behind them, and a man in an expensive suit walked into the room. A lawyer. Judah didn't even need to ask who he was to know that. "You're free to go, Ms. Hatcher, Alice was simply a friend who stayed with you and unfortunately passed away. And Detective Hatcher-Barlow's abduction is nothing to do with you and Mr. Landry. He informed me that the limousine is waiting for you outside and that he will be with you shortly," the man said.

Emerald nodded and took a step toward the door, then paused. "Please keep me updated on Sapphire, we really don't have anything to do with this which means she's in danger."

Judah nodded, and the woman walked quietly away.

"Mr. Landry is also leaving," the lawyer informed them, "and if you have any further questions, you can direct them to me and not my client."

"He bought himself a ticket out of here," Zeb muttered as they followed the lawyer out of the interview room.

"He did," Judah agreed. It was frustrating, mostly because while he believed that Emerald wasn't involved in Sapphire's disappearance, he believed that Noah was. Noah had probably told Emerald that he had released her sister but instead spirited her away someplace else.

"We're not done with you, Mr. Landry," Zeb said when they saw him walking away with the lawyer.

"Emerald has this whole beautiful story about how you two are just kind philanthropists helping poor dying Alice, and how you have nothing to do with Sapphire going missing, but we're not buying it," he said.

"You kept Sapphire behind Emerald's back because she wouldn't agree to keep quiet, you think that you're protecting Emerald, but you're only making things worse by keeping Sapphire prisoner," Zeb said.

"Your prerogative to believe whatever you choose." Noah shrugged disinterestedly like this whole thing bored him. "You can address us in the future through our lawyer, but I do not want you, under any circumstances, approaching Emerald. She's been through enough, and I won't have *any*one hurting her." The threat hung in the air, and he fixed them with an icy blue stare before turning his back on them and walking away.

"He knows more than he's saying," Zeb said.

"They admitted that they're responsible for Alice's death which means they were the ones who wanted us to believe that Emerald was dead. They're the ones that paid Bobby to kill her, and they took Sapphire to try to get her to keep quiet and stop investigating this case. But why? What are they afraid of? Why go to all of this trouble when Emerald was already as good as dead hiding out on Noah's estate?"

He knew if they'd had a little longer with Emerald, she would have spilled everything, if they could just get to her again then they could get the answers they needed, but Judah knew that Noah would never allow them to see Emerald again.

～

1:26 P.M.

Neither of them spoke on the ride back out to the house.

Noah was angry, Emerald could tell that, she just wasn't sure if his anger was directed at the cops, her family, or her.

She was trembling.

She hadn't been able to stop since she learned that Sapphire had never arrived home like she should have. Noah was supposed to drug her again, then have her driven someplace quiet, but where someone would find her relatively quickly, and leave her there. Although she didn't like the idea of drugging her sister again, if they didn't, then Sapphire would have fought them, and she'd been worried that she'd wind up getting herself hurt.

Where was she?

Had Alfie gotten his hands on her?

They knew that Alfie knew where they lived and he knew that she was there and not dead like they had hoped, so it was possible that he—or some of his people—were watching the house. Maybe he had figured out who Sapphire was and thought that taking her would give him a bargaining chip to try to get his hands on her.

The thought terrified her, but it wasn't the only possibility.

There was also the chance that ...

No.

She couldn't think like that.

Noah said that he would let Sapphire go and she believed that he had done so.

The limousine turned into the driveway, and for the first time she didn't feel safe here. She didn't feel *un*safe, but she didn't get that warm, cozy, cocooned feeling being here usually gave her. Maybe it was because she had finally found the courage to leave, maybe it was because she wasn't afraid of the world anymore, maybe it was because she had seen her sisters again after so many years.

As soon as the limo stopped Noah bounded out, he didn't pause to offer her his hand, and they didn't walk up to the front door together, by the time she climbed out of the vehicle Noah had already disappeared inside.

Well, that definitely answered one of her questions.

Noah was angry with her.

She supposed she couldn't blame him. He had provided a safe place for her here, he had looked after her, taken care of her, held her while she shook and cried, been patient with her when she was so scared she couldn't even go to the bathroom without permission. He had never done anything but support and love her and how did she repay him? She got him dragged down to a police station in handcuffs. If she was him she'd be angry with her too.

Feeling lost and more alone than she ever had before, Emerald wandered slowly up the steps and through the front door. She didn't know where to go. She didn't feel like going down to the horses, and she didn't want to go to her and Noah's room, she didn't want to play music, she didn't really want to do anything.

Although it wasn't a conscious decision, Emerald walked through the halls and eventually found herself standing at the door to the room where she had been kept when Noah and Alfie thought she was their willing sex slave. Her hand shook violently as she placed it on the door handle and she wanted to turn around and leave, but her feet wouldn't move.

Not sure why she was doing this, Emerald pushed the door open and stepped into the room.

It had been cleared out and was now nothing but an empty space, bare walls, no furniture, no signs of the cage she had been put in or the objects that had been used to torture her.

Emerald walked across the floor and stopped right where the cage had been, she remembered how terrified she had been when they had put her in there, as soon as they had left the room she had cried herself to sleep. She remembered them coming back, and then they had started with their games.

Those days had been so dark, and they had seemed never ending, she'd thought that would last forever, that it would go on and on until either they killed her or they got bored and sold her on to someone else.

It had seemed like a vicious circle that she would never be able to break.

She'd just get sold on from one perverted monster to another until eventually her luck ran out and she was killed.

Tears built up, and when she blinked, they began to trail slowly down her cheeks. She sunk down to the floor and curled up, letting herself cry as though by doing so she might be able to rid herself of some of her pain.

No matter what she did it never seemed to work out.

Hiding hadn't helped, but going back to her family hadn't either.

The door to the room slammed, and she heard footsteps storm toward her. "What are you doing in here?" Noah growled at her.

Emerald shrunk away from him.

He was angry.

Angrier than she had ever seen him.

She knew that anger was directed at her, and she didn't know what he was going to do to her.

"Get up," Noah ordered. When she didn't move quickly enough he bellowed at her, "Get up."

With a terrified whimper, she scampered to her feet, keeping her gaze firmly on the floor. She didn't want to see the fury in Noah's eyes. He stepped closer, close enough that she could feel him vibrating even though he wasn't touching her. She braced herself, expecting a blow even though Noah had never hit her before, or at least not since he learned the truth about how she came to be in his house.

But Noah didn't hit her.

In fact, he did the opposite.

He reached for her, wrapped her up in his arms, and drew her in, holding her firmly but gently.

His hand stroked her hair, and fresh tears began to flow as she clung to him. How could she have thought he would hurt her?

"I'm sorry." She wept into his chest.

"Shh," he said with uncharacteristic tenderness. Noah had been patient with her, supportive, but he wasn't usually tender like this. It fueled more tears, and she wasn't sure how long she held onto Noah and cried.

Although she knew that she would ruin the moment by asking, she had to know for sure. "Noah, did you take Sapphire? Do you have her stashed away somewhere? I'd understand if you do that you were doing it to protect me, but if you do have her, then please tell me."

"I don't have your sister, Emerald," he told her. "I thought about it, you were making an emotional decision when you wanted to let her go, not a logical one, and I believed it was the wrong one. But it was what you wanted, and you were so sure about it. I let Sapphire go exactly the way we discussed."

She believed him.

There was something in his voice that convinced her he was being truthful.

"Sorry for doubting you," she said.

"It was those cops who put the idea in your head. Putting you in handcuffs, taking you down to the police station like a common criminal, they put you in a cage, they upset you." He was angry again, she could feel it flowing through him, and she wanted to take it away, but she didn't know how. She wasn't used to being in this position, usually it was Noah who was calming her when she was a mess, but Noah was so strong, so confident, he was never a mess, until now anyway.

"It's okay, I'm okay," she assured him, taking his arms and tightening their hold on her.

"You're not, you're in here, in this room, crying. It's *their* fault," he spat. "After everything you've been through that they would treat you like that is ..." he trailed off as he physically shook with rage.

"They don't know," she reminded him. "They don't know what happened to me."

"They know you were sold."

"But they don't know any details, and they're worried about Sapphire." She wasn't worried about what Sapphire's family had done. She was glad that her sister had people who loved her enough to do whatever it took to try to find her. She just wanted to know that Sapphire was okay, and then she and Noah could go back to their lives. She wasn't sure that there was still a place for her in the Hatcher family, but there was always a place for her here. "You were right. We shouldn't have gone there today. I'm glad we did because if we hadn't, I wouldn't have known about Sapphire, but I don't belong there. I belong here."

"You will always belong here," he said, lifting her feet off the floor and touching a very light kiss to her lips. "You will always be mine."

That safe feeling was back, cocooned in Noah's arms, she knew that she was home.

～

5:57 P.M.

"Can we make pizza for dinner?" Archie asked.

"I think your mom went to pick up ingredients," Zeb told his nephew. They were spending the night at Gideon's house again tonight, he wasn't sure that their presence was doing much to console his brother-in-law besides reminding him that they were still together and his wife was gone. But Amethyst wanted to be here for her nephew, and the sisters seemed to need to be together, now more than ever.

Emerald turning up on the doorstep this morning had been a shock none of them were anticipating.

While they had surmised that given someone went to such lengths to convince them she was dead that she was probably still alive, but still being alive and turning up at Sapphire and Gideon's house were two completely different things.

"Goodie," Archie clapped excitedly. "And can we make cookies for dessert?"

"Sure can, why don't you choose what you want to make," Ruby handed Archie a cookie recipe book, and he started to flip through the pages.

"Shouldn't Diamond be back by now?" Amethyst asked as she turned away from the stove where she was making homemade pizza sauce.

"When did she leave?" he asked, touching the screen of his phone so that he could see the time.

"Almost an hour ago," his wife replied. "And the supermarket is only five minutes down the road. She should be back by now."

Zeb stood and walked over to give Amethyst a kiss. "I think you're just letting the stress of the last few days get to you. There is no reason that anything should have happened to Diamond, it's probably just busy, she'll be home soon."

"I hope so," Amethyst muttered, then turned her attention back to the stove.

He understood his wife's stress, first they'd thought Emerald was dead, then found out she probably wasn't, then Sapphire had gone missing, and then Emerald had turned up, and they had learned that she had deliberately stayed away. If he was her, he'd be stressed out too. Maybe hanging out together was what she needed, they'd make pizzas, bake cookies, watch movies, maybe play a board game or two, then they would all try to make it an early night. All of them, kids included, needed a good night's sleep.

Zeb was about to go check on the younger kids when his phone began to ring. He snatched it up, hoping it was news on Sapphire. "Detective Tuck."

"Detective, this is Officer Breslow, we have a potential abduction at the supermarket on Dworn Street."

"Why are you calling me? I'm homicide."

"Because the car is registered to a Diamond Hatcher-Newton, your sister-in-law."

Guess Amethyst's instincts were spot on. "I'll be there in five minutes." He hung up the phone and any attempt he might have made to downplay the call until he got more information was gone when he saw everyone looking at him.

"News on Sapphire?" Ruby asked.

"No," he sighed and knew he may as well just get it over and done with. "It's Diamond."

"What about her?" Elijah asked, rising from his chair at the table where he was rolling out pizza bases.

"Is she hurt?" Amethyst asked.

"Potential abduction," he replied.

"Abduction?" Judah echoed.

"First Sapphire, now Diamond, and right when Emerald comes back into our lives," Ruby said.

"Noah Landry," Elijah growled. "This has his name written all over it."

"But what would taking Diamond do to help his case?" he asked. There was an important piece of the puzzle missing, and until they found it, they weren't going to get anything useful to find where Sapphire, and Diamond, were being held.

"We need to call his lawyer, set up a meeting for tomorrow, he's going to tell us what we need to know," Judah said.

Zeb agreed, but right now they needed to work this scene. "We need to go down there, see what we have, maybe if we can find something on who committed the abduction—because we know it's not something Noah would do himself—then we might be able to get him to flip.

Bobby Tompson is still keeping his mouth shut, but assuming Noah paid someone to abduct Diamond, then they might be more willing to talk."

It was a long shot, but the way things were working out it might be the only shot they had.

"Let's go," he said, already grabbing his phone and keys. Judah, Elijah, and Gideon all stood. "We can't all go. Someone should stay here, if Noah is responsible for both Sapphire and Diamond's abductions, then there's a chance he might come after Amethyst and Ruby next." There was no way Zeb was going to risk his wife's safety, she was not about to become Noah's next victim in whatever twisted game he was playing. "Elijah, you should stay here. Gideon too." There was no reason that Elijah should have to go to the scene of his wife's kidnapping.

"I'm coming," Elijah said firmly.

"No," he shot back, just as firmly. "You should stay here with the kids. We need to work this as quickly as we can, and you can't be objective."

Although it looked like it just about killed him, Elijah nodded and sat back down.

"We'll let you know when we know something," he said, giving his wife a quick kiss before hurrying out the door.

"You think he's going to go after Ruby and Amethyst next?" Judah asked as they got in the car.

"I hope not." He *hoped* not, but since they didn't know what angle Noah was working, it was hard to figure out what he was going to do next. "Taking Sapphire was because of the case, they wanted to try to convince her to keep quiet about Emerald, write the case off as closed and just lay it all on Bobby Tompson's feet. They realized she wouldn't do that, so Noah goes behind Emerald's back and keeps Sapphire. That makes some measure of sense, but going after Diamond doesn't."

"Unless he plans on getting all of the sisters back together again," Judah said quietly.

Unfortunately, that could be a possibility.

And would Noah stop with just bringing Emerald her sisters?

He could go after the kids next, if he wanted to please Emerald, then having her sisters there without their children wasn't going to do it.

His partner must have been thinking along the same lines because neither of them spoke the rest of the short ride to the supermarket. There were three police cruisers and a crime scene van already in the parking lot, and he parked the car next to the others and got out with a heavy step. He had lost his family when he was a child, but when he and Amethyst had gotten together, her family had become his family, and that someone was messing with the people he cared about was enough to fuel him to do anything, he had to close this case.

"What have we got?" he asked as he approached the hubbub.

"Victim's car is here," an officer told them. "Shopping cart still there, half the bags in the trunk, half—including her purse—in the cart, and one spilled on the ground, presumably she dropped it when she was grabbed."

"We have any witnesses?" Zeb asked. Just because he couldn't think of any other logical reason for Diamond to walk off and leave her purse, and phone, and car, and a shopping cart full of food behind while she went off to do something else, knowing it would worry them, didn't mean there wasn't another explanation.

"Several," the cop replied. "All report the same thing. A woman's screams alerted them, they turned, saw a brunette being grabbed by a masked man, and pulled into the back of a van. A couple even got the license plate of the van, it was reported stolen earlier this morning, so I'm guessing this wasn't spur of the moment and she wasn't a random victim. Chances are they transferred to another vehicle as soon as they got away from the scene, and we'll find the van torched at the side of the road or in a parking lot somewhere."

"What's this?" Judah asked, crouching on the ground beside the bag of groceries that Diamond must have been loading into her car when she was grabbed.

"What is it?" he asked, squatting beside his partner.

"Looks like a syringe," he said, using a pen to move a bag of grapes out of the way so they could get a better look.

"They drugged her so she wouldn't be any trouble while they were transporting her," Judah said.

"Stole a vehicle, came prepared with drugs, parked beside her car, waited until she was distracted, this wasn't some random abduction. They wanted her specifically, and there is only one person that has any motive for going after the Hatcher sisters. Noah Landry."

The man could hide behind his lawyer all he wanted, but they needed answers, and Noah had them. The man *would* talk, and if he went after Amethyst next then he wouldn't be spending the rest of his life in prison, he'd be spending it in a coffin.

∼

9:38 P.M.

She had been angrier enough before, but now she was fuming.

Noah had taken this too far.

It was one thing to keep her here, they thought she was a threat because she was a cop, which she supposed was well founded because she was going to do whatever it took to make sure Noah rotted in prison, but messing with one of her sisters, that was taking it to a whole different level.

Diamond had been unconscious ever since an armed guard carried her in here a couple of hours ago. While Sapphire knew that her sister had just been drugged because the first thing she had done once the guard left was give Diamond a thorough examination and hadn't found any injuries, it didn't stop her from worrying. She wasn't a doctor, she had no idea how long was an appropriate time for Diamond to be unconscious. What if Noah had had his men give her too high a dosage for her size and something was wrong?

"Argh," she yelled in frustration. This was so annoying, she wanted to be home with her family, she wanted to be working this case, she wanted to be finding all the evidence she needed to make sure Noah ended up where he belonged. A jail cell.

But she wasn't home.

She wasn't with her family, and she wasn't working this case.

Instead, *she* was the one stuck in a jail cell.

At least that man hadn't been back, she didn't know who he was or why Noah had allowed him to come in here and touch her, but she was sure that sooner or later he was going to return. Her instincts were telling her that the man and his visit meant something, she just didn't know what. There didn't seem to be any logical reason for Noah to send him, okay, so he wanted to keep her prisoner so she didn't have him arrested, but to have her assaulted, she wasn't sure that was Noah's style.

As much as she hated that she had let Noah into her home and around her family, she had, and that meant she had spent time around him. From what she knew about him, he was a businessman and a smart one at that. He made sound, logical decisions and this didn't seem to be one. He was letting his emotions lead him, and she hoped, now more than ever since Diamond was stuck here with her, that those emotional decisions were going to have him make a mistake.

Who was coming next?

Ruby?

Amethyst?

Would he stop there, or would their husbands and their kids be next?

A moan on the bed drew her attention, and she hurried over just as Diamond blinked open heavy eyes.

"Hey," she said, perching on the edge of the bed and putting a hand on her sister's shoulder. "You okay?"

"Sapphire?" Diamond groaned again and then lifted a hand to rub her eyes. "My head feels like it's full of cotton wool."

"I know the feeling. Unfortunately."

"Am I with you or are you home?" Diamond asked the question, but the look on her face said that she already knew the answer.

"You're with me. Unfortunately," she said again. "Are you hurt anyplace? I checked you out when you arrived, but you might have some internal injuries I couldn't see."

"Other than my head I'm okay, they drugged me. But you're not okay." Pushing herself into a sitting position, Diamond reached out and touched the gash on Sapphire's cheek. "What happened?"

"I made one of my captors angry."

"And this?" she asked, touching the cut on her temple.

"The car accident when Noah's men ran us off the road. Is Elijah okay?" She had been worrying about her partner ever since she woke up here.

"He's fine," Diamond assured her. "And we met Noah."

"You did?" she asked, surprised. She had thought that Emerald was happy enough with her decision to stay away and keep her freedom a secret forever. Obviously, she had been wrong.

"Emerald came around, seeing her again was a ... shock. But finding out that she stayed away on purpose was ..."

"Like getting stabbed in the heart," she finished.

"Yeah, like that. We got a bathroom around here?"

"Through there." She pointed to the door.

"I'll get some water and clean you up, did you even tend to those cuts at all?"

"Not really," Sapphire replied. She didn't need her sister to clean up the wounds, but she knew that Diamond was the big sister and the kind of big sister who liked to fuss, so she didn't put up a fight when she returned with a towel and some antiseptic cream.

"Do you know where here is?"

"Nope. Ow." She jerked when Diamond touched the wet cloth to the cut on her cheek.

"Sorry. Hold still."

"I'm trying."

"So, you don't know where we are?"

"I don't know, but I assume we're still at Noah Landry's house, that's where he took me at first. They were watching us, the security systems, Noah had set them up so he could access them, and watch us."

"For how long?"

"I'm guessing since we had them installed, so years."

"There we go," Diamond said, putting some cream and then a Band-Aid on each of the cuts. Then she met her gaze. "Seeing Emerald again was, odd."

"She's not the same as she was before."

"None of us are," Diamond reminded her. "What we went through changed all of us, me, you, Ruby and Amethyst, we can't be angry that it changed Emerald too."

"But she stayed away," Sapphire said. "None of the rest of us did that. We were there for each other, we helped each other, we supported and encouraged one another. When I needed someone you were all there for me, I love you guys. But Emerald didn't care, she didn't care that we were missing her or that we were worried about her. All she cared about was herself. You know that's not Emerald, in fact it's the very opposite of Emerald."

"It is," Diamond agreed, moving to sit beside her on the bed. "And I know that it hurts, it hurts all of us, but our Emerald is still inside there somewhere."

"How do you know that? It didn't seem like she was still there, whatever happened to her made the old Emerald disappear."

"I don't believe that. Did she tell you anything about what happened to her?"

"A little, I think, I don't know I was still in shock, and angry, I probably shouldn't have been so angry." The anger was still there, but she did feel bad about yelling at her sister. Emerald was messed up, but she blamed Noah for it. Noah should have made her come home, he should have made her get counseling, proper counseling, not his own warped version.

"It's okay." Diamond slipped an arm around her, and Sapphire rested her head on her sister's shoulder.

"Emerald said that she didn't want them to keep me a prisoner, I want to believe that Noah kept me behind her back, but I don't know."

"I do. When Emerald showed up, it was at your house, we were all there with Gideon and Leo, she expected that you would be there too, she thought we'd be putting up the Christmas tree because it was December first. If it is Noah that has us then Emerald doesn't know about it."

That made her feel better.

Marginally.

Maybe Diamond was right, and there really was a piece of the old Emerald left.

"How's Leo?" she asked, her voice trembled a little as she said her son's name. She missed him so much it hurt.

"He misses you, but he's okay, everyone is looking out for him."

"And Gideon?"

"He's holding it together, mostly for Leo, but he's okay."

Hearing that her husband and son were okay was a weight off her mind, and it rejuvenated her a little, giving her a boost when she was starting to run dry. She would hold on, she would fight, she would do everything she could to get home to them, but she had an extra reason for wanting to get home—a reason that no one but her husband knew about.

"Diamond, we weren't going to tell anyone because we were going to wait another month, but I'm pregnant, about eight and a half weeks," she said, a hand moving to rest on her stomach. She had to get home because there was no way she was having her baby here. If Noah did decide to sell them, then she knew he wouldn't pass up selling a baby, he could get a lot of money for it, and there was no way in hell she was letting her child be sold.

"I'd say congratulations, but ... given that we're here, I'm not sure it's appropriate," Diamond said and gave her a hug.

"We have to get home, Diamond, I want my husband and my son, and I cannot, *cannot*, have this baby here."

CHAPTER
Twelve

December 2nd
8:47 A.M.

"He was supposed to be here nearly twenty minutes ago," Elijah said with an annoyed sigh. If Noah Landry had his wife, then the man better enjoy the outside world while he could because once he got here, he wouldn't be leaving.

"You can't be here when we interview him," Zeb said.

Elijah just glowered.

"If he has Diamond, then you can't work this case," Judah said. Clearly, they were both on the same page.

"Well, I'm not leaving." That was that as far as he was concerned. This case was going nowhere. They had Bobby who wouldn't speak, they had the real Dean Winters' body found buried in a shallow grave under an oak tree on his property, and the fake Dean Winters in the wind. They had no prints, fibers, or DNA on Sapphire's car, the one they had been in when someone ran them off the road then driven to the parking lot with him in the trunk. They had the van—with

Diamond's scarf in it—that had been used in the abduction yesterday, it had been driven a few blocks then dumped, but there was no forensics in it.

They had nothing.

Just two missing sisters.

And a dead woman.

Alice Lincoln was connected to Noah and Emerald, and they were the only ones with something to gain by kidnapping Sapphire and Diamond. They had called Noah's lawyer and told him to produce them both at the police station at eight-thirty this morning.

It was now eight forty-seven.

Forty-eight, he amended when his clock-watching noticed the second hand ticking past twelve.

"You think they've run?" he asked. Elijah didn't think that it was particularly likely because Noah didn't have all the sisters yet. He believed that the man was going to make a play for Ruby and Amethyst next, then when he had all five of the Hatcher sisters together, he might disappear.

If he stopped there.

Elijah was afraid that the end game was that Noah would get all the sisters together, and then he'd come for the children. It was like his obsession with Emerald was compelling him to do whatever it took to make her happy. He had organized Alice Lincoln's murder to make them think Emerald was dead, that way he could keep her all to himself and get Sapphire off his tail. Now he was getting her sisters for her, probably because he knew that despite her decision to keep her distance —if it really *had* been her decision—she still loved and missed them.

But if he took her sisters, then they were only going to be angry with Emerald for taking them from their children.

That was an easy fix.

Take the kids too.

Then Emerald would have her whole family around her.

As far as Noah was probably concerned, that was problem solved. His precious Emerald got what she wanted, and he got to keep her. He probably preferred to keep her all to herself, but given the choice of losing her or sharing her, Elijah was sure the man would compromise.

At least for a time.

But if Diamond, Sapphire, Ruby, Amethyst, and the kids eventually became a nuisance, then he was sure that Noah would eliminate them.

Permanently.

There were two easy options, kill them or sell them. They already knew he had been involved in trafficking so it wasn't a stretch.

"No, they didn't run," Judah said, and it took Elijah a moment to realize why he was saying that. He'd asked the question but already decided on an answer.

"Not until he has them all," Zeb said tightly.

Just because Judah and Zeb still had their families intact didn't mean they weren't every bit as emotionally invested in this case as he was. Diamond was close with her sisters, and Ruby and Amethyst were out of their minds with worry, and he knew that both Zeb and Judah were worried that their wives would be next. They had officers on Zeb and Amethyst's house—since it was the one with the saferooms—and everyone was supposed to be staying there until they had this sorted out.

"He's here," Zeb announced.

Elijah looked up and saw Noah and his lawyer striding toward them, but no Emerald. "They didn't bring Emerald because they know she's close to cracking," he said, annoyed. He was sick of being railroaded, this whole case had been one long nightmare, and there didn't seem to be an end in sight.

"Morning, Detectives." Noah Landry smiled at them as he entered the room. He looked like a man without a care in the world. That was more frustrating than anything else. Noah was at the center of this, and it was time for him to start talking.

"Where's Emerald, Mr. Landry?" Elijah asked.

"You don't need to answer that," the lawyer, a Mr. Mellstrom, told his client, and Elijah already knew that this interview wasn't going to go anywhere. The lawyer was going to tell Noah that he didn't have to answer every time they asked a question, and Noah would no doubt follow his lawyer's advice, getting them nowhere.

"That's okay," Noah said, taking a seat, crossing his legs, and then folding his hands in his lap. "Emerald was exhausted from the emotional upheaval of the last few days and took a sleeping pill so that she could get the rest that she needs. You can speak with her at a later date."

Yeah right.

No matter how many times they asked for Emerald to be brought down to the station for them to speak with, Noah would have some excuse as to why she was unable to come that day.

"We *will* speak with her," Elijah warned.

"Of course." Noah nodded amenably. "I would never do anything to impede a police investigation."

"If that's true, then tells us where Sapphire and Diamond are," Judah said.

"You don't have to answer that," Mr. Mellstrom said.

Noah waved him off. "I have no idea."

"Why bother coming if you're not going to tell us anything?" Zeb asked.

"Because you asked," Noah said with a shrug. "I don't have any information on Emerald's sisters, but I do have this for you." He nodded to his lawyer who produced a memory stick from his pocket.

"What is that?" Elijah asked.

"It's proof," Noah answered.

"Of what?"

"That Alice Lincoln was a guest at our home. It's the security footage from the months that Alice was with us. You can see for yourselves that she was no prisoner, that we took care of her, and that she wanted to help us."

"She didn't die of a brain tumor," Elijah reminded him, although the medical examiner had confirmed that she had one and that it was terminal.

"You don't have to give any information on Alice Lincoln's death," the lawyer said.

"Bobby Tompson was with Alice when she died, you'll have to speak to him about specifics," Noah said.

"But you and Emerald were the ones with something to gain if we believed Emerald was dead," Zeb reminded him.

"Which means that you had a reason for setting us up," Judah added.

"We want to know what that reason is," Elijah said, staring the man down—or attempting to. But Noah Landry just met his eyes and didn't look away. He wasn't rattled, he wasn't scared, he wasn't worried that they were going to find something that would land him in prison because if he was, he wouldn't have come down here. He was sure of himself and irritatingly confident, there was no way that they were going to get Noah to tell them anything useful. But that didn't change the facts. Noah had Alice killed to try to trick them, and whether she was a willing participant in the game or not, there had to be a reason why he did it.

"You don't have to answer that," Mr. Mellstrom said.

"This time I think I'm going to listen to my lawyer," Noah said. "We came down here to give you the security footage, now that we've done that we're going to be on our way."

"We're not going to stop, Mr. Landry. We have a dead woman, an abduction, and a missing cop. All of those lead back to you, until you give us an explanation that satisfies us we're not going away," he warned.

"Then until next time, Detective," Noah said with another one of those smiles.

"If you hurt my wife you won't ever smile again," he threatened.

Noah just winked and turned his back on them, strolling out of the room like he was enjoying a meander through the park.

"What do we do next?" he said, barely resisting the urge to slam his fist into the nearest wall only because it wasn't going to serve any purpose, and all that mattered right now was getting his wife home to him and their kids, where she belonged.

"We watch the footage," Judah replied, picking up the memory stick. "Hope it gives us something we can use."

Pray it gave them something they could use because that was about all they had left. Prayers.

∿

10:34 A.M.

. . .

Behind her on the bed, Diamond yawned and slowly sat up, rubbing at her eyes. "I can't believe I fell asleep."

Sapphire paused briefly in her circuit of the room. "You needed the rest. The drugs were still working their way out of your system."

"Yeah, I guess," Diamond shuffled over to the edge of the large bed and stood up. "Did you sleep at all?"

"Not really," she said, resuming her pacing.

"You know you need sleep, especially given that you're pregnant."

Pregnant.

She'd been so excited that she had managed to fall pregnant quickly, practically as soon as she and Gideon had started trying. But before Leo had been born she'd had several miscarriages, and the fear that she would lose this baby had been strong. As much as she had wanted to tell her sisters, she and Gideon had decided that waiting until they were at least to the twelve-week mark was the best idea.

Now she was torn.

She wanted her baby more than anything, but if it was just going to be kept here in this room for the rest of its life, or worse, be sold into sexual slavery then maybe it was better if she didn't carry it to term.

"The baby is why I can't sleep," she told Diamond. "I have to figure out a way out of here."

"I don't think there is one."

"There has to be," she insisted, anything else was unacceptable.

"Sapphire." Diamond came and stood in front of her, stopping her from her near continual circling of the room, and put her hands on her shoulders. "Elijah and the others aren't going to stop until they find us. You know that every cop in the city is looking for us."

"Doesn't mean they'll find us, they don't even know about Noah's ex-partner, that he's the one who wants Emerald and that's why they killed Alice Lincoln," she protested. Right now she wasn't sure that they were even still in Noah's house, so even if they knew to be looking into Noah and Emerald, there was no way they would find wherever he had stashed them. Noah was smart, and he wasn't going to put them someplace where anyone could ever find them.

"They were already looking into Noah and Emerald," Diamond reminded her. "Emerald admitted that they were the ones that took you and left Elijah in the trunk of the car, they took them both down to the station in handcuffs."

Her sister in handcuffs.

That was something she hadn't thought would ever happen.

But Emerald wasn't the same Emerald she had been back when they were kids. As hard as it was to accept, it was what it was, and they couldn't count on Emerald coming through for them and convincing Noah to let them go. And that was even if she knew that Noah still had them.

"What do you know about this partner of Noah's?" Diamond asked.

"Not much, his name is Alfie, and he and Noah decided together to buy Emerald, only they believed that she was part of some group that trained women who wanted to be someone's sex slave. According to Emerald, when Noah realized that something was wrong, he got the truth out of her then faked her death so Alfie wouldn't hurt her again. I don't know how much of it is true, but apparently this Alfie figured out that she was still alive and—"

"And that's why they killed that woman and tried to make us think it was Emerald," Diamond finished.

"That's what they said." Sapphire wasn't sure how much they could believe that Noah and Emerald told them, the two of them were only interested in covering themselves, and they didn't care who they had to hurt to do it.

"It sounds true," Diamond said.

"Even if it is, unless Noah tells them why they did it, then they're never going to know anything about Alfie." With a frustrated sigh, she tugged herself free from Diamond's grasp and began to walk again.

"I'm surprised you're not dizzy yet, you've been pacing the room all night."

"I don't get dizzy," she said. "Except when I'm ..." she trailed off and touched her stomach. "Except when I'm pregnant." This time around, she hadn't suffered much from morning sickness, but when she'd been pregnant with Leo things had been pretty bad in the first few months. It seemed to run in the family, both Ruby and Amethyst had suffered from bad morning sickness as well.

"They'll find us before that little baby of yours is ready to come out," Diamond told her, but Sapphire knew it was her sister just trying to reassure her. Neither of them could know whether that would happen or not, and she preferred not to let herself get her hopes up. For now, she had to proceed under the worst-case scenario.

The sound of the door being unlocked had her head snapping toward the door. "Get over there," she told her sister, pointing to the far side of the room. "Don't say anything and try not to draw his attention your way."

"Is this the man who hurt you?" Diamond asked, doing as she'd said.

"Breakfast was brought while you were sleeping and it's too early for lunch, so I'm guessing it is. Let me deal with him."

"You're pregnant," Diamond reminded her.

"But I'm also a cop, I want to keep his attention on me in case I can figure out a way to get a jump on him."

The door opened, and the same man who had hit her walked into the room. He had that same annoying smile on his face, and he was relaxed like he had been looking forward to coming in here.

"Why don't you just let us go," she demanded, crossing over to him. "I'm a cop, that means the entire police department is looking for me. You may as well just make things easier on yourself and let us go now before they find wherever Noah has us."

"But if I let you go I wouldn't be able to enjoy your charming company," the man winked at her.

"I'm not charming, and we both know it," she said, wanting to keep his attention on her however she had to. She was a cop, it was her job to protect people, and that went double when the person who needed protecting was her sister, there was no way she would let this man lay a hand on her Diamond.

"You are amusing," he said, taking a step close so he was right beside her. "And beautiful," he said, running a hand over her hair.

"Don't touch her," Diamond yelled.

"Stay over there," she told her sister, why was Diamond drawing attention to herself when she had the man's attention focused firmly on her?

The man laughed. "You're a pretty one too. Maybe once I finish with your sister you and I can get better acquainted."

"You leave her alone, leave both of us alone, does Noah know that he hired such a pervert to keep an eye on Emerald's sisters?" she asked.

"I'm not a pervert," the man said, anger flashing through his eyes. He didn't like it when she implied that he was depraved, it had made him angry earlier, and again now, that was something she could use to her advantage. The maid that brought the meals never spoke so there was no way to get to her, but this man was attracted to her, and that was something else she could use. If she could let him get close enough and distracted enough, then maybe she could slip the keys out of his pocket. Then she could wait until he was about to leave the room and hit him with something, knock him out, then she could deal with whoever was outside the room.

"Not a pervert?" she said with mock shock horror. "What would you call a man who wants to sleep with someone who is being held prisoner? I don't want your disgusting hands touching me, and yet that's not stopping you. I'd call that a sexual predator."

The man growled like some sort of wild animal, then threw her up against the wall, holding her in place with his body while he crushed his mouth against hers and his hands groped her body.

Perfect.

Not the kissing part. The man tasted like smoke and evil, but she had achieved exactly what she wanted. All she had to do was find something in this room that she could use as a weapon, then next time he came in here goad him into assaulting her so she could snag the keys.

Next time she would be ready for him.

But this time she wasn't going to let him do any more to her than he already had.

Sinking down her teeth onto the man's lips, she smiled when he screamed and pulled back, blood dribbling down his chin.

Seeing the fury on his face was worth every bit of pain as he hit her in the face.

~

11:51 A.M.

Emerald woke slowly.

She felt groggy like she had been drugged, and it took her sluggish mind a moment to remember that she had taken sleeping pills before going to bed last night.

She didn't really like to take them, but Noah had persuaded her that she needed the rest and was unlikely to get any sleep if she didn't. Since she had been stressed, and she had been worked up, she had reluctantly agreed. Seeing her sisters again, being dragged down to the police station, her emotional afternoon with Noah, she had been on a roller-coaster that didn't seem to have an end.

So she'd gone along with it.

Noah could be very persuasive when he wanted to be.

With a yawn, she rolled over, wondering whether she might keep her eyes closed and go back to sleep, but she could already tell that her mind was crawling out of the hole and was waking up whether she wanted to be or not.

Blinking, she fought back another yawn—she might be awake, but she suspected she was going to feel wiped out and sleepy for the remainder of the day—and opened her eyes.

A smile broke out on her face when she saw that Noah was sitting in an armchair beside her bed.

Back when she was a traumatized mess that he was trying to help, she spent a lot of time in bed. Her mind and body were so drained that she found she could hardly stay awake for more than a couple of hours at a time. She was afraid to be on her own, and Noah had already been her safe place, he knew that, and he would often sit beside her bed while she slept, keeping watch over her.

Just like he was now.

He was sitting in an armchair, his legs crossed, a newspaper in his hands, busily reading. He hadn't noticed that she was awake yet, and she took a moment to just look at him. That chiseled jaw, the blond hair, those piercing blue eyes, he was so handsome, and despite what he thought of himself he had a good heart. He could be controlling, and he believed that he was right in every situation, but it was that very confidence that was what had attracted her to him in the first place.

When she had needed something strong and sure in her life, Noah had been there. When she had needed someone to take control and help her rebuild her life, Noah had been there. When she had needed someone to love her and make her feel like something more than a toy you pulled out when you were bored, Noah had been there.

She still needed all those things.

And Noah was still there.

"Hey," she said. Her voice was a little gravelly from the sleeping pills, and she wondered how long she had been out.

"Hey, yourself," he said, looking up. Noah folded the paper and set it on the nightstand, then moved to sit on the edge of the bed, cupping her face in his palm and brushing the pad of his thumb across her cheek. She wasn't used to such uncharacteristic displays of tenderness from him, but something seemed to have changed, he was different somehow. There was a lot about his past that she didn't know, but she *did* know that his childhood hadn't been an easy one or a happy one.

"What time is it?"

"Nearly midday."

"Wow," she said surprised, it had been before midnight when Noah had finally gotten concerned by her constant tossing and turning and suggested she take something to help her sleep. "I can't believe I slept for twelve hours."

"You needed it."

She had.

And it was sweet that Noah knew what she needed and made sure that she got it.

"Is there any news on Sapphire?" she asked.

"Emerald," Noah said slowly, reaching for her hands, "while you were sleeping the cops called, they wanted to speak with us. I thought it best to take them the security footage from when Alice was here, so they could see that she wasn't our prisoner, I didn't want them putting you in handcuffs again." As he said the word handcuffs, his grip on her tightened convulsively. She knew how angry it had made him when her brothers-in-law had dragged them down to the station, he could be possessive, but it was only because he loved her, and he had seen her at her lowest and helped her claw her way out of that deep, dark hole.

"It's okay, I'm okay," she reminded him. "What did the cops say when you took them the footage?"

"They wanted to know why we did it."

"Did you tell them?" Emerald was torn between wanting the cops' help in finding Alfie, but also terrified that their interference would push him to do something drastic.

"No. And I won't. But they did tell me something."

"Oh?" She arched a brow, wondering why he was dawdling, usually if he had something to say he just said it. That he was procrastinating meant that it was something he didn't really want to tell her. That meant that this was bad news.

Was it Sapphire?

Was her sister dead?

Had her body been found?

If Sapphire was dead then she was never going to forgive herself. If she and Noah hadn't brought her here in an attempt to convince her to let her stay dead, then she would never have gotten into the hands of whoever had her now.

Not *whoever.*

She was sure she knew who had her sister.

Alfie.

Who else could it be?

"There's no easy way to say this, Diamond is missing as well."

Diamond.

Missing.

Two of her sisters gone.

The world began to spin around her.

How could this be happening?

Her life had been going smoothly, her and Noah, the horses, the peace and quiet, and now Alfie had come back, and everything had fallen apart. Alice was dead, Sapphire and Diamond were gone, what was going to happen next?

"This is not your fault," Noah said, roughly grabbing her shoulders and sitting her up.

He could say that all he wanted, but it didn't make it true.

It was her fault.

Their fault.

They had set this chain of events into motion that meant that this was their fault.

"Do I need to say it again?" he asked, shaking her.

"Noah, it's Alfie," she said, her voice strained.

"I would assume so."

"This is because of me, because he wants me. He's going after my sisters one by one because he's trying to force our hand, he's hurting them to hurt me. They're in danger now because of me. Diamond and Sapphire's children are scared and grieving and missing their mommies because of me. Are Ruby and Amethyst going to be next? Will he stop there or will he go after their children next? They're so young, just babies, if Alfie gets his hands on them you know what he's going to do to them," she rambled, tears began to flow down her cheeks.

"He'll sell them or he'll keep them for himself," Noah said bluntly. "He'll do the same to your sisters."

She flinched at his words.

Not because she disagreed with them or hadn't thought of that herself, but because they suddenly became very real.

She and her sisters had already experienced that, she did not want her nephews and nieces to live through it as well.

"This is all our fault, we have to do something," she said, frantic now. She couldn't let her other sisters or her innocent little nephews and nieces become Alfie's next victims.

"Do what?" Noah asked. "What do you suggest we do? Hand you over to Alfie on a silver platter?"

"N-no," she stammered.

"Then what? You're what he wants, you're *all* he wants, he's not going to make a deal, and even if we hand you over, he's not going to let your sisters go. You know that. There isn't anything we can do. We need to leave."

"Leave?" she shrieked. How could they leave now? Alfie had two of her sisters, and he was just going to keep going after them until he had them all, and that still wouldn't be enough.

"He knows we're here, he's abducting your sisters to try to get to you, and sooner or later he's going to make a move to grab you. We need to leave." The look on Noah's face said he was already forming a plan, but there was no way she was running and leaving her family to pay the price of her freedom.

"I'm not leaving, Noah, I can't. They're my sisters."

"And you're mine," he hissed. "And I won't stand by and let Alfie get his hands on you."

He said it like it was a done deal.

But as far as she was concerned it wasn't.

She wasn't making another mistake, and running and letting Alfie get her family.

She couldn't.

She wouldn't.

∾

4:47 P.M.

She hated being cooped up like this.

It reminded her of the years she had spent as a captive, used to make money for the people who had bought her.

Ruby felt like she was going to lose it.

She had battled depression and suicidal thoughts ever since she escaped, and although they had faded a lot, she could go days at a time now without any of those dark thoughts, at times like this they resurfaced.

Emerald coming back, and first Sapphire and then Diamond going missing, and now being a virtual prisoner because the same person who took her sisters might come after her next, was enough to have her teetering on the edge again.

What if she fell off the edge?

Ruby was so afraid that she would, that she would fall back into that dark place, get stuck, be unable to climb out. And this time it wasn't just about her, now she had a husband and a two-year-old little girl who needed her. She couldn't go back to that place. She couldn't.

But how could she stop herself?

Her phone rang, and a sense of dread washed over her. Was this going to be bad news? All day she and Amethyst had been on edge, trying not to let it show so that they didn't worry the kids who were already worried enough, particularly Leo, Archie, and Oscar who missed their moms and didn't understand what was going on. This could be the moment they got the news they had been dreading, the moment they learned that Sapphire and Diamond were never coming back.

"Who is it?" Amethyst demanded.

"Judah."

"Answer it," her twin sister ordered, "he's not going to tell you that they're dead over the phone so it has to be something else."

"Yeah, you're right," she said with a small exhale of relief. Quickly, she snatched up the phone before it got to voicemail and Judah worried that something had happened to her. "Judah? Do you have news?"

"No, I just wanted to let you know that we're going to be late home, we're at the house of Dean Winters, seeing if we can find anything on the man impersonating him."

Ruby shook her head at her sister to let her know it was nothing bad, and Amethyst headed off with the big bowl of slime they'd just made for the kids to play with.

"You okay?" Judah asked.

"Yes, of course," she replied automatically.

"I meant, are you *really* okay."

"I'm ..." she paused as she searched for the right words, finally settling on, "holding on."

"I guess that's the best you can do given the circumstances," Judah said, his voice full of the kind of empathy that could only come from having walked the same path. "Call me if you need me."

"You're working," she protested. She didn't like to bother her husband at work, especially when he was working a case that hit this close to home.

"But nothing is more important to me than you and Chloe. Call me if you need me," he said again.

"Okay," she relented. "I will. Keep us updated when you can."

"I will. Don't bother with dinner, Zeb, Elijah, Gideon, and I will grab something quick while we're working. Give Chloe a kiss for me."

"I will."

"Love you."

"Love you too."

Ruby disconnected the call then stood for a moment staring at the phone in her hands. She had a bad feeling. A feeling she couldn't quite put a name on, but she felt like something was going to happen.

Something big.

She knew that Judah was always as careful as it was humanely possible to be when he was at work, but some days cops didn't come home no matter how careful they were being.

She prayed today was not that day for her family.

Setting the phone down, she pasted on a smile and turned to see the kids, Amethyst, and the nanny laughing and chatting away at the table. They'd moved from Gideon and Sapphire's house to the house that she used to share with her sisters. It was odd being back here with it no longer being her home, this place held so many memories, some good, some not so good. This was where she had slowly learned to live in the real world again, it was where she and Judah had taken the first steps in their relationship, and now it was where they were keeping their little girl safe.

When she and her sisters had designed this place, they had put in five safe rooms. It was a paranoid decision, she acknowledged that, but they were four young women in their twenties who had been sold—by their own parents—to human traffickers, they'd needed the reassurance of knowing that if something bad should happen again they had a safe place to hide. One of those safe rooms had saved her life once before, and it was reassuring to know that should Noah Landry come after her and Amethyst that they had a place to hide.

Not that she thought he would be stupid enough to try that.

It was different with Diamond, none of them had realized he was a threat to them, but now that they did, there were a couple of cops sitting in a car outside their house.

That should make her feel safe, but …

But she had been through enough in her life that she knew safety was an illusion.

No one was ever truly safe.

She didn't mean it to sound as pessimistic as she knew it did, but it was what it was. It was hard admitting that she was raising her daughter in a world where monsters walked around—sometimes in plain sight— but she couldn't let that knowledge wipe away all the magic and whimsy that still existed. The colors a sunrise painted the sky with, the tiny wings of a butterfly, the way a drop of water could hang on the branch of a tree, the sound a baby made when it laughed. There was so much good that it undid a little of the bad.

Laughter reached her ears, and she looked at the pure joy on her daughter's little face as she put her hands in the glittery pink slime they'd just made. It was the simple things in life that got little ones excited, she missed that innocence and having Chloe had helped her touch it again, it was one of the things she loved most about being a mom.

Ruby picked up a pack of spaghetti and was about to carry it toward the stove so she could make a start on dinner for the kids. They'd asked for pizza again, but they couldn't eat junk every day just because they were all stressed, so she had offered spaghetti and the kids had jumped on the idea. She remembered how much she had loved spaghetti and meatballs when she was a little girl, and she loved the way Chloe called it 'psghetti,' it was so adorable.

She was reaching for a pot when something exploded.

It sounded like it was right outside the house.

Amethyst jumped to her feet, the kids screamed, and she dropped the spaghetti on the floor.

Before they could do anything else she heard another loud crash, this one seemed to shake the entire house, and she knew it was someone trying to break in.

"Brooke, Tillie, get the kids in the safe room," Amethyst screamed.

Another crash made the house shake again, and then there was a bang, and the room filled with smoke.

Not just smoke, it was mixed with something that made her eyes sting and tear so badly she couldn't see even if she could manage to open her eyes.

"Amethyst?" she called out. Where was her sister? Had Brooke and the nanny gotten the kids to the safe room in time?

"Ruby?" Amethyst called back.

Footsteps sounded.

Then she was grabbed roughly.

She fought as hard as she could, swinging her fists, trying to do what Sapphire had taught her, aim for the groin, eyes, or throat, but she couldn't even see let alone do anything coordinated enough like fight off an attacker.

So much for thinking they were safe here because there were cops watching the house. Noah was determined to get all of them, and it seemed like he was going to get what he wanted. Ruby wasn't sure what he had done to the cops, but they had likely been eliminated in the first explosion, and now his men were here to get her and her twin sister.

"Ruby?" Amethyst yelled again, and she could hear the sounds of a scuffle.

She wanted to call out, but something shark pricked the skin on her shoulder, and the world around her began to go fuzzy.

She clawed at the hands holding her, she tried to grab hold of consciousness and cling to it, but despite her efforts, she was fading. She lost control of her body, her limbs hanging uselessly by her side, her mind floating away.

Further and further away.

Until she fell into some deep, dark place.

CHAPTER

Thirteen

December 3rd
12:19 A.M.

Everything was in order.

Noah closed the study door behind him and headed for the bedroom. There was nothing in this house that he was worried about anyone seeing so if the cops decided to come here in an attempt to arrest him and prove he had done something wrong, they wouldn't find anything incriminating.

Not that they would care.

They believed he was a monster who had hurt Emerald, had Alice tortured and murdered in cold blood, and then kidnapped the Hatcher sisters.

They weren't the only ones who believed he was a monster.

He believed it too.

He *was* a monster.

He always had been, and he always would be.

The only good thing he had ever done in his life was helping Emerald. He should never have allowed her to come back here. It had been selfish. When she had shown up on his doorstep, begging and crying to be allowed to come back, he should have turned her away. He should have convinced her that he didn't care about her, that he didn't love her, and that she was better off with her family than she was with someone like him.

But he hadn't done that.

He had allowed his own selfish needs and desires to take precedence over what was best for her, and because of that, she was now in trouble with the law. The video footage that he had given the cops clearly showed that Alice Lincoln was no prisoner here, she had come to them because she wanted to. Because she had wanted a safe place to hide out, away from the man who had abused her, where she knew she would be safe.

Monster or not, it seemed he was good at providing a safe haven to abused women.

The idea to have her pretend to be Emerald when the time came, and she passed away from her brain tumor had been Alice's. She had been here when Alfie had contacted him and said he knew that Emerald was alive and that he wanted her back. Alice had seen Emerald's terror firsthand and had wanted to help them. She was dying anyway, that's what she'd said, and if she could do one last thing for someone else then she would do it. That was all clear on the security footage, but it was up to the cops whether they wanted to see what was right in front of them or not.

And he suspected it was not.

If they wanted to punish someone for Alice's death then they could punish him, but not his sweet, pure, innocent Emerald.

They shouldn't have brought Bobby into this. That too had been Alice's idea, since they needed someone who wasn't him to dump the body. Bobby was ambitious, and promises of money and a chance to rise in the ranks at his company had been enough to persuade the man to do it. After all, it was only strangling, beating, and mutilating an already dead body. Alice had died of her tumor, they hadn't killed her, they had just made it look like she'd been murdered, hoping it was enough to fool the cops.

It might have been if it wasn't Sapphire herself who had found the body.

That was a coincidence they hadn't anticipated.

Or wanted.

He wasn't out to traumatize Emerald's sisters, he just didn't care if they got hurt along the way. His only concern in life was Emerald.

Which was why they were leaving.

Noah walked through the house to the bedroom he shared with Emerald, expecting to find her out on the balcony, staring up at the sky, lost in thought. The same place he found her practically every evening. Rain, snow, hail, or storm, she went out there. She said it was because watching the stars made her think of her sisters and a time in her life when she had been free, not tied down by the bonds of the trauma she had endured.

He wished he could give her that piece of herself back, but it was gone forever.

Much like the pieces of himself that he had lost along the way.

Money didn't buy your health, and it certainly didn't buy you safety.

Monsters came from monsters, and that was certainly true in his case.

He didn't know who his mother was, as far as the legality of the world was concerned he didn't have one, there was none listed on his birth certificate, and while he suspected he knew why, he had no proof.

His father had died when he was an infant leaving him in the care of an uncle who had no use for children.

Raised by a nanny—Alice Lincoln's grandmother—who cared only for his physical needs, making sure he was fed and bathed and supervised, she had no part in disciplining him.

That was reserved for his uncle.

He was tutored on this very same estate he had inherited upon his uncle's death, and rarely allowed to leave. The few friends he had were the children of his uncle's friends. Children who were raised in much the same way he was.

Daily punishments for the small infractions every child made, were standing in the corner with his nose to the wall for hours at a time, running laps in the middle of the night in the pouring rain until he collapsed and could not physically continue, beatings, and whippings. That was how you became a real man, his uncle always said. A real man was tough, he was strong, he took what he wanted without caring who he hurt to get it.

On his thirteenth birthday, his uncle brought a young woman to the house and made him have sex with her. That was what men did, he was told, they used women for their own pleasure and whether the woman wanted it, or derived any pleasure from it, was immaterial.

When you lived in the darkness you never learned what the light was like.

And that was his world.

Darkness.

With his money, power, good looks, and charm, he never failed to have a plethora of women falling at his feet, eager to get a piece of him. But that became dull. He craved the complete power and control over another human being that his uncle had had over him.

So when Alfie had shown him the website, it had seemed like a win-win. He got the chance to be in control over someone's every move, when they spoke, when they ate, when they used the bathroom, whether or not they received pleasure or pain, and that person got whatever sick pleasure they received out of the arrangement.

It should have been perfect.

It should have been everything he wanted.

It shouldn't have mattered that Emerald *wasn't* a willing participant.

But it did.

Because she was light.

And light eradicated darkness.

He was never going to be the kind of man Emerald deserved, but neither was he the same man he had been before he met her. He no longer used other people to get what he wanted, well not like he had before anyway. But deep down inside he was still selfish enough to want Emerald all to himself, he wasn't sharing her with her family, and he wasn't allowing her to go to prison.

So they were leaving this house for good.

Tonight.

Emerald wasn't going to like the idea, she was too good, too kind, too compassionate. She would worry about her sisters, and what would become of them, she would worry about Alfie hurting them because of her, and she would want to do something about it.

That he couldn't allow.

Pulling the small vial from his pocket, he prepared the syringe with sedatives. She wouldn't notice him walking up behind her as she stared up at the stars, she never did. He would have the drugs in her system before she even realized what was happening, and then he would spirit her away from here and take her someplace safe. Someplace where neither the cops not his ex-partner would ever find them.

Then their lives could go back to the way they had been before.

Just the two of them.

Noah walked into their bedroom, and when he saw that the doors to the balcony were closed, he knew.

Emerald was gone.

Her good heart was going to be the death of her.

With a scream of agony as all the things that Alfie was going to do to her ran through his head, he threw the vial and the syringe at the wall.

He had to find her.

He had to stop her before it was too late.

He spun around and ran through the house, he knew her, he knew how she thought, he knew what her next move would be, and he had to get to her in time.

He wasn't paying attention, and when he flung open the front door he came face to face with the cops.

Zeb Tuck grabbed him roughly and shoved him up against the wall. "Noah Landry, you are under arrest for the abductions of Amethyst, Ruby, Diamond, and Sapphire Hatcher, and the murder of Officer Todd McIntire and Officer Richard Pell. You have the right to remain silent, anything you say can and will be used against you in a court of law. You have the right to an attorney, if you cannot afford one, one will be provided for you. Do you understand these rights?"

Understand these rights?

All he understood was that Emerald was out there and they were preventing him from finding her.

If Alfie got his hands on Emerald he would hold these cops personally responsible, and they would pay the price.

～

12:52 A.M.

The breeze whipped through her hair, the sky was clear, and the moonlight bright enough that she could see where she was going even though it was the middle of the night.

Emerald couldn't believe she was doing this.

For the last fifteen years she hadn't been in control of herself and her decisions. She had been a prisoner, beaten and brutalized, then she had been a scared girl trained not to think for herself to the point that she had let Noah make her choices for her.

But it was time to stand on her own two feet.

It was time to take control of her own life, to do what she knew was right, and to take responsibility for this mess that she had set into motion.

This was her fault.

She was the one that Alfie wanted, not her sisters, and yet it was her sisters who were the ones paying the price. She couldn't tell Noah what she was going to do because he would have stopped her. He loved her too much to let her put herself in harm's way, but this was the right thing to do.

Pulling on the reins of her horse, she led Storm through the woods. It was so quiet out here, the only sound was the rustling of the breeze through the last of the leaves left on the trees. Most of the deciduous trees had lost their leaves already, leaving behind a carpet of yellow, orange, and red covering the ground. There were a few evergreens dotted about, but soon they would be covered in a dusting of snow.

Winter was just around the corner, and usually it was her favorite season, she loved the sight of the landscape covered in white, sparkling magically in the sun, like something out of another world. But right now, there was nothing special about the upcoming winter, all it served to remind her of was how bleak she had let her life become. Instead of trusting in her love of Noah and the support he had steadfastly provided her with throughout the years, she had hidden away, she had let fear rule every aspect of her life.

Now she knew she should have done more with the second chance she had been given. She should have embraced her relationship with Noah, they should have gotten married, had children of their own. She should have built up her confidence, gone out and gotten a job, started the animal shelter she had always wanted. She should have reconnected with her sisters, rebuilt and strengthened their bonds.

So many years had been wasted.

Well, not wasted, she had loved every minute of the time she had shared with Noah, and she couldn't think of a more beautiful place to live, but there were so many things she should have done differently.

If she could have, she would have rectified that, but it was already too late.

The only way to save her sisters was to give Alfie what he wanted.

Her.

That was why she had snuck out of the house while she knew Noah was busy in his office. She'd come straight down to the stables because the horse was the only option besides walking that she had. She'd been fifteen when she was sold and had never gotten a driver's license, Noah had offered to teach her how to drive, but she had never wanted to, that time in her life was gone.

She wished she could get those years back.

If she could get them back she would still keep Noah in her life, but she would have done all those things that normal people did. Her sisters had husbands and children, and it had her thinking that maybe she would have liked to become a mother. Only she couldn't imagine herself being one. Maybe she was just too damaged to care for a small child, but ...

No.

There was no point in thinking about it.

What she was going to do there was no coming back from. Even if she had decided to marry Noah, have his baby, and start her animal shelter she would never get a chance to do that.

She was going to give herself to Alfie.

Sacrifice herself in the hope that he would let Sapphire and Diamond go once he had what he really wanted. If he wouldn't agree to do that, then at least he would have no reason to go after Ruby and Amethyst. If all she could do was keep two of her sisters safe, then it was a sacrifice she was well and truly ready and willing to make.

So this was it for her.

This was the last time she would be free, the last time she would sit on the back of her powerful horse and ride through the woods, it was possibly the last time she would feel the wind on her skin, and breathe in fresh air.

She was handing herself over to a psychopath she was already well acquainted with.

He was going to torture her.

He was going to do horrific things to her.

Things she still had nightmares about the last time he did them to her.

But it was worth it.

Anything was worth it to save her sisters.

And Noah.

Emerald was very afraid that if Alfie continued to make threats directed at her, and continued to make plans to come after her, then Noah was going to do something drastic. Something that would end up putting him in danger, and she couldn't live in a world that didn't have Noah in it.

He had suffered as a child, and he suffered as an adult, he had a darkness inside him, darkness that had been placed there by his uncle. He thought that she didn't know about it, but Noah talked in his sleep, and she had heard a little of what he had endured, enough to have her heart break for the small, terrified child he must have been.

He was going to be so devastated when he realized what she had done.

Angry too.

Furious.

He would no doubt try to come after her, but it would be too late, by then she would already be Alfie's.

It was odd, before she had been sold, she had never even thought of herself as belonging to another human being, not even her parents, but ever since, she couldn't help but think of herself as a possession. She had been Richard Curtwood's, then she had been Noah and Alfie's, and then she had been Noah's.

No, she would *always* be Noah's. It didn't matter if she gave herself to Alfie, it didn't matter what he did to her, nothing could change the fact that her heart and her soul belonged to Noah.

Since she had no idea where Alfie was or how to find him, she had to just hope that his men had been watching the house, waiting for an opportunity to get to her. It had to be how he got Sapphire, he must have seen Noah's men driving away with her, followed them, and then taken her when they had left her somewhere she would be found.

She prayed her plan worked because she didn't know what else she could do.

Lights.

Up ahead she could see a light.

This was it.

She was about to step back into Hell in the possibly vain attempt to protect her sisters and Noah.

Emerald pulled on the reins, and the horse stopped walking and stood, awaiting its next command. Forget butterflies, there was a herd of rhinoceros in her stomach.

Just because she was doing the right thing didn't mean this was easy.

It was the hardest thing she had ever done in her life.

This wasn't like last time when she hadn't known what to expect, or what was going to happen to her. Then her imagination had run wild, conjuring up scenarios of what they would do to her, but this time she didn't have to imagine, she already knew, and that made it so much worse.

Like he had stepped right out of her nightmares into reality, Alfie appeared through the trees, walking toward her, that awful smile on his face, and stopped right in front of her. The horse, as though sensing the evil, began to snort, and she could tell it was going to bolt at any moment. Not wanting the animal to get hurt if it annoyed Alfie, she leaned over and stroked Storm's mane, then quickly swung her leg over and dropped down. Emerald tied the reigns to the nearest tree and hoped that it wouldn't take Noah too long to find the horse.

Then she turned around, ready to face her destiny.

Maybe this was always how she was supposed to die.

You couldn't really cheat death, she'd been given a reprieve and enjoyed a decade of good years with Noah, but now the grim reaper had come for her, and this time there would be no one to save her.

~

3:30 A.M.

"You signed Emerald's death warrant," Noah growled at the cops as they came into the interrogation room they had put him in hours ago.

All this time he had been sitting here seething with rage because anger was so much easier to deal with than abject terror.

He didn't do terror.

At least not anymore.

He had set aside fear when he became a man and took control of his own life. He was never going to let anyone else control him ever again, and if these cops thought they had the upper hand, they were sorely mistaken.

"Because of you, Emerald is gone," he snarled. Anger burned so brightly inside him, he was almost surprised that he didn't burst into flames. The cops had cuffed him and dragged him down here, giving Emerald the time she needed to give herself up as the sacrificial lamb in a misguided attempt to save her sisters' lives.

It was never going to work.

If Alfie knew that hurting her sisters was going to cause her pain, then he would do it just for fun. Then he would go after her nephews and nieces, and possibly the imbeciles standing in front of him. They would pay for what they had done, likely with the deaths of their wives, but if he could get away with it he would rip them to shreds as punishment for preventing him from stopping Emerald in time, if for no other reason than it might abate some of his anger so he could think clearly and come up with a plan.

"Maybe Emerald ran because she found out that you kidnapped her sisters," Zeb said, taking a seat at the table in front of him. Looking at the man was like looking in a mirror, seeing his own anger reflected back at him.

"I. Didn't. Kidnap. Anyone," he ground out. How stupid were these cops? If he had to rely on them to find Emerald on their own, it was never going to happen.

"So, it's a coincidence that right when you and Emerald come back into the picture, all four of her sisters go missing?" Judah demanded.

"No, of course not," he rolled his eyes. He really didn't have time to babysit a bunch of idiot cops, he needed to get out there, figure out where Alfie was hiding and go and get Emerald back. He didn't care if Alfie killed him, he didn't care about anything but making sure Emerald was safe.

"Then care to explain what's going on?" Elijah asked.

"No." They were responsible for Emerald getting herself abducted, and there was no way he was bringing them in, they were only going to mess things up more.

"Then you're not going anywhere," Elijah growled.

"You have nothing to hold me on, my lawyer will have me out of here within the hour," he said. He'd already called his lawyer, and the man was on his way here, at the latest, he would be out of here by sunrise. Not in enough time to save Emerald, but he knew Alfie wanted to torture her not kill her right away, so he still had time to get her back.

"You killed two cops when you abducted Ruby and my wife." Zeb glowered at him.

"I didn't kill anyone, and I'm sick of repeating myself. This is *your* fault, you wouldn't leave well enough alone, and now Emerald is gone."

"Maybe, if you hadn't kept Emerald away from her family for the last decade, then none of this would have happened," Judah shot back.

"There was nothing else to do," he muttered. While it was true that he wanted—and still did—Emerald all to himself, keeping her a secret had had practical applications as well. If Alfie had found out about Emerald, he would have done exactly what he was doing right now.

That couldn't happen.

But now it had, and the only way to rectify it before things got too out of hand was to get out of this police station.

ASAP.

Which meant he had to try to keep his anger under control because the angrier he got, the more he was going to provoke the cops and the angrier they would get. The angrier they got, the more likely they were going to get stubborn and insist on keeping him here.

Play nice, he thought to himself.

"Emerald wanted to stay away, continuing to harp on that isn't going to change it. I know that it hurt your wives' feelings, but it is what it is."

"No."

They all turned as the door to the interrogation room opened, and Gideon Barlow walked in. He was the shrink, married to Sapphire, and while he admired anyone being able to deal with her on a daily basis, he certainly didn't want to have to deal with the shrink.

Shrinks knew things they shouldn't.

That unnerved him.

"Keeping Emerald a secret was what *you* wanted, not what she wanted. You convinced her to stay away, and while I want to hate you for that because I know how many sleepless nights Sapphire had trying to find her sister, and how much guilt she carried around because she couldn't, I think you did it because you were trying to protect her."

He wasn't the only one who looked at the shrink in surprise.

That wasn't what he had expected the man to say.

"You really love Emerald, she's the most important thing in your life, and I believe that every choice you make is because you believe you're doing what you have to do to keep her safe. But we don't have time for you to think you can do this on your own. You know where she is, you know where my wife is, and her sisters, and like it or not, we're not going anywhere, so the quicker you accept that and just tell us what is going on, the quicker we can find them."

Work with the cops?

The idea was so absurd he very nearly laughed in their faces.

He did not need their help. He had this under control, he was going to find Emerald, and he was going to save her. If he could, he would free the others as well, but that wasn't his priority.

Emerald needed him, and he wasn't there for her.

He had been there for her every other time she needed him, and this wasn't going to be the exception.

"You were abused as a child." Gideon strode over and took a seat at the table. "Not by a parent, but by the person who raised you. Physical abuse, probably sexual abuse as well—"

"I wasn't sexually abused," he recoiled at the very notion.

"Maybe not by whoever raised you, but you were exposed to prostitutes, or possibly since we know that you bought Emerald, human trafficking victims. You were forced to have sex with them to prove your manhood, and that developed a need to control others because you need to feel powerful since growing up, you had your power stolen from you. That's part of the appeal of Emerald. She's traumatized by what she went through, and you were her savior, she clings to you, and she needs you to be in control because it makes her feel safe. It's a win-win, you both get what you want. You took Sapphire, and you intended to keep her so she couldn't tell anyone that Emerald was alive, but Emerald wouldn't go along with it, so you let her go, and someone else got her before she could be found."

Well, that was unsettlingly accurate.

Since he couldn't think of a comeback, he just glared at the man. This was exactly why he hated shrinks. They thought they knew everything, and they didn't care that they invaded your privacy or made you think of things that were better left buried.

Deeply buried.

"We don't have time for this, Noah. Every second that ticks by just gives this man more of an opportunity to hurt them. To hurt Emerald."

The man was trying to emotionally blackmail him into giving them what they wanted.

It wasn't going to work.

"Say we let you go, and you find this man on your own, what's your plan?"

His plan?

He didn't have a plan.

Yet.

But he would figure something out.

"See? You don't know what your next move is, but you know what your goal is. It's the same goal that all of us have. If we work together, our chances of finding them before they're killed are much higher." The shrink's eyes grew stark, and his voice took on a pleading tone, "Sapphire is pregnant. You know who has my wife and unborn baby, so I'm asking you, please, to tell us who he is and help us find them. All of them."

Noah groaned inwardly.

Great, they were manipulating him with innocent unborn babies now.

As much as he wanted to do this his way, maybe the man was right, maybe if they worked together, they would find Emerald and the others quicker. Or at the very least, if he told them what they wanted to know they would let him go, and he could go after Alfie himself.

"Fine," he nodded. "You want to know who has Emerald, I'll tell you."

～

5:24 A.M.

Voices.

She heard whispered voices.

But they weren't male voices they were female.

Familiar female voices.

Emerald struggled to get her stuffy head to focus, she knew it was important that she get it together as quickly as she could because time was not on her side.

Not on *their* side, she amended when she pried open her eyes—which felt like they had been superglued shut—and saw that the voices around her belonged to her sisters.

All her sisters.

Ruby and Amethyst were here too, she had hoped to hand herself over to Alfie before he went after them, but she was too late.

Too late.

If seemed she was always too late.

If she had learned that she couldn't live her entire life letting fear guide her before now, then she could have avoided all of this.

But right now, she didn't have time for regrets, they needed to figure out a plan.

With a moan as her stomach churned, Emerald pushed herself into a sitting position and immediately drew the attention of her sisters who turned to look at her.

None of them smiled.

They were angry and hurt, and she couldn't blame them. She had betrayed them by keeping herself a secret, and she wasn't sure that it was something she could undo, even if they did survive this.

"You're awake," Diamond said, taking a step toward her but not coming all the way over to the bed. "Are you okay? Did he hurt you?"

Thank goodness her oldest sister couldn't help but mother them, even if she was angry. "I-I'm okay," she stammered, wanting so badly to fix things but having no idea how. A simple apology didn't seem like enough, but what was enough? Was anything enough? Was there a way to fix this? Could things go back to the way they had been before? She wanted so badly to believe that they could, but she felt so lost, she didn't know what to do, she wished that Noah was here. He always knew what to do.

"He drugged you," Diamond said, taking another step closer. "That's what he did to all of us."

"I'm sure she knows that already," Sapphire snapped. "She and Noah probably planned it together."

"We didn't—" Emerald broke off when she looked at her sister's face. Her sister's battered and bruised face. Alfie had hurt her. Her guilt surged, almost incapacitating her. All her life had consisted of for the last few years was Noah, the horses, music, drawing, reading, she had pushed away the violence that had ruled her life while she had been a prisoner, but now she was back in that very same place—as were her sisters. "I'm so sorry."

"See," Sapphire said triumphantly. "I told you that she and Noah were in on this."

"We're not," she said, ignoring her swirling stomach to stand up. "We didn't do this, I swear, Saph, I told Noah that we couldn't keep you a prisoner, we shouldn't have taken you in the first place. I'm sorry," she said again, wishing it was enough.

"I believe her," Diamond said, turning to face the others.

"Why would you believe her?" Sapphire demanded. "You heard what she said, she admitted to abducting me. Why should we believe her when she says that she and Noah aren't the reason we're all here?"

"Because if its Noah, then why is she here?" Diamond asked.

"I don't know," Sapphire shrugged, clearly convinced she was right.

"Do you know who brought us here?" Amethyst asked, stepping up beside Diamond.

"It's Alfie," she shivered as she said his name. Even thinking about him was enough to make her break out in a cold sweat.

"That partner of Noah's," Sapphire said, narrowing her eyes. "The other man who bought you."

Emerald nodded.

"This Alfie person, is he why you stayed hidden all these years?" Ruby asked, stepping up to join Amethyst and Diamond so only Sapphire stayed away now.

She wanted to say yes because she knew that would give her sisters a reason to let go of some of their anger, but in truth, Alfie was only part of the reason she had stayed away. "I stayed away because I was afraid," she said honestly. These were her own sisters, if she couldn't be honest with them, who could she be honest with? "What happened, it changed me, I was afraid of everything, even myself. With Noah was the only place that I felt safe. I know maybe it doesn't make sense since he was one of the people who bought me, but Noah makes me feel safe. I let my fears control me, I let them keep me away from you, and I used them as an excuse to keep hiding. But I shouldn't have. I shouldn't have stayed away, and I shouldn't have let fear rule my life. I know it doesn't make up for everything, but I'm sorry, I really am." Emerald reached up to brush away the tears that threatened to spill down her cheeks.

"You don't have to apologize for letting fear rule your life," Ruby said. Her sister came over, then hesitated for a moment before throwing her arms around her and hugging her tight.

Emerald let a sob escape as she wrapped her own arms around her sister and clung to her tightly. Maybe there really was a way to get back to the way things had been before. It wouldn't happen overnight, but it might happen.

If they lived long enough that was.

"Can you forgive me?" she asked through her tears.

"Ruby is right, there's nothing to forgive," Diamond said, coming to join them. "We all know about fear ruling our lives."

Two down two to go.

"I'm not going to say I'm not hurt," Amethyst said, "but I'm also not going to be so stubborn as to not be thrilled that you're alive, or to admit that I understand why you stayed away even if I don't like it."

That was three now. Emerald cast a glance over at Sapphire, who remained where she was, the angry glower firmly stuck on her face.

It would take time to win over Sapphire, and she prayed she got it.

She and Sapphire had been the closest growing up. As the two youngest, they had shared a room, and for a while as kids, they had been virtually inseparable. Emerald remembered the night they had been taken, Sapphire had fought to try to save them, and if she knew her sister, Sapphire had been beating herself up for failing ever since.

"So you think it's this Alfie who brought us here?" Amethyst asked.

"Yes, he somehow found out I was alive, and he wants me back, he's angry that Noah cut him out and kept me to himself. He probably thinks that Noah has been doing the same things the two of them did to me while I was their prisoner all these years. I think that he brought you all here to try to bring me out of hiding because he knew he could never get to me at Noah's house."

"Then how did you get here?" Ruby asked.

"I ran," she said simply. "I didn't know that he already had you and Amethyst and I thought if I gave myself to him, he might leave you alone, but I was too late."

"You were going to trade yourself for us?" Ruby asked.

"Of course."

"You didn't have to do that," Amethyst said.

"I wanted to." What else would she do? Stand by and do nothing while this man hurt the people she loved? "I just wish that I had gotten here in time because now that we're here, I don't know how we're ever going to get out."

"Sapphire has a plan," Diamond said.

"One that we don't need her help for," Sapphire inserted.

"Five of us is better than four," Amethyst reminded her.

"Not if we can't trust all five of us."

"We can trust her," Ruby said.

"You're hurt and angry, we all get that," Diamond—ever the peace-maker—said, "but right now the five of us are stronger together than we are apart. I know you don't like it, but we have to work together. With all of us, we have a better chance of getting out of here. So are you able to set aside that hurt and anger, at least for now, and tell Emerald your plan?"

Sapphire stayed where she was, not coming over to join the rest of them, but the look on her face said she was wavering, she had always been the most stubborn of the five of them. Despite Sapphire's anger, Emerald knew her sister still loved her, she wouldn't be this angry if she didn't still care.

"You want to go home, for Leo's sake, and that little baby you have inside you," Diamond said. "Let Emerald in on your plan if for no other reason than to get you home to your little boy."

"Fine," Sapphire said with a sigh, "it's clear I'm outvoted anyway. Emerald can help, but I don't like it." With that, she finally crossed over to stand with them, and the five of them took seats on the bed. "Tell us everything that you know about Alfie so we can use it to our advantage."

A small smile touched her lips. She might be about to face torture and death, and she was still more afraid than she could stand, but at least she had her sisters back. Now if Sapphire's plan worked and they survived this who knows, maybe she could have a real life with her family and the man she loved.

∾

7:46 A.M.

"There has to be something we're missing," Judah said.

"Of course there's something we're missing," Noah snapped. If they had all the pieces of information they needed, then they would already know where Alfie was hiding with Emerald and her sisters.

"You're the one who knows this man, where do you think he is?" Elijah asked.

They'd already asked him that a dozen times over the last couple of hours since he had told them everything about Emerald and how she came to be with him, and Alfie, and everything that had happened all the way up until they came and arrested him. While he didn't think he was still under arrest and he was sure that they now believed he didn't have their wives, he wasn't sure how things would go if he just up and left.

Besides, he had reluctantly accepted their help.

He was putting his trust in them.

For him that was huge because he didn't trust people.

The only reason he was doing it was for Emerald. He needed to find her, and they had resources at their fingertips that he didn't, and they were every bit as motivated as he was to find Alfie because their loved ones' lives hung in the balance as well.

"If I knew where Alfie was I wouldn't have tried to convince him Emerald was dead," he reminded the cops. Going over and over the same thing wasn't getting them anywhere, he wanted to get out there and start searching, knock on every door in the city if they had to.

"How did he know where Diamond was going to be, and when she would be there?" Zeb asked, looking thoughtful. "And how did he know that there were cops outside the house but not inside? And how did he know that both Ruby and Amethyst would be together? We'd been staying at Gideon's house after Sapphire disappeared, so how did he know that had changed?"

As far as he was concerned, he didn't care how Alfie had been watching Emerald's sisters, all he cared about was where they were now.

Apparently, the cop minds of the room's other occupants disagreed.

"We assumed that it was Noah using the security system he had installed to watch us, and that was how he knew what was going on, but now that we know Noah isn't the one who kidnapped them it can't be that," Judah said.

"Is there anyone in your company who might have found a way to hack your system and access the cameras?" Zeb asked.

"No. You asked me that already, and I said no."

"What about this Dean Winters guy? We know the real Dean Winters is dead, and this imposter started working with you about two years ago, not long before Alfie came back. Could he have hacked your system?" Elijah pressed.

"Dean was just in marketing, he didn't have access to any of the security systems."

"But you didn't know that there was anything odd about him," Elijah said, like a dog with a bone he couldn't let go. "So maybe he found a way to get access."

"He didn't," Noah insisted. "I set it up so I would know if anyone gained access. And this Dean Winters imposter isn't Alfie, I would have known if he was."

"But chances are he is a spy of some sort, someone Alfie sent in to watch you. So what if he did the same with us?" Zeb asked.

"Sent in someone to spy on us?" Elijah asked.

"Why not? If he did it to Noah, then it stands to reason he would do the same to Emerald's sisters when he realized they might be a way to track her," Zeb said, getting excited now.

"But we would notice if someone came into our lives for the purpose of spying on us," Elijah didn't look convinced. "You, Judah, Sapphire, and I are cops, Diamond, Ruby, and Amethyst have all been through something traumatic so they're aware of their surroundings, and Gideon is a criminal psychiatrist, there's no way someone could fool all of us."

"What if it's someone we would never suspect?" Judah asked slowly.

"Who are you thinking?" Zeb asked.

"Where's the footage from when Ruby and Amethyst were taken?" Judah asked, standing and going to the computer. He sat down and began to fast forward through the footage, stopping it right before the explosion outside that killed the two cops who had been assigned to watch the house. "Look, there," he said, pointing to the corner of the screen where a blonde woman who appeared to be in her mid-twenties was visible.

On the screen, he saw Ruby hang up the phone, then walk over to the stove with a pack of spaghetti in her hand. The blonde woman had picked up her cell phone as soon as Ruby hung up hers, and then she started looking about nervously.

She looked jumpy.

Abruptly, the woman stood and picked up one-year-old Lucy Tuck.

Then the explosion went off.

Although it wasn't visible on the footage, you could tell by the way both Ruby, Amethyst, and Brooke all jumped and turned in the direction of the explosion.

The blonde woman had already grabbed Leo Barlow and was taking both children toward what he knew was the safe room before the teenager grabbed the other remaining children.

"She knew the explosion was coming," Noah said. "She texted whoever set it off to tell them that everyone was there and they could come in. Who is she?" When he got his hands on this woman, he would do whatever it took to get her to talk. He needed to know if she knew where Alfie was hiding out.

"It's the nanny," Judah said quietly.

"Where is she?" he growled, anger coursed through his body.

"She's here," Zeb replied. "With the abductions, we were worried that you were going to go after the kids next, so we brought them here last night. Tillie came by this morning to look after them."

That was all he needed to hear.

Noah stood and headed for the door, if that woman was here he was going to find her, and he was going to make her talk.

"Where are you going?" Elijah asked, moving to block his path.

"To find this Tillie woman, make her tell me where Alfie has Emerald."

"No," Elijah shook his head. "You're not going in there, not like this, she'll take one look at you and clam up."

"Well, I'm not staying here," he fumed. "And you think she'll talk to you? She looked after your children, you see her as a warm, caring, compassionate woman that you trust, she'll play on that. I'd say right now that this girl needs a dose of fear. If you want her to talk that is," he added, and stared the man down.

"I agree," Gideon spoke up. "Tillie is more likely to talk if she's afraid. Let Noah go with us to talk to her."

Elijah sighed but opened the door, and the five of them walked through the police station.

"Let me get the kids out before you go in there," Judah said.

As much as he wanted to storm right in there, it wasn't like they had a lot of time on their hands, he nodded and waited while Judah went into the room. The moment he exited with the small children in tow, Noah threw open the door, hard enough that it slammed into the wall, and then he grabbed the woman, yanked her out of her chair, and shoved her up against the wall.

"Where is Alfie?" he demanded, the fear in the woman's eyes abated some of the anger inside him, power and control were like a soothing balm to him, and this was the first time he had felt even a little of either since he realized Emerald was gone.

"I-I don't k-know what you're t-talking about," the woman stammered, her gaze darting around the room, not settling on any one thing for more than a split second.

"I don't have time for lies," he snarled, holding his face just a millimeter away from hers. "You told the man who set the explosion yesterday when to do it, we know you're involved, denying it is only wasting time. Time we don't have," he roared. "Now tell me where they are."

"I-I can't," Tillie stammered.

"Why can't you, Tillie?" Elijah asked before he could demand once again that she start talking.

"I-I-I," she stuttered helplessly.

"Are you afraid of him? Did he threaten you?" Elijah asked.

The girl burst into tears, sobbing so hard that she shook in his grip, and he knew. He had seen those tears before. "Alfie bought you. You're a human trafficking victim, he tortured you, and then he threatened that if you didn't get the job as the Hatcher family nanny he would punish you, and if you didn't give him the information he wanted he would punish you."

"I-I'm sorry," Tillie sobbed. "I didn't want to do it, but I was afraid."

Noah released the woman, and she slid to the floor, curling herself up into a ball as she wept. He could imagine the scars and broken bones the examination of her would turn up. He knew because he'd seen them on Emerald.

The cops moved to offer comfort to the woman, but he stopped them with a single glance. He still needed information.

"How long were you his?"

"S-seven years," she hiccupped through her tears.

Seven years, he would love to say he couldn't imagine what she had gone through, but unfortunately, he could. "So, you know where Alfie is."

"N-no. We-we moved when he wanted me to be-be the nanny, every time we met it-it was at a hotel."

"Do you know the name of the hotel?" he demanded.

"Y-yes, it's the Grand Palace Reuss."

That was a start, the cops would search Alfie's room maybe find something that would point them to where he had Emerald.

"Why didn't you run away, Tillie?" Elijah asked, crouching beside the crying woman. "When Alfie let you out of his house why didn't you go to the cops? Tell someone what he did to you? You could have come to us, we would have helped you."

"I-I couldn't, he has my brother and my sister," she said, lifting her head to look at them, her face wet with tears. "He made my brother pretend to be this man that Alfie killed, he made him go and work at your company," she said, nodding at Noah. "He said if we didn't do what he wanted he would kill our sister. Slowly."

This was more information than he needed.

He didn't care about this woman and her family—although he wished them no harm—he only cared about Emerald, and her time was running out.

She needed him, she thought that she was saving him, but he would give his life in a second for her, he would do anything for her.

She was his life.

Without her, he was nothing.

～

10:09 A.M.

"I hear someone coming," Sapphire said.

Emerald looked over at her sister. Sapphire had stood determinedly over by the door while the rest of them sat on the bed and caught up on each other's lives. She had learned a little of what had happened to them after their parents had sold them, and a lot about their lives since.

The more they talked, the closer she felt to them.

It wasn't exactly like it used to be, but it was getting there, she just wished they had the time to get to know one another properly again, become sisters again. She wished they had more time. Even a few hours would be better than nothing, just a little time to try to make inroads with her sisters. She wanted them back, all four of them, and their families too. She didn't want to be lonely anymore, and she didn't want Noah to be lonely anymore, they had a family, and she wanted them to be close.

Maybe if Sapphire's plan worked, they might get that chance.

Even if this was it, even if they would soon die, or live out the rest of their lives here, then at least she'd had these last couple of hours with them. It was better than nothing.

"Diamond, go stand over there," Sapphire ordered, pointing to a spot where Diamond would be able to see out the door when it opened, and Alfie came in here. "Just like we discussed, remember. You get a quick look, find out how many men are out there, confirm they're armed, then when Alfie comes in here, and I call you over here you hold up the number of fingers of how many men there are."

"I remember what to do," Diamond said, moving to stand in the spot they had chosen when they had practiced this earlier.

"Everyone else know what they're supposed to do?" Sapphire asked.

"I know, I just don't like you playing bait." Amethyst frowned.

"He's already hit me a few times, I annoy him, he's attracted to me, this is just the easiest option," Sapphire said, the same thing she'd said before when she came up with the plan.

Emerald was with Amethyst, she didn't like the idea of Sapphire deliberately provoking Alfie into hurting her, she was pregnant, and this was dangerous. They had no idea just how dangerous Alfie was, the man was evil personified. She had met a lot of evil men, she knew her sisters had too, but Alfie was something else.

He was a monster.

He had no soul.

"Let's do this," Sapphire said, and for a moment their eyes met, Sapphire's were cold, but then they softened, warmed, and Emerald saw her old sister in there. Maybe she wasn't the only one who had changed because of what their parents had done to them.

The door to their room swung open, and she wondered why Alfie had kept them together. They were more dangerous together than if he had kept them in separate rooms. Alfie had to know that there was a chance they would try to jump him, especially since Sapphire was a cop, he was probably just too cocky to believe that anyone was able to best him.

"Good morning," Alfie singsonged as he entered the room, then closed and locked the door behind him. Emerald gave him a quick onceover but didn't see a gun, that was good for them. She still wasn't sure about Sapphire's plan, but her sister was smart, and this was her job, so she trusted her.

"What's good about it?" Sapphire asked. "Diamond, get away from him."

Diamond nodded, and quickly hurried across the room, holding up two fingers so only they could see.

Alfie chuckled, and a million flashbacks ran through Emerald's mind. He would always laugh like that when he got done hurting her. Noah had never been like that, even when he believed she was part of the sex slave game, he didn't get any sick pleasure from it, he didn't really like hurting her, and when he knew she wasn't in it willingly any pleasure for him was gone.

But not for Alfie.

He hurt people because it amused him.

"Thinking about old times?" Alfie asked her, that manic smile on his face.

"She told us about you." Sapphire shot a haughty glare Alfie's way. "You won't get away with what you did. Monsters never do."

Alfie stiffened. "You're a slow learner."

"I'm not a slow learner, I'm just not afraid of you. You think you're some big man, you feed off your victim's fear, it gives you the high you need, but you won't be getting your next fix from me. I lock guys like you up for a living, and guess what, you're not the scariest I've ever met, not even close."

"Guess what, princess? This isn't about you, this is all about my pretty little Emerald. She's the one that got away. Well not *got* away, more like snatched away from me before I was finished with her, and I was taught to *always* finish with things before throwing them away. We have unfinished business, you and the others are just here to teach her a little lesson." He turned and met her gaze, holding it as though his eyes were magnets. "She's going to watch while I kill each one of you, then it will be her turn. And you can all look forward to a slow death."

Emerald couldn't help but shudder.

No matter how many years passed, this man would always terrify her.

Alfie was her own personal bogeyman.

Ruby and Amethyst moved closer to her, flanking her sides, and she drew strength from them.

This time, she wasn't a terrified teenage girl, traumatized and alone, now she was a twenty-nine-year-old adult with her sisters by her side.

"I think you'll find Emerald isn't the same kid you knew back then, and now you have to deal with us. Five good princesses against one ugly monster, my money is on us." Sapphire winked.

Alfie sprung at Sapphire, hitting her in the face and shoving her up against the wall, fresh blood blossomed where he'd hit her, and Emerald had to clench her hands into fists and force herself to stay still.

Follow the plan.

How many times had Sapphire said that in the last couple of hours?

If they didn't stick to the plan, then they might not get out of here alive.

Emerald still only rated their chances at maybe twenty to eighty, in Alfie's favor, but she was going to give this everything she had.

"You can hit me all you want, Alfie, I'm still not scared of you," Sapphire goaded.

"You will be," he snarled. "You think all I'm going to do is hit you a few times? I'm going to do so much more. Princess."

Alfie shoved his hand down Sapphire's pants, and she took the piece of the mattress spring they had prepared earlier and shoved it into Alfie's cheek.

He screamed and staggered backward, his hand flying to his face, blood gushing through his fingers.

Before he had time to recover, Sapphire had stabbed him again, in the side of the neck. Alfie screamed again and dropped to his knees, but there wasn't enough blood for him to be bleeding out.

"Here's the thing, Alfie." Sapphire leaned over so she could look him in the eye. "The princess always wins. We leave him in here, drop the two men outside, then we get out of here. I want him alive so he can live out the rest of his life in prison, and we can find every one of his other victims."

Sapphire turned her back on Alfie to get the strips of sheet they had ripped so they could restrain him while they found a way out of here. Alfie took advantage of her momentary distraction and launched at her before any of them could stop him.

He grabbed her wrist and shoved the hand that still held the sharp piece of metal down, sending it plunging into her leg.

"Don't you know the monster always comes back one last time?" He laughed as blood flowed down Sapphire's leg. He released her and she sunk to the floor, her hands pressed to her wound, trying to stem the flow of blood.

Alfie bent down and pulled a small gun out of his boot, then he leaned back and smiled at all of them.

Emerald's stomach sunk.

They had tried, and they had failed.

Their plan hadn't worked which meant their fates were sealed.

They would remain here as Alfie's prisoners, he would rape, torture, and then kill each of her sisters one by one, making her watch every single thing he did to them.

Then it would be her turn.

She knew that whatever Alfie was going to do to her sisters was nothing compared to what he would do to her.

Fear chilled her to the very bone.

~

10:27 A.M.

"So much for your good versus evil theory," Alfie said as he watched the faces of Emerald and her sisters fall as they realized that their little plan hadn't worked.

He loved it when things went his way.

Things *always* went his way.

Well, almost always anyway.

Except with Emerald.

But that was Noah's fault. His friend had turned on him, told him that Emerald was dead, that a game had gone too far, but that was a lie, he had wanted to keep Emerald all to himself.

Now Emerald was all his.

And he was going to enjoy the time they spent together.

Not here though. There was a chance that Noah—or he guessed the cops—might figure out where he was hiding out and come after him. So he was going to pack up Emerald and her sisters and leave, he had enough money to go anywhere he wanted, maybe a tropical island would be nice. No more snow, he could swim all year round, and he'd choose someplace remote, where no one would hear the screams.

Screams.

He loved the sound.

Some people liked to listen to the sound of ocean waves, some people liked the sound of birds chirping, some people liked the sound of laughter, but he liked the sound of screams.

Alfie didn't see himself as a monster, in fact he hated that word. It was so ... silly. Monster made him conjure images of a big furry creature with fangs and claws, and big googly eyes, but he didn't have any of those things. He was a human being, an attractive one at that, he had blond hair and green eyes, a smile that could—and did—charm the panties off any woman he turned it on. He was no monster, he was simply a man without a soul.

It wasn't anyone's fault, it certainly wasn't because he'd had a bad childhood, or been abused, or any such thing. On the contrary, he'd had a fabulous childhood. A wealthy family, a father who traveled a lot but also tried to spend time with him when he was around, a mother who doted on him, spoiled him, he had everything he ever wanted.

But he had known even back then that he wasn't like most people.

He craved power and control like other people craved water and food. He didn't hurt animals, there was no reason to, he was already superior to them. It was people who he wanted to harm, specifically women.

Women served one purpose; to please a man.

That was his mother's only purpose in life. She didn't work—she didn't tend to the house—they had a maid for that—she didn't cook—they had a chef for that—she didn't look after him—they had a nanny for that—all she did was work out at the gym to keep her figure, go shopping to buy nice clothes, go to the salon to have her hair dyed an unnatural shade of blonde, and dress up in her pearls and her pretty dresses—with plenty of cleavage showing—and look beautiful.

Women were entertainment, so he let them entertain him.

And now he had five very pretty new pieces of entertainment.

Ignoring the pain in his face and neck, he looked down at Sapphire. "You, princess, are going to be my first. As soon as we get somewhere a little more private, I'm going to set you all up in cages, one beside the other. Don't worry, the cages are high class, aren't they, Emerald?"

Emerald stared at him, but there was something different about her. She was looking at him. *At* him. No more gaze fixed on the floor, no more cowering, no more trembling when he spoke her name.

She was different.

Stronger now.

That would make this even more fun.

"Let's—" Alfie broke off when two shots were fired off in rapid succession, and then a moment later, the door was broken down, and a man stormed in. "Ah, Noah," he said, holding up his weapon, pointing it directly at Emerald so the man knew that doing anything stupid was out of the question. He would shoot Emerald if he had to, he wanted her back but more than that, he wanted to win, and so long as he was the one to end Emerald's life then it was a win as far as he was concerned.

"Emerald, did he lay a hand on you?" Noah asked, his own weapon aimed squarely at Alfie's head.

"I'm okay," Emerald assured Noah. "But he hurt Sapphire."

Alfie knew that Noah didn't care about the sister, he was here for Emerald and Emerald alone. He wouldn't be surprised if the man tried to bargain for Emerald's freedom, offering to walk away and let him keep the sisters.

"Don't worry, he'll pay for that," Noah said, his voice was low and deep, like the angry growl of a bear or a lion.

"How exactly are you in a position to do anything about it?" Alfie asked. "Anyone in this room moves and I blow off your precious Emerald's pretty little head."

"The girl is bleeding badly," Noah said, nodding at Sapphire who was now sitting in a large pool of blood. "She's pregnant you know, so you might not want to let her bleed out. You lose her, you lose the baby, and pretty white babies with big green eyes sell for a bundle."

A baby.

He hadn't known the woman was pregnant, his little Tillie hadn't told him that, she would be punished for keeping that a secret. Noah was right, he would get a bundle selling the infant, he better make sure he kept the woman alive until she gave birth.

"You," he nodded at the oldest sister, "go to her, make sure she doesn't bleed out."

The woman crossed the room, trying to keep as far away from him as she could, then dropped to her knees at Sapphire's side, grabbed the strips of sheet, and wrapped them around the wound, pressing her hands to her sister's leg to keep pressure on the cut.

"Thanks for the heads up." He nodded to Noah. "How'd you finally find me?" He had been sure that Noah would never discover where he was hiding out and yet here was his ex-partner—his ex-friend—standing before him.

"I stopped living in the past and realized that you're looking to the future," Noah replied. "This house is on Emerald Grove, and it's number one thousand and two, Emerald's birthday is February tenth. Rebirth, you want to start over, you think that Emerald can be yours, but you're too late, she's already mine."

"Not anymore." That Noah had turned up here was a stroke of luck, his friend's betrayal had cut deeply. It was a pure fluke that he had found out that Emerald was alive, he'd come to Noah's place one day, intending to ask him if he wanted to enter a business venture with him, and he'd seen her walking through the grounds.

He would recognize her anywhere.

And in that moment, he knew he had been played.

Emerald had never died, Noah just wanted her all to himself, and he would bet his bottom dollar that Noah was responsible for the sudden lost funds from his account, and the demise of the website they had bought Emerald from. Noah thought he was so much better than him, but they were the same, he just wore his darkness on his sleeve instead of hiding it away.

"You lost, Noah. There's no way that you are walking out of here with Emerald. You can either put your gun down and Emerald lives, or you can keep it pointed at my head and I kill her, then you, and then every one of these beautiful women. If you shoot me, my finger still pulls the trigger, and Emerald dies, then you'll wish I'd killed you. Your choice."

"You forgot the third option," Noah said with a smug smile.

"Oh?" Whatever game the man was playing wasn't going to work. He knew Noah couldn't risk Emerald's life so he would lower his weapon, leaving him the victor.

"I didn't come alone," Noah told him.

"You brought some of your men? That's irrelevant, my men can take yours, and besides, they're never going to get in here before I kill her."

"Not my men, theirs," Noah replied, gesturing at the sisters. "I let the cops put a tracking device on me when I figured out where you were and came here, that means they'll be here any minute. You can kill everyone in this room, but you still won't be walking out of here any other way than in a body bag or in handcuffs. I think that means *I* win."

The smug tone made him snap.

I win.

Those two little words he despised.

Monster.

Pervert.

Those were the words his father had uttered when he'd walked in on him at age thirteen with his girlfriend tied to the bed while he hit her over and over again as he pounded into her.

He'd killed his father that day, then his girlfriend, and then his good for nothing mother.

He should have spent the rest of his life in prison, but he had inherited a lot of money, and his lawyer had gotten him off with an insanity plea, and he'd spent only a couple of years in a psychiatric facility, his record expunged given he was a minor.

I win.

That's what the lawyer had said like his life was some sort of game.

But now life was *his* game, and he wasn't going to let anyone beat him, not ever again.

If he wasn't walking out of here a free man, then he wasn't walking out of here at all.

He pulled the trigger, but Noah, apparently sensing what he was going to do a split second before he did it, sprung straight into its path.

10:39 A.M.

"Noah," Emerald screamed.

A shaft of pain sliced through her heart as the bullet sliced through Noah, and he landed with a thud.

He wasn't moving.

Was he dead?

She wanted to run to him, check on him, press her hands to his wound, and force him to live because she couldn't exist without him.

But she didn't.

Because Alfie still stood with a gun in his hand.

"I always win," the man said with a smug look on his face. "And since Noah stupidly led the cops right here, we need to get moving. Noah killed my men so I'll have to wait for others to arrive, then we can go, get settled someplace where no one will ever find you again. Oh, we'll get a doctor for you, Sapphire, don't want you dying on me before that baby of yours is born."

Alfie pulled out a cell phone, and the second the gun was no longer pointing at anyone, and he was distracted, Emerald pounced on him.

They all had sharp pieces of the metal mattress springs, and as her body slammed into his she wasn't shy about using it.

This man had just shot the love of her life, Noah might be dead, or he might die from his wound, he could be bleeding out at this very second.

Although her body was smaller, Alfie wasn't expecting her to throw herself at him, he thought that he had already won, and that things were going to go his way because that was what he was accustomed to. He was too cocky and overly confident to believe that a bunch of women were capable of doing anything to take him down. Since he wasn't expecting her to do it, they had tumbled to the ground, and now she was on top of him slicing the metal through his flesh over and over again.

Alfie tried to fight her off, but it was like she was possessed.

She stabbed at him again and again, all the times he had hurt her ran through her mind, and with each blow a little of that pain vanished.

Emerald was aiming for major arteries, she wanted Alfie dead.

She *needed* him dead.

As long as he was alive, she was never going to be able to move on with her life.

And for the first time she *wanted* to move on.

She wanted what her sisters had. A husband, children, a family of her own, a job that she loved, surrounded by those she cared about.

And she wanted it with Noah.

So Alfie had to die.

It was the only way.

The *only* way.

"It's okay, Emerald, it's okay," a soothing voice whispered, and arms closed around her, a hand grasped her wrist stilling it from its frantic slashing at Alfie's body. "He's dead."

"He's dead?" she echoed. Her vision was blurred by tears, and all she could see was red.

Blood.

So much blood.

"He's dead, honey," Amethyst said, pulling the metal from her hand and drawing her up onto her feet and away from the body.

"I killed him," she said, not quite able to believe that this was real.

She should feel shock, horror, remorse, something appropriate given she had just taken a life, but she didn't.

Emerald felt free.

"He deserved what he got," Amethyst said firmly. "He was going to run and take us with him, he hurt Sapphire, and he shot ..."

Noah.

Alfie had shot Noah.

Wrenching herself out of her sister's arms, she flew across the room and dropped down at Noah's side.

"He's still alive," Ruby told her, "but he's losing blood quickly."

Too quickly.

She pushed Ruby's hands away and pressed her own to Noah's chest. His heart still beat beneath her hands, but his eyes were closed, his lashes fanned out on cheeks that were virtually colorless.

"Noah," she whispered. She wasn't used to seeing her big, strong savior lying still and quiet like this. Holding one hand against his wound, she ran her fingertips over his face. "Don't leave me. I need you."

What would she do without him?

He had been the only person in her life for a third of it. He was the center of her world, he basically was her world, and she couldn't imagine her life without him.

She didn't want to imagine her life without him.

"Someone's coming," Amethyst called out from over by Alfie's body.

"It's either Alfie's people or ours," Sapphire said, her voice weak and heavy with pain, and Emerald felt her anger toward Alfie flare. He had hurt her sister, and he had hurt Noah, she wished that she could bring him back to life just so she could kill him all over again.

Anger was a new emotion for her.

She hadn't felt anger, not once since she had been sold. Well, at least not toward the men who had hurt her. There was some anger toward her parents and their betrayal, but the only thing she had felt for the men who hurt her was fear.

So much fear.

It had ruled her life, it basically *was* her life.

It was all she knew.

Until now.

Now there was so much anger inside her.

At Richard Curtwood, at Alfie, at herself.

The only fear inside her was that she was going to lose Noah, and that was just too much to cope with.

"Close the door," Sapphire ordered. "If it's Alfie's men they'll be armed, but we're not going down without a fight. That's not what Hatchers do."

A smile tugged at her lips despite the dire situation they were in. Her sister was right, they weren't going down without a fight, and they never would. It might have taken time for them to get their feet back underneath them, but they were strong, they had survived hell, and they were still here to tell about it.

If these were Alfie's men on their way here, then they weren't going to make it easy on them.

Amethyst and Ruby stood near the door, Diamond stayed beside Sapphire, her hands on the wound on her leg, and Emerald stayed with Noah, she wasn't sure she could leave him even if she wanted to.

The footsteps got closer, and Emerald held her breath.

A moment later the door swung open, and her breath whooshed out in relief. It was her sisters' husbands.

"Sapphire," Gideon said, running to her side, gathering her into his arms. "We need an ambulance."

"Two," Emerald said, choking on a sob. Now that it was over she could feel herself crashing, Noah wasn't moving, he hadn't opened his eyes, he hadn't said anything, he hadn't stirred, she was losing him.

"Is anyone else hurt?" Elijah asked, wrapping his arms around his wife. "You have blood on you."

"It's Sapphire's," Diamond replied.

"Amethyst?" Zeb asked.

"It's Alfie's," she told her husband.

"And this is Noah's," Ruby said.

"What happened here?" Elijah asked.

"Alfie was going to shoot Emerald, but Noah jumped in the way, then Alfie was going to take us all and leave, but Emerald stopped him," Ruby explained.

"Please," Emerald begged when Elijah and Judah squatted beside her. "Please help him."

She wasn't sure that anyone could help Noah.

Blood continued to seep between her fingers, staining her hands and mixing with Alfie's blood that also covered her hands.

The blood of her tormentor and the blood of her savior.

One was dead, and one was dying.

"An ambulance is on the way," Zeb assured her.

"What if it doesn't get here in time," she said, tears blurring her vision again. "He did it for me. Alfie was going to shoot me, but Noah jumped in the way, took the bullet meant for me. Now he might die for me."

Her whole world was hanging in the balance. She and Noah had committed crimes, they'd let the cops think that Alice was her and messed with their investigation, they'd kidnapped Sapphire and inadvertently gotten her in Alfie's hands, they'd had Elijah drugged and left in the trunk of a car. And she had slaughtered Alfie in cold blood.

Not self-defense.

It had been anger, punishment, retribution.

If the cops decided to charge her with murder, she would be looking at spending the remainder of her life locked up in a jail cell.

And she might lose the one person who had been there for her no matter what. Noah was a complicated man, molded by the uncle who had raised him, determined to have his way, confident, and yet underneath that calm, cool exterior, there was a vulnerability that he didn't want anyone to see, even her.

Especially her.

But she did see it, and it was that vulnerability mixed with strength that had drawn her to him and gained her trust.

She loved this man.

More than anything.

He had saved her life, and it killed her that there wasn't anything she could do to save his. All she could do was kneel beside him, her hand pressed over the bullet wound on his chest, her fingers on his cheek, her tears splashing down onto his deathly pale face.

Sapphire sat in her husband's arms, her eyes closed as her head rested on his shoulder, his hands clamped around her wound. Ruby knelt beside her, her arms entwined with Judah's. Amethyst was standing held against Zeb's chest, and Diamond was clutching at Elijah's hands.

Her sisters all had the men they loved, she prayed she wasn't about to lose hers.

~

7:46 P.M.

The beeping of the machines was driving her crazy, and yet also keeping her sane.

Emerald had been sitting here, next to Noah's hospital bed, for hours.

The cops had taken her clothes as evidence, and the hospital had given her scrubs to wear. They were thin, and she was cold, but not enough that she was going to do anything about it.

She didn't want to do anything but sit here.

She had to be here when Noah woke up.

If he woke up.

The doctors had told her that there was only a fifty percent chance that he would live. They said that he had lost a lot of blood, and that even though they had given him transfusions while he had been in surgery it might not be enough.

Right now, she couldn't accept that. The last few months had been such a rollercoaster, and the last couple of days had been filled with so many ups and downs that she was struggling not to shut down. Shutting down, retreating inside herself, had been the only way she had survived what Richard Curtwood and Alfie had done to her, and old habits were gnawing at her now when she had pretty much reached her limit, but she couldn't do it. It wasn't what Noah would want her to do.

Noah would want her to remain the person he had helped her become, and she had fought so hard to get here. It was because of Noah that she was a semi-functioning person, and now that Alfie was gone and that last tie to her horrific past was severed, she felt like she was on the verge of becoming fully functioning.

But what was the point if she lost Noah?

"Knock, knock, can we come in?"

Emerald turned toward the voices and saw that the doorway was full of people. She had expected her sisters to come sooner or later, but they weren't here alone, their husbands were with them, and she couldn't help but wonder if it was because they were here to arrest her.

"You can come in," she said softly, returning her gaze to Noah. She hated seeing him like this, it was so unnatural, she wanted him back, but she knew that she was going to have to prepare herself for the possibility that it would never happen.

"How's he doing?" Diamond asked.

"The same, the doctors said fifty-fifty he survives. But I know you don't really care either way," she said. She didn't mean it as an accusation, she wasn't angry with them for not caring about Noah, it was what it was.

"That's not true," Ruby said. "I think he proved that if nothing else, he really loves you. He took that bullet for you."

He had.

And the guilt of knowing that he had died in her place would eat at her every second of every day for the rest of her life.

"Are you here to arrest me?" she asked, looking away from Noah to where the others were standing. No one was holding handcuffs, but she wasn't necessarily basing her assumptions off of that, maybe they just thought they'd be nice to her given the situation and lead her away without cuffing her.

"No," Judah replied.

"You're going with self-defense?" she asked, it seemed unlikely that anyone would believe that given the number of times she had stabbed Alfie.

"Something to do with extreme emotional distress. Sapphire tried to explain it, but she was high on painkillers and not making much sense," Amethyst said with a smile.

"I make perfect sense," Sapphire contradicted as Gideon pushed her into the room in a wheelchair. "And I didn't take any of the painkillers they offered me."

"You're okay?" Emerald asked, giving her sister a visual once over. She seemed okay, she was pale, but her eyes were alert, and her face had been cleaned up, a couple of the cuts had been stitched, the rest covered in white bandages. Her leg was heavily bandaged, but it was clear that she was going to be okay, even if she'd have to be off her feet for a few days.

"I'm okay." Sapphire met her gaze, held it for a long moment, and then turned to the others. "Can Emerald and I have a moment alone?"

"*One* moment," Gideon said, taking her chin between his thumb and forefinger he tilted her face up and kissed her. "One moment," he repeated. "Then I'm taking you home so you can get some rest."

Nervous to be alone with her sister because she knew that Sapphire was still upset with her, Emerald returned her gaze to Noah. She wondered if it was possible to will someone into living.

In a way that was how Noah had saved her.

He hadn't given up on her, and that had been what eventually led her out of the dark hole she had been trapped in. If he had doubted her, even just one time, it would have changed everything. She had needed his belief in her because she hadn't believed in herself. With no one to believe in her, she would have been lost.

But Noah had been there for her.

He hadn't left her alone, he had remained by her side, and now she was going to do the same for him.

"I'm never going to like what you did," Sapphire said, wheeling herself over toward the bed.

"You mean nearly getting you, and our sisters killed? Is your baby okay?"

"My baby is fine, and I'll be fine too. And no that's not what I meant. I mean staying away, letting us think you were either dead or still someone's prisoner. You aren't responsible for what Alfie did. But you are responsible for your choices, and I'm never going to be okay with it. It hurts, Emerald. It hurts that you let us believe we had lost you, it hurts that you let *me* believe I'd lost you. You and me we used to be a team, sisters and best friends, without you I felt like a piece of me was gone. I don't know how to be okay with that. But ..."

"But?" She looked up with hopeful eyes.

"But, we're family, and I love you, Emmy," Sapphire said, reaching out and taking her hand. "I don't like what Noah did either. He knew who I was and he deliberately kept you away from us while invading my privacy and the privacy of my family by using the security systems to watch us. But ..."

"But?" she prompted when Sapphire didn't finish her sentence.

"But, I can't deny the fact that he loves you, and that in keeping your existence a secret he was trying to keep you safe, and that I understand. And then today, he told Alfie I was pregnant because he was trying to keep me alive, and he helped Gideon and the others find us. He knew that I still had the piece of wire because I showed it to him while he was talking to Alfie, he jumped in front of that bullet because he knew that Alfie would rather have you dead than lose you again to anyone else. He also knew that even if he was dead, we could kill Alfie before he took us away, we only had to hold out until Gideon, Elijah, and the others got there. He was prepared to die so long as you could live, and I guess it's kind of hard to hate someone who would do that for my sister."

Tears blurred her vision for about the hundredth time today, and Emerald squeezed her sister's hand, she was so glad that she had all four of them back in her life. "I'm so sorry for letting you believe that I was dead or still in trouble. I love you, and I missed you, Saph," she murmured. "I used to go out onto the balcony every night to look at the stars because it reminded me of how we used to wait for the stars to come out each night to make a wish."

"I always won," Sapphire said with a teary smile of her own.

"Because I always let you win," she teased.

"No way, I won because I was the big sister and big sisters always win. I missed you so much, Emmy. I blamed myself because I didn't save you that night."

"That's not your fault. We were just girls, they were men, men with guns. You tried, and you've been looking for me all these years, haven't you? You never gave up on me."

"I would never give up on you, not for anything."

"I'm so sorry I made you go through that. I was so afraid, I felt different, not the same person I was before, and I didn't want you to see me that way, but it was wrong, I made a mistake, and I wish I could take it back but I can't," she implored.

"Noah was good to you? He looked after you? He made you happy?" Sapphire asked.

Emerald reached over and curled her fingers around Noah's. "He was everything to me. He saved me literally and figuratively. He gave me horses because he knew I loved animals, he bought me instruments because he knew I loved to play music, he bought me beautiful clothes and jewelry and took care of me. He would sit beside my bed at night, he would read to me, he would hold me when I cried, he told me that I was strong enough to survive anything but ... I'm not sure I'm strong enough to survive losing him."

"Noah is right, you're strong enough to survive anything," Sapphire said firmly. "And even if you do lose him—and I honestly hope that you don't—it doesn't mean you're alone. You still have us."

Her life kept teetering so close to being normal, but it kept falling out of her grasp. She was closer than she had ever been to having it all, but not if Noah died. She wanted her sisters in her life more than anything, but she wanted Noah too.

If it was possible to will someone into remaining alive then she was going to do it.

She wouldn't lose Noah.

11:11 P.M.

Emerald was crying.

That was the first thing Noah registered.

It was enough to prompt him to gather his strength and open his eyes, if Emerald needed him, then he had to be there for her.

When he opened his eyes, he saw Emerald sitting in a chair beside his bed. She had her knees pulled up to her chest, her arms wrapped around them like she was trying to hold herself together, and her face was buried in her knees. The sound of her quiet weeping filled the room, and the knees of the blue scrubs she was wearing were wet from her tears.

"I hope those tears aren't over me," he said, his voice was croaky and insubstantial, but it was the best he could do given he had just been shot in the chest.

"Noah," she squealed, she darted off the chair and threw herself into his arms.

Pain knifed through his chest as she jostled him, but he would take all the pain in the world if it offered Emerald even a molecule of comfort.

"You're alive," she said, her wet face pressed against his neck and her thin arms clung to him as a fresh batch of tears seized her.

"I'm alive," he said, lifting a hand and awkwardly patting her back, ignoring the tugging on his skin from the needle that was stuck in the back of his hand.

"I thought I was going to lose you, I was so scared," she wept. Then abruptly, she straightened and punched him in the shoulder hard enough to hurt. "Don't you *ever* do that to me again."

"What? Save your life?" he drawled, amused by her little temper tantrum.

"You didn't have to do that, you should have just kept him talking until the cops arrived."

"If I did that, he would have shot you the second the cops walked through the door." He had done what he had to do to make sure Emerald walked out of that room alive. That was all that had mattered to him, if he had died in the process he would have died content. He knew Sapphire had a weapon, she'd shown it to him, and in doing so, he assumed she was also telling him that the rest of her sisters also had weapons. He'd ensured that Alfie had reason to keep Sapphire alive, and he'd made sure that Alfie made his play before the cops got there so he had a chance to make sure the man wound up dead.

He wanted Alfie dead.

He should have killed him a long time ago.

That he hadn't done what he should have had led to a lot of people getting hurt.

It had led to *Emerald* getting hurt.

"Are you okay?" he asked her, taking her hand, then he sat up, barely registering the resulting pain. "Your hand," he said, turning it over to reveal a deep, bloody gash on her palm. "What's this from?"

"I think it's from when I was stabbing Alfie," she replied.

"*You* killed Alfie?" he repeated, he had thought the sisters had done it together, or Sapphire had found a way to do it.

"He tried to kill you," she said fiercely, her green eyes taking on a glint he hadn't seen before. Something inside her had changed, she had finally found her power again.

Noah cupped her cheek in his hand. "I'm so proud of you."

Her cheeks went pink, and she smiled and tilted her face into his hand. "I'm just glad that you're okay."

"But you're not," he said, lifting her hand. "This looks painful, and there are a lot of tendons in your hand, you should have had a doctor look at it. What kind of hospital is this if they let you sit here in pain and injured?"

"I wouldn't let them look at it. I didn't want to leave you. They said there was only a fifty percent chance that you would live, I had to stay here, I had to be with you. When I needed you, you were there for me, I wanted to be there for you too." Tears welled in her eyes, hovering on her eyelashes but not falling down her cheeks yet, and this time he had to admit that he had no one else to blame for Emerald's tears but himself.

"You go and get this looked at now," he ordered.

"No." Emerald shook her head.

This was new.

Emerald never usually went against anything he said to her. And yet she had gone off on her own after Alfie, and she had just told him no, his Emerald was definitely gone and he knew she was never coming back.

"No?" he repeated.

"I want to be here with you." She smiled and gently tugged her hand from his and pressed against his shoulders, easing him back against the mattress. "Do you need anything? Water? Are you cold? Do you need more pain medication? I should go and get the doctor so they can check you out."

Her fussing was sweet, and Noah knew that his Emerald wasn't gone, she had just changed.

But how much?

"You want to be here?" Noah made his voice cold and detached because he would never beg Emerald to stay with him no matter how much he loved her. "For how long?"

"What do you mean?" Emerald's brow creased quizzically.

"You're different, you've changed, you got control of your life back when you killed Alfie. Your sisters are back in your life now, that means that you don't need to hide away from the world."

Emerald nodded slowly. "I am different now," she agreed, and those words tore through him more deeply than any bullet ever could. "But I don't want to leave you," she said, her hand resting lightly on his head, her fingers threading through his hair. "Noah, I love you. I *love* you. I don't even want to imagine my life without you. I still want to be with you, I still want to live with you, I want to spend the rest of my life with you. But I do want to have my sisters in my life too. They're warming up to you, you know," she said with a smile.

"Not Sapphire though."

"Even Sapphire. You jumping in front of the bullet meant for me kind of sealed things in their minds," her smile grew bigger. He loved to see her smile, her whole face lit up, her eyes sparkled like real emeralds, and her cheeks went a pretty shade of pink. There was a lightness to her that hadn't been there before, the heavy burden that had been holding her down had been removed, and now she was free to fly.

To fly away from him.

"No, Noah," she said as though she read his mind, these drugs they were pouring into him must be messing with his ability to keep his thoughts to himself. "I would never leave you, why won't you believe me? Because you think I'm not yours anymore, now that there are other people in my life? I love my sisters, and I want my family back, but I still want you. You are the center of my world, and nothing will ever change that. But I *do* want other people in my life. I want us to get married and have babies, have our own little family."

Marriage?

Babies?

He balked at the notion.

Emerald sat beside him on the bed, her hands rested on his stomach, below his heavily bandaged chest. "Noah, I know you never had a family, and my family was messed up, but we can change that. We can make our own family. I love you so much." She leaned over and touched her forehead to his. "I don't want to hurt you, but I want to kiss you," she whispered.

Whatever Emerald wanted she got.

If she wanted marriage, then he would buy her the biggest diamond he could find and propose.

If she wanted children, then they would have a baby.

And if she wanted a kiss, then she would get a kiss.

Curling a hand behind her neck, he drew her lips to his and kissed her.

"You're too good for me," he murmured against her soft lips.

"That's not true. You are a good man who made some mistakes, but that doesn't change who you are in here." She held her hand to his chest with a featherlight touch. "Bad men don't take bullets for other people. Bad men don't become a virtual recluse for a decade because the person they love can't face the world. Bad men don't love other people, and you love me. This is our chance to put the past behind us and have a future. A real future. A happy future. I think we both need a little happiness in our lives. Don't walk away from this chance. Don't let fear control you like I did for all those years. I'm stronger now, Noah, strong enough to be there for you like you've been there for me. Don't shut me out. I want us to be a couple, a *real* couple, a partnership. You're not alone, I'm right here."

What could he say to that?

This woman was an angel.

His beautiful, sweet, innocent, pure angel.

His.

She might have changed, but nothing could change that.

They were two souls tied together for all eternity.

Epilogue

December 25th
10:02 A.M.

This was chaos.

Loud, laughing, talking, merry chaos.

Emerald sat in one of the sitting rooms at her and Noah's house, there was a fire raging in the fireplace, a huge Christmas tree in the corner, and at least a hundred gifts wrapped in brightly colored paper sitting underneath it.

She *may* have gone a little overboard with her Christmas shopping this year.

She and Noah weren't alone this Christmas, her sisters, their husbands, and their children were all here. The kids were hyped as only children on Christmas morning could be. There was a huge dinner cooking in the kitchen, the table was set, there was enough candy here to start their own store, and being surrounded by so many laughing, happy people warmed her from the inside out.

They would exchange gifts after lunch, but she already had exactly what she wanted. It was sitting around her, full of Christmas spirit, she had her family back, Noah had proposed to her the day he had been released from the hospital, four days after being shot, they had set a wedding date—New Year's Eve, just six days away because neither of them wanted to wait—and she wanted to start trying for a baby immediately—if she wasn't already pregnant.

Her life had changed a lot in just one month.

She felt like a new person, not quite the person she had been before she'd been sold, and not the person she had been for the last decade and a half, but someone new, kind of in between the two.

Her life was bright and colorful again, she was reconnecting with her sisters, she was getting to know her nieces and nephews, she was taking classes to finish high school and then she planned to go to college. While she studied, she was working on setting up an animal shelter here on the estate, and she couldn't wait to start caring for animals that needed help and a safe place. And what better place to run it than right here? Where she had found the safe place she needed to heal.

Things with Noah were wonderful too.

She had doted on him while he'd been healing from the bullet wound that nearly took him from her, and being forced to take things easy had mellowed him a little. Emerald knew he couldn't wait to get back to work, and back to full strength, he loved to be in control, and right now his body was failing him, and he couldn't be. But that had formed a closeness between them that hadn't been there before. Their bond had grown and developed, it was so wonderful to be able to be there for Noah like he had been there for her.

"Mommy, can we go outside and have a snowball fight?" four-year-old Archie asked Diamond.

"I don't see why not," Diamond replied. "Let's all go."

"Family teams," competitive Sapphire said, pushing to her feet, a little slowly in deference to her leg that hadn't yet fully healed. "And Gideon, Leo, and I are going to win."

"No way, little sister, your leg still isn't one hundred percent," Amethyst—who was just as competitive—said. "Lucy, Zeb, and I are going to beat your little booties."

While they got their kids into coats, mittens, and scarves, Sapphire and Amethyst continued to bicker, and Emerald couldn't help but laugh.

This was nice.

This kind of silly family bickering and teasing, and she was so glad to have her home filled with love and joy this Christmas. Last Christmas had just been her and Noah, they had spent the day snuggled together in front of the open fireplace making love, reading, and eating way too much turkey, it had been a lovely day, but this was better.

"We're going to win, Aunty Sapphire," Archie was saying. "Because we have daddy and mommy, and Brooke, and Oscar, and me. That's five people."

"Maybe we should loan someone to Aunt Emerald," Diamond suggested. "So they're not outnumbered. This year at least," she added with a wink.

"I'll be on Aunt Emerald and Uncle Noah's team," Archie said, but then his gray eyes grew concerned. "But Uncle Noah still has a sore chest."

"Uncle Noah is tougher than Superman," Noah said, and Archie's eyes grew round. "And you know what?" he asked as he crouched down to Archie's level. "Since this is Uncle Noah's house, I know all the best places to hide."

"Yay," Archie clapped his hands then shrugged into the coat Elijah held out for him.

Emerald couldn't wipe the smile off her face as she watched Noah. Bit by bit, the more time they spent around her sisters and their families, his rock hard armor was beginning to get chinks in it. She knew he was never going to be mister warm and fuzzy, but she didn't want him to be, she just wanted him to be happy, and he was. They both were.

Dressed in a brightly colored array of beanies, jackets, mittens, and scarves, they bundled out into the cold winter morning. A fresh layer of snow covered the ground, it had been snowing all Christmas Eve, but this morning the sky was a clear blue, and the sun shone brightly, making the snow sparkle.

The whole world looked magical.

Tonight, when the sun went down, the fairy lights that had been strung around the huge fir trees lining the driveway would turn on, making them look like giant Christmas trees, and she wanted to bring the kids back out for a game of hide and seek before they went home to bed.

Everyone was chattering over the top of each other as they came up with rules for their snowball fight, it seemed the grown-ups were a lot more excited about it than the kids were. The kids were already running about, grabbing handfuls of snow and tossing them at one another.

What could be better than this?

Christmas Day with her family, and maybe by this time next year she and Noah really would have a little addition to their team for whatever game her competitive sisters came up with.

Their parents had tried to destroy them, but she and her sisters had come out of it stronger than ever. In life, you couldn't go backward, you could only keep moving on, they could never be the people they had been as teenagers, but she thought they had all turned out okay despite all the odds.

"Oh, Emerald," Noah sang as he sidled up beside her, and the next thing she knew a shower of snow was raining down on her as Noah threw a snowball at her.

"Hey," she exclaimed. "I thought we were supposed to be on the same team. You are going to pay for that."

"We got your back, sis," Sapphire said, reaching down to grab a handful of snow.

Grabbing her own handful of snow, she molded it into a snowball, then surveyed her own little army, as her sisters and their husbands and kids began throwing a bevy of snowballs at Noah, who was laughing and making and throwing his own snowballs as quickly as he could.

Snow flew everywhere.

Laughter filled the air.

And Emerald knew she had finally found peace.

The Hatcher sisters might have found love and happiness now meet their cousin Marigold and continue with the final book in this gripping romantic suspense series now!

. . .

Salvaging Marigold (Broken Gems #6)

Also by Jane Blythe

CRUSHED RUBY

FRACTURED DIAMOND

SHATTERED AMETHYST

SPLINTERED EMERALD

SALVAGING MARIGOLD

River's End Rescues Series

COCKY SAVIOR

SOME REGRETS ARE FOREVER

SOME FEARS CAN CONTROL YOU

SOME LIES WILL HAUNT YOU

SOME QUESTIONS HAVE NO ANSWERS

SOME TRUTH CAN BE DISTORTED

SOME TRUST CAN BE REBUILT

SOME MISTAKES ARE UNFORGIVABLE

Candella Sisters' Heroes Series

LITTLE DOLLS

LITTLE HEARTS

LITTLE BALLERINA

Storybook Murders Series

NURSERY RHYME KILLER

FAIRYTALE KILLER

FABLE KILLER

Saving SEALs Series

Prey Security Series

Prey Security: Alpha Team Series

Prey Security: Artemis Team Series

IVORY'S FIGHT

PEARL'S FIGHT

LACEY'S FIGHT

OPAL'S FIGHT

Prey Security: Bravo Team Series

VICIOUS SCARS

RUTHLESS SCARS

Christmas Romantic Suspense Series

CHRISTMAS HOSTAGE

CHRISTMAS CAPTIVE

CHRISTMAS VICTIM

YULETIDE PROTECTOR

YULETIDE GUARD

YULETIDE HERO

HOLIDAY GRIEF

Conquering Fear Series (Co-written with Amanda Siegrist)

DROWNING IN YOU

OUT OF THE DARKNESS

CLOSING IN

About the Author

USA Today bestselling author Jane Blythe writes action-packed romantic suspense and military romance featuring protective heroes and heroines who are survivors. One of Jane's most popular series includes Prey Security, part of Susan Stoker's OPERATION ALPHA world! Writing in that world alongside authors such as Janie Crouch and Riley Edwards has been a blast, and she looks forward to bringing more books to this genre, both within and outside of Stoker's world. When Jane isn't binge-reading she's counting down to Christmas and adding to her 200+ teddy bear collection!

To connect and keep up to date please visit any of the following

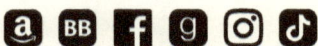

www.ingramcontent.com/pod-product-compliance
Lightning Source LLC
Chambersburg PA
CBHW031942240626
47153CB00003B/831